T0343583

"Texas is neither southern nor western.

Texas is Texas."

—Senator William Blakley

LOVE'S A MYSTERY

LOVE'S A MYSTERY

in

CUT AND SHOOT
TX

JANICE THOMPSON &
RUTH LOGAN HERNE

Published by Guideposts
100 Reserve Road, Suite E200
Danbury, CT 06810
Guideposts.org

Cover and interior design by Müllerhaus.
Cover illustration by Dan Burr at Illustration Online LLC.
Typeset by Aptara, Inc.

ISBN 978-1-961441-36-1 (hardcover)
ISBN 978-1-961441-37-8 (softcover)
ISBN 978-1-957935-49-2 (epub)

Printed and bound in the United States of America

LOVE PIECED TOGETHER

by

JANICE THOMPSON

*There is no chasm in society that cannot be
firmly and permanently bridged by intercession;
there is no feud or dislike that cannot be healed
by the same exercise of love.*

—CHARLES BRENT

CHAPTER ONE

Cut and Shoot, Texas
Saturday, December 14, 1912

"Why didn't you tell me Gilbert Sutton was coming home for Christmas?"

Patience Cochran ducked behind a mercantile shelf filled with lanterns and peered out from behind them. Across the room, she caught a glimpse of Gilbert. Her Gilbert.

Well, not hers anymore, though years of childhood friendship had led everyone in the town of Cut and Shoot to believe they would one day marry. Of course, that was before the big uproar last summer. These days, she wouldn't be caught dead speaking to him, for fear of what folks would say.

"What are you doing, Patience?" Her cousin Adeline planted her hands on her hips and shot a glance her way. "Why are you hiding back there behind those shelves?"

"Shh!" Patience put her finger over her lips and reached out to pull her cousin closer. "You know perfectly well. The Cochrans and Suttons haven't spoken since that awful day last summer. I can't let Gil see me."

"Well, that's just plain silly." Adeline brushed a loose blond hair from her face. "You and Gil have been best friends since you were little. You can't let a little thing like a town feud come between you."

Patience adjusted her position so that she could see between a couple of the beveled glass hurricane lanterns. She observed Gil chatting with a handsome young man with dark, wavy hair.

She turned back to face her cousin. "Easy for you to say. You don't live here anymore. You have no idea how bad things have been. The whole town is split right down the middle. And Gil has been living and working in Conroe, so I've barely seen him." Until now.

With a wave of her hand, Adeline appeared to dismiss any concerns. "It's just stuff and nonsense. And I refuse to have my Christmas visit spoiled by childish squabbling. I've come all the way from Houston to be with my cousins for the holidays, and I won't have something as silly as a misunderstanding ruin my visit."

"It was a bit more than a misunderstanding, Adeline," Patience said. "There were knives and guns involved."

"Pooh. No one got hurt, right?"

"Not physically. But my little brother was traumatized."

Adeline batted those big brown eyes of hers and reached for Patience's hand. "Ernest will be fine. Now come on out of there, and let's say hello. That's the proper thing to do when you run into an old friend in a public setting, is it not?"

Patience swallowed hard and summoned the courage to face Gilbert. She took that first step, but then someone else caught her eye, and she ducked behind the lanterns once again. "Oh no! He's with his grandmother." She peered across the store at Florence Sutton and noticed how frail the elderly woman looked. "This is dreadful! I knew we were taking a risk, coming into town on a Saturday."

"For pity's sake." Adeline reached for a tiny perfume bottle and gave it a closer look. "That's ridiculous. A person should be able to come to town whenever they like without having to worry about what anyone else thinks of it." She placed the bottle back on the shelf. "Now, come on out, or I'll drag you out. And I assure you, that would not be pretty."

"But you know me, Adeline," Patience said. "I can't abide feuding. No doubt any encounter between the Cochrans and Suttons would end poorly. I can't risk that."

Adeline seemed perplexed by this statement. "But you've always loved Florence Sutton. She's Granny's best friend, after all."

"Not anymore. They don't speak."

Adeline's eyes widened. "I don't believe you! I thought you were just exaggerating in those letters you sent last summer."

"I wasn't exaggerating, trust me." Patience took hold of her cousin's arm and pulled her a little closer as Florence and Gilbert filled a basket with items for purchase. Her heart thumped in her ears as Gil's jovial voice rang out just a few feet away from her. She ducked down a bit lower and tried to make herself invisible.

That's when she heard a little girl singing. The youngster trilled a familiar Christmas carol. Patience peeked out once more and saw that Gil's younger sister Violet had arrived. The whole family must be here. Violet made her way to the candy counter, where Florence—ever the doting grandmother—offered to purchase licorice sticks. Then Florence turned her attention to a shelf with homemade preserves. A shelf that happened to be just a few feet away from where Patience now stood.

She had no choice but to plan an escape, to get out of the mercantile while the gettin' was good, as Granny Cochran was prone to say. Patience took a couple of steps in the direction of the door, tiptoeing across the creaky, wood-planked floor. Unfortunately, she was so busy making sure Gilbert didn't see her that she bumped into a bin that was balanced precariously on the edge of a table. It came crashing down, creating quite the stir. Potatoes rolled across the floor and under the shelves. In her attempt to fetch them, she tripped and fell headfirst into a stack of flour sacks, breaking one open.

Patience sprang up as quickly as she could and brushed the white powder from her hair and skirt, doing her best not to groan aloud.

"That's one way to hide from your enemies." Adeline giggled and faced Gilbert, who was rushing their way. She greeted him with a smile and a friendly, "Hello, stranger!"

He responded with a rushed, "Hello," then turned his gaze to Patience.

"I had no idea we were expecting snow." A smile tipped up the edges of Gilbert's lips. "That's a first for these parts."

"Very funny." Patience straightened her skirts as she stepped across the busted flour bag, then did her best to brush the white powder from her blouse. She must look absolutely ridiculous.

He brushed flour from her cheek. "I won't ask how this happened."

"Thank you."

"But were you here all along? I didn't see you when we came in."

"Well, I—"

"Were you hiding, by chance?"

"Who, me? Hiding? Now why would I need to do that?" She turned her attention to a display of baking powder on a nearby shelf. "I was just giving the baking supplies a closer look."

"Since when have you had an interest in baking? Your granny tried to teach you to make biscuits a dozen times, and you were a sensational flop."

"I was no such thing. It just so happens I excel at biscuit-making. Ask anyone in town."

"I would if I could, but half the town isn't speaking to me." He gave her a knowing look. But did he have to be handsome while doing it? Did those bright blue eyes of his have to twinkle with such merriment? They captivated her, just as they always had. And his honey-blond hair still fell fetchingly over his forehead.

How could she avoid staring? And how could she get past those old feelings that threatened to creep up, even now?

"Only half the town?" Adeline chuckled as she rested her hand on Gil's arm, a move that rankled Patience. "I'd think you would have more enemies than that, Gilbert Sutton. As I recall, your antics turned nearly every townsperson against you, back in the day."

"I've grown up since then." He smiled. "And I can't remember the last time I pulled a prank on anyone."

Patience wasn't so sure about that. The lawsuit he had helped the Suttons file against her family came off as the worst prank ever. Only, it happened to be real. Very, very real.

Suddenly he didn't look so handsome anymore. He was the enemy, after all, as were all the Suttons and their crew.

"Well, I'm glad to hear those days are behind you." Adeline leaned in a little too close to him. Was she flirting?

On the other side of the store, the handsome stranger with the dark wavy hair was asking Mr. Pepperdine about the grocery items he wanted to purchase. Adeline must've decided she was the perfect person to answer his questions, because she strolled in his direction and engaged him in conversation.

In her nervous state Patience began to finger the products on the shelf, finally grabbing hold of a book.

"What's this?" Gil quirked a brow. "You're reading dime novels now?"

"I am?" She glanced down, and heat rose to her cheeks when she saw the title. *Knickerbocker's Sixpenny Tales.* "No, no. This is for Granny Cochran. A Christmas gift."

"I see." He took the book and flipped it over, skimming the back cover copy. "Your granny is now reading salacious tales of intrigue and romance?"

"Yes, well, she might enjoy it."

Violet was now singing "O Little Town of Bethlehem." This afforded Patience the perfect opportunity to change the subject.

"I hear the children are caroling tonight."

"Violet has asked me to transport several of the carolers in my motorcar. Are you coming?"

"Heavens, no." She shook her head. "There's no telling who will be there, and I can't risk—"

"Singing? You can't risk singing the praises of God with your fellow men? And women? And children?"

"No, I can't," she responded.

"That's just silly." Adeline reappeared, just in time to interject her thoughts on the matter.

"I agree." Gilbert gave her a pensive look. "After all, the town that sings together, stays together."

"This, from the man who helped the Suttons file a lawsuit against the Cochrans?" She didn't mean to mention that, but the words were out now, and she couldn't unsay them.

His smile immediately faded. "Patience, you know I had no choice. My uncle's law firm took the case. He put me on it. I had to—"

"Had to hurt the very people you'd spent most of your life claiming to care about." She shoved the dime novel back onto the shelf. Knickerbocker could wait.

"*Claiming* to care about?" The pain in those beautiful blue eyes was undeniable.

"I heard you were working with a big law firm over in Conroe," Adeline crooned. "I'm so proud of you."

"Proud of him?" Patience could hardly believe her cousin's response. "He represents the people who sued us after the feud." She still couldn't believe he had betrayed her family in such a way. Was nothing sacred anymore, even a friendship that went back twenty years?

"Well, not your family specifically," he said. "And to be fair—"

"There was nothing fair about it." She planted her hands on her hips and glared at him, determined to lower her voice so as not to draw attention. "And we shouldn't even be speaking about such things, especially in public. If you came around more often, you would know that. But you don't come around anymore, do you?"

"What are you saying, Patience?" His eyes narrowed, and she could read the concern in his expression. "That we're supposed to be sworn enemies just because our people aren't speaking?"

"Our *people*?" She shook her head, agitation setting in. "Don't you mean our *families*?"

"Well, yes, but the lawsuit involves a lot more people than just your family."

"And yet, you took it on, knowing my pa would be named in it. And my grandmother. How could you, Gil?"

"I told you, I didn't have a choice. My uncle—"

"Pulls the strings and you snap to attention." She paused as heat filled her cheeks. "Yes, I know. He's the most important attorney in the county, and you're proud to be working for him."

"Well, I—"

Heat washed over her cheeks as embarrassment set in. "I'm sorry, Gil. I didn't mean that. This whole thing has me very—"

"Worked up. I know. I feel the same."

An awkward silence grew up between them.

Violet stopped singing, and Patience saw her lift her hand in a friendly wave. She wasn't sure how to respond. These days, even the simplest gesture could be misconstrued. She offered a hint of a smile and a tiny wave... until Florence noticed her. Then she turned back to her cousin. "I think we should go now, Adeline. Let's pay for Granny's baking supplies and get out of here."

"If you say so." Her cousin's gaze was firmly planted on the handsome stranger, who wrapped up payment for his goods.

Patience tugged at her sleeve. "Granny wanted my help with dinner tonight, and I promised. Besides, I need to check on Goldie. She's due to have her puppies any day now, and I want to make sure she's comfortable in the barn. So let's pay for our items and go. Please."

Adeline sighed. "Sure."

"Great to see you," Gil said. "If you change your mind about the caroling—"

"I won't." She turned and headed toward the counter, where she paid for the items they had placed there earlier. Then they gathered their baskets to leave.

When they reached the door, the handsome stranger approached. In true gentlemanly fashion, he held the door open for them and tipped his hat as they walked by.

"Who is that?" Adeline asked as soon as they were outside. "Is he new to town?"

"No idea." Patience glanced back over her shoulder and noticed the man was peering at them through the paned glass in the mercantile door.

"I tried to strike up a conversation with him." Adeline reached into her basket and came out with a stick of candy. She took a bite of it.

"More than *tried*, I'd say."

Adeline offered an exaggerated pout. "Now, don't be like that. I was just being hospitable. He's mighty handsome, wouldn't you say?" She took another bite of the candy.

"Is he?" Patience cleared her throat. "I hadn't noticed."

"Sure you hadn't." Adeline laughed. "I very nearly lost control of my senses when I laid eyes on him. I cannot be held responsible for what happens when I'm under the spell of a handsome young man like that. Can you?"

"It's not something I think about."

"Then why did your cheeks turn such a delightful shade of pink when Gilbert Sutton walked up?"

"They did no such thing."

"Mm-hmm. Sure they didn't. And you weren't glued to his baby blues either."

"I...well..."

"As I said." Adeline paused and glanced down the street, looking a bit perplexed. "I meant to ask you this earlier, but why is only one side of the street decorated for Christmas?"

"The Suttons couldn't seem to get in the Christmas spirit, I suppose you could say. We Cochrans did our part." Patience shifted the basket to her other arm and kept walking.

"Oh, I see." Adeline gave the decor a closer look. "Well, that's sad. Why didn't you just decorate the whole thing, then?"

"Pa said we should give them the benefit of the doubt. He thought if we did half, they might do the other."

"But they didn't."

"No, but that's life in Cut and Shoot for you, at least these days."

"I still can't get over the name you all have given this once fair town." Adeline shook her head. "'Cut and Shoot'? Sounds ominous."

"Well, after what we've been through, it's fitting. But the name was actually just an expression from Ernest on the day of the big feud."

Adeline looked intrigued by this idea. "Are you telling me your eight-year-old brother named the town by accident?"

"Yes. In his haste to leave the terrifying scene going on at the church, he said he was going to cut around the corner and shoot through the bushes in a minute."

"My goodness. And such a silly little phrase stuck?"

"Yes. Though, to be honest, I've heard more outsiders use it than locals. I don't think folks here want to be remembered for the one day that drove us apart."

"Understandable." Adeline reached into her bag for a handkerchief, which she used to cover her nose as dust from the road blew into their faces. She pulled the handkerchief away and said, "I simply don't understand people who kick up a fuss and then refuse to forgive one another."

"It's more complicated than that, Adeline."

"But doesn't the Bible say we should offer forgiveness?"

How could she explain that some situations required more time and effort to get there?

They passed a man with a matted, shaggy beard and dirty, long hair. His clothes were in need of a good washing, and his boots were worn almost through. Patience's heart twisted as their eyes met. He coughed and kept moving, diverting his gaze to the far side of the street.

Adeline clutched Patience's arm and whispered, "Who is that man? Do you know him?"

"No." She shook her head. "But I heard there was a drifter in town. Jeb, the foreman at the mill, said he's been stealing from folks. Jeb said we should watch out for him."

"That's terrible! What has that awful man stolen?"

"One of Granny's pies, for one thing."

"What?" Adeline tightened her grip on Patience's arm. "Are you saying he's been on the family's property?"

Patience's gaze shifted back to the man, who shuffled down the road, moving toward the meetinghouse. "We think so. Granny set her pies out for the sawmill workers yesterday afternoon, and one of them went missing before they got there. Jeb is sure it was the drifter. He was on our property earlier."

"Why?"

"Who knows. Maybe hoping for a job?"

"What kind of pie did he steal?"

"Apple."

Adeline sighed. "That's my favorite."

"It's everyone's favorite. No one tops Granny Cochran when it comes to apple pie." Patience lowered her voice as she watched Gil, Violet, and Florence leave the mercantile, headed toward his car. She turned back to face her cousin. "But don't tell the Suttons. There's an ongoing feud between Florence and our grandmother over that."

"I've never tasted one of Florence's pies, but I can't imagine anyone would come close," Adeline said. "It's a shame that awful man took off with the pie before the workers could eat it."

"Agreed." Her gaze traveled behind them once again to the man, who hobbled, hunched over, down the road. She only hoped he would hop on board the next train and leave Cut and Shoot once and for all, before something even worse happened.

Gilbert watched as Patience and Adeline walked down the street in the direction of her family's home, just a few blocks away. Should he offer them a ride? No doubt Patience would turn him down. She seemed very out of sorts today. Not that he blamed her, of course. The lawsuit had driven an even larger wedge between the townspeople, and he was at the very center of that, though he had little to do with the feud.

"Gil, can you help, please?" He looked back to see his grandmother trying to juggle her basket while attempting to open the passenger door of his Model T.

"Coming, Grandma. Sorry." He raced to her side of the car and opened the door, then took the basket from her and put it in the rear.

He diverted his gaze to the Cadillac Touring Car that buzzed by with Daniel Jennings behind the wheel. He knew the man from Conroe and didn't trust him as far as he could throw him. Daniel's over-the-top articles for the *Tribune* were nearly as salacious as those dime novels Patience seemed to be interested in.

"Was that a Cadillac?" his grandmother asked from her spot in the passenger seat.

"Yes, ma'am."

"My goodness, I've heard such stories about them." She pulled her coat a bit tighter to ward off the cold. "They don't require a crank to start?"

"No, ma'am." Which served as his cue to move to the front of his vehicle to crank his Model T into motion. Seconds later the Walkaround's engine sprang to life.

Violet climbed into the rumble seat, and Gilbert climbed into the driver's seat. They were soon on the road, headed to the family's property on the south side of town.

"I feel so special, tooling down the street in a Walkaround. No one else in town has one." Violet giggled as she waved at a friend standing in front of the post office with her mother. She let out a gasp. "Gil, slow down! I want Margaret to see me. She'll be green with envy."

"Is that the goal here?" he asked. "To make people green with envy?"

"Of course. Honk the horn, please!"

He obliged, grabbing hold of the rubber ball and giving it a squeeze until a honk rang out.

Violet leaned out of the open window and hollered, "See you tonight, Margaret!"

Violet's friend turned to face them, her mouth falling open at the sight of the car moving down the road. Violet made quite the production out of greeting everyone who happened by, but Gilbert shifted his gaze back to the road, his thoughts still in a whirl after his run-in with Patience. Clearly, she was angry with him. That much was evident. And he didn't blame her. Not really. Besides, what could he do this late in the game? Nothing would change the past, so why even bother?

CHAPTER TWO

As he passed the Cochrans' sawmill, Gilbert's gaze traveled to the spacious property. He slowed the vehicle down as the mill came into view and then strained to get a better look. The whirring of the log carriage filled the air and, off a bit farther, the familiar whine of the saws as they did their work. Above all, he could smell the pine, strong and earthy. That scent brought him back home in every respect. He slowed, almost to a stop.

"Everything all right, Gil?" his grandmother asked.

"Yes, ma'am." Still, he couldn't manage to speed up, not just yet. And with no other cars on the road behind him, what did it matter?

In the rearview mirror he caught a glimpse of Patience and Adeline approaching the house, and he felt overcome with guilt for having caused Patience so much pain with that ridiculous lawsuit. If only he'd had the courage to tell his uncle he couldn't take it on. But turning down Frederick Sutton was next to impossible. The man was his mentor and guide, after all. And his employer.

Gilbert's gaze traveled up to the ever-present pine trees, their barren branches stretching out in every direction. "I had almost forgotten," he said after reflecting on his surroundings.

"Forgotten what?" His grandmother shifted in her seat.

"How thick the pine trees are. How tucked away in the woods everything seems. I had almost forgotten that in the winter some of the green hangs on to the trees, but most are bare."

"There is no shortage of pine here, that's true."

Gilbert's gaze traveled to the mill, where the workers were busy, the whine of the blades as they bit into the wood ringing out in the otherwise still environment.

That could have been me. The words flitted through his thoughts, though he would never voice them aloud, at least not in front of his grandmother and little sister. No doubt they would be thrilled to have him back at home every day, working at the mill and helping out around the house.

Not that his parents would agree. They were adamant that he make something of his life—something beyond what this little town had to offer. The legal field had called his name, and he'd responded. With great joy and satisfaction, no less. Other than the one infamous lawsuit, his days of writing legal briefs were nothing but pure joy.

And he knew his parents were right. Cut and Shoot had little to offer in the way of employment outside of the lumber business. A few of his friends had ventured down to places like Humble or Spindletop to get into the oil business. But most folks hung tight to their hometown, like children clutching their mothers' apron strings.

He wasn't one of them.

Patience and Adeline rounded the turn onto her property, the hum of the mill's large saws sounding in the distance. It was a familiar sound, a comforting sound.

"A penny for your thoughts," Adeline said as they walked up the drive toward the house.

"Just remembering simpler times, when half the boys in this town ended up working for Daddy at the mill. Now we've lost several of our crew."

"You have?" Adeline paused from walking to give the mill a closer look. "I still see quite a few fellas out there."

"But we've lost enough of them to make things hard on Pa. He told us at dinner last night that Jimmy Durham is headed north to Dallas to be with his mother. She's a widow now, you know."

"I don't remember her, sorry. My summers here were mostly spent playing with you and the other Cochran cousins. And Gil, of course."

"True. Well, I can tell you that Cut and Shoot isn't the simple place it once was. Not even close."

"Small-town drama." Adeline laughed.

"Yes, but I still wouldn't trade it for all the big cities in the world."

"Well, I can tell you—living in the big city myself—that there's a marvelous world out there, Patience." Adeline's eyes lit up. "Ask Gilbert. He'll tell you."

"Gilbert." She did her best not to sigh as she walked toward their expansive white house with its deep green shutters. "What's he got to do with any of this?"

"You know as well as I do that he would have ended up working for your daddy if he'd stayed. He's blessed to get away and work for his uncle in Conroe. You should be happy for him."

"Adeline! I can't believe you're saying that." Patience spoke in a carefully controlled tone to keep the situation from escalating into an argument. "Why does everyone want to leave home?"

"Because we've seen the world and love what we've seen, that's why." Her cousin sniffed. "You haven't experienced it, Patience. I have. I've traveled. I've seen the fashions. The new parasols. The latest model cars, for heaven's sake! There's a new world out there, ready to be explored."

"If you dislike our little town so much, why are you here?" She paused just short of her home's front steps and planted her balled fist on her hip.

"To see you, silly." Adeline transferred her heavy basket to her other arm. "I would cross the Atlantic to spend time with you."

Patience relaxed a little. "Even if it's a tiny town in the boonies?"

Adeline shrugged. "You have to admit, there's not much to recommend the area. Pine trees. The world's smallest and most ill-stocked mercantile. A shocking lack of transportation."

"We have a new post office, and a restaurant just a few miles away. And the Community House is—"

"Worth fighting over, apparently." Adeline made her way up the front steps. "Isn't that where the big shoot-out took place?"

"It wasn't a shoot-out." Patience sighed.

"But you said yourself there were guns drawn."

"Yes. Could we change the subject, please? I don't want to talk about any of this in front of Granny. She gets so upset."

"I won't," Adeline promised. "But I want you to know I don't blame Gil for leaving."

"Well, I do." But Patience didn't want to argue about it.

She opened the front door of the house, and they stepped inside. At once she noticed the quilt slung over the banister railing. The

Round Robin. The one the town's women had started before the big quarrel. Granny must've pulled it out for some reason, but it wasn't like her to leave things lying around like this.

As they crossed the parlor headed toward the kitchen with the groceries, Adeline stopped abruptly. "Oh, Patience! I've had the best idea ever. It's the only way to convince you."

"Convince me of what?"

"That there's a bigger world out there. After Christmas, you simply must come to Houston with me. Stay for a few weeks, or even a few months. You'll see!"

"Me? In Houston?" She fought the temptation to laugh at such a notion.

"Yes! We have the finest department stores in the state of Texas, you know."

"I'm not much for shopping."

"You will be. And besides, what kind of fella are you going to find in a place like this, anyway?" Adeline asked.

"I'll have you know Jimmy Durham invited me to sit next to him at the fall festival."

A playful look came over Adeline's face. "Isn't he the boy who used to eat bugs?"

"Well, yes, but that was a long time ago."

"And didn't you say he's about to move to Dallas to be with his widowed mother?"

Patience sighed. "Yes."

"Well, there goes the town's most eligible bachelor."

"Very funny." She moved toward the kitchen door.

Adeline didn't budge. "Honestly? I cannot understand why some handsome fellow hasn't marched in here and swept you away to a life of marital bliss."

"What?" Patience stopped short, shocked by her cousin's words.

"No worries! I'll find you a husband in no time in Houston."

"I really don't think I—"

"*Mmm.* Granny's making chicken and dumplings. I'd recognize that smell anywhere." Adeline pushed the kitchen door open and stepped inside. Patience followed on her heels.

They found their grandmother rolling out dumplings on the floured workspace on her counter. Patience set the groceries down and filled her in on the latest happenings in town, sharing about their encounter with Gilbert and his family.

"I was afraid of that," Granny said as she reached into the basket to unload the groceries. "If I hadn't needed extra flour and baking powder so badly, I never would have sent you. I'm sorry if it was uncomfortable."

"It was delightful!" Adeline beamed. "We met a handsome stranger."

"Did he, by chance, have remnants of my apple pie?" Granny continued emptying the basket.

"Not that I recall," Adeline said. "When I saw him, his hands were empty. He didn't look at all like a pie thief."

"This was a young man, well-dressed," Patience explained. "He was in the store making some purchases. But we saw the drifter too. The one Pa suspected of stealing the pie. He was walking down the road all by his lonesome."

"With a pie in hand?"

"No, ma'am." She shook her head. "Maybe Goldie got to your pie. Did you think of that?"

"No, but that pooch has never stolen food in the past." Granny reached for Adeline's basket. "Oh, speaking of Goldie, she had her puppies while you were gone."

"What?" Patience gasped. "And I missed it."

"She's doing fine. Ernest hasn't left her side. He's like a doting mother."

A sad way to describe a boy who had spent most of his life without a mama.

"I haven't been out to see them yet, but Ernest tells me she had six of them," Granny explained. "Four males and two females. One of them—the runt—isn't doing well. We'll be hard-pressed to pry your little brother away from them, even for my chicken and dumplings."

"I'll go get him and check on the pups. And I can take some warm milk for Goldie." Patience pulled out a pan and filled it with milk, then set it on the stove. She turned back to her cousin. "See, Adeline? Exciting things happen here too. Not just in the big city."

"Who's talking about the big city?" Granny asked.

"Adeline was trying to convince me that Houston has more to offer than Cut and Shoot," Patience explained.

"And I was doing a fine job of it too," Adeline countered.

"Houston. *Humph!* The devil's playground! Why, the big city has nothing to offer but crime, greed, and degradation!" Granny moved the empty baskets off the counter.

Adeline looked shocked. "That has not been my experience at all, Granny."

"I've read the papers. The big city is a seedy place, riddled with pickpockets and thieves lurking in dark alleys, ready to pounce on the first unsuspecting victim."

"My stars." Adeline giggled. "You make it sound so exciting, Granny. Maybe you really have been reading those dime novels, like Patience said."

Granny's eyes grew wide. "Patience said I've been reading dime novels?"

Oh dear.

Adeline nodded, clearly amused with herself for telling on Patience. "She told everyone in the mercantile all about it."

Patience jabbed her cousin with her elbow.

"Patience Noel! Whatever would possess you to say such a thing?" Her grandmother's cheeks flamed pink.

"I'm sorry. It was all a big misunderstanding," she said.

"There's no shame in reading, and I highly recommend dime novels. They're loaded with adventure." Adeline turned to face Patience. "You should read a few before coming to live with me in Houston. They will prepare you."

"You're moving to Houston?" Their grandmother did not look pleased with this news.

"No," Patience said. "Just wishful thinking on Adeline's part."

"Don't you dare," Granny admonished. "I don't think my heart could bear it. Not after all we've been through this year."

"I'll convince you," Adeline whispered. "Just wait and see."

Patience refused to respond. Instead, she poured the warmed milk into a bowl, ready to head out to tend to Goldie. Only then did she realize her grandmother had grown quiet.

"Are you all right, Granny? I'm not really leaving, you know."

"Well, that's good. But I'm still not sure I'll feel up to celebrating this Christmas season, even with the whole family gathered around." Granny turned her attention back to the pot of chicken and dumplings.

"Why?" Adeline asked. "Christmas is your very favorite time of year. I've always loved coming to visit for the holidays because you make them so special."

"Used to be my favorite." Granny rolled out the dumplings.

Adeline reached to take a pinch of the dough, but Granny slapped her hand away.

"Why are you so down in the dumps?" Patience asked.

Granny sighed and plopped a couple of dumplings into the pot of boiling chicken broth. She brushed her hands on her apron, then turned to face them. "I've been quilting all afternoon. I decided I'd finally finish my bluebonnet square on the Round Robin."

"We saw it on the banister," Patience said. "It's beautiful."

"I haven't set eyes on it since last summer. Mine was the only block unfinished." Granny's words drifted off, and she plopped a few more dumplings into the broth. "But after everything fell apart, I didn't see the point in finishing it. So I put it in my cedar chest. Out of sight, out of mind."

"Until today?" Adeline asked.

"Yes." Granny nodded.

"I'm glad you're working on it," Patience said. "About time, I'd say."

"It was a bad idea." Granny shook her head and returned to her work. "I thought my heart was ready, but clearly it's not. Working on it has made me sad. Very sad. So I set it aside."

"But it's beautiful, Granny," Patience said again. "I love all the wildflowers."

"Each woman chose her own flower to embroider," Granny explained. "And, like I said, I chose the bluebonnet."

"Your favorite." Patience smiled at her.

"But it's too much for me to handle. I can't bear to look at it. I plan to take it back upstairs after supper. I'll return it to the cedar chest, where I don't have to look at it or think about it."

"You should finish your square," Patience encouraged her. "Even if it's difficult. I think it will do you good."

She thought about her grandmother's words as she and Adeline made their way to the barn with the warm milk. They visited with Ernest and spent several minutes with the pups, making sure they were clean and warm, then headed back to the house to see if their grandmother needed help in the kitchen.

Patience's father arrived just as they set the table. Ernest showed up a couple of minutes later, at five o'clock straight up. The Cochrans were nothing if not prompt. Supper was served every evening at five, rain or shine.

As they took their seats at the table, a knock sounded at the door. Granny tried to rise from her chair, but Adeline gestured for her to remain seated.

"I'll get it, Granny." Adeline sprang up and bounded to the door. A moment later she arrived back in the room, eyes wide as she led in their guest—the handsome stranger from the store.

"I hope you don't mind that I showed up unannounced." He pulled off his hat and held it in front of him. "I was headed back home to Conroe, but my Cadillac broke down on the side of the road. Just a flat tire, but it's so dark I can't see to change it. I was hoping you might have a lantern I could use."

"It's mighty cold to be out on a night like this," Pa observed. "Come on in, and I'll help you with that tire after supper."

"Yes, could we offer you something warm to eat?" Adeline's lips curled up in a smile. "We were just about to enjoy some chicken and dumplings. Granny makes 'em extra special."

"Well, sure, if you don't think it would be an inconvenience. A few minutes in a warm house sounds mighty good right about now." He extended his hand. "Daniel Jennings. I write for the *Conroe Tribune*."

"You've come a few miles for a story, son." Pa gestured to the empty spot at the table.

"Not that far by car," he countered, "though I did see a drifter walking just up the road a piece. I'm sure he's wishing he were someplace warm about now." He reached for the back of the chair, his gaze on the pot of chicken and dumplings.

During their meal, Daniel regaled them with tales of stories he'd written for the *Conroe Tribune* over the past few months. Was it Patience's imagination, or was he gazing directly at her as he carried on about his exciting job?

Adeline must've assumed the same thing about herself. She elbowed Patience and whispered, "Look at what heaven just dropped on our front doorstep."

"And you thought nothing fun ever happened in a small town," Patience whispered in response.

Granny seemed a bit confused by this stranger at their table. More than once, she referred to him as Gilbert. Patience would have to explain her grandmother's forgetfulness later.

After they'd finished up the dumplings, Granny rose and took the bowl to the kitchen. No doubt she would return momentarily with dessert.

"Tell me about that beautiful quilt I saw on the banister," Daniel said. "My grandmother is a quilter, and I recognize a Round Robin when I see it."

"The women of the town started it last summer," Patience explained. "Each one chose a different flower to embroider."

"Granny is the last to finish hers," Adeline said. "But she was working on it today. Hers is the bluebonnet square."

Patience spoke before she thought. "I hope this isn't the last one the women do together."

"Oh?" Daniel looked surprised. "Is there a reason it would be?"

"Well..." She'd better not go into detail about how the ladies felt about each other now.

Unfortunately, Adeline didn't hesitate to tell him about how the quilt had been used to wrap knives and guns on that infamous day and how the women took sides and no longer spoke to one another.

"So, what you're telling me is, a quilt that was supposed to bring them together actually tore them apart?" Daniel leaned back in his chair. "Interesting."

"It wasn't the quilt that tore them apart," Patience said. "But I'm afraid it has a place in the disagreement."

Her pa cleared his throat, and she decided she'd shared enough of their story with this man. After all, they barely knew him.

Just as Granny brought out a beautiful coconut cake and set it on the table, a rap sounded at the door. Patience rose to see who else might be stopping by on this very busy night. She passed by the quilt on the banister, wishing Adeline hadn't shared so much of its story with Daniel.

Patience reached to open the door and discovered a small group of the town's children outside. The moment they saw her they burst into a rousing chorus of "O Come, All Ye Faithful."

Patience saw that Gil was standing in the midst of them. He glanced her way. My goodness, he looked pleased to see her. His boisterous baritone voice rang out above the others. She tried not to react, but she knew the edges of her lips betrayed her.

Adeline and Daniel appeared next to her moments later. Daniel stood beside the banister, his gaze shifting back and forth from the quilt to the crowd of children. Moments later, Pa, Ernest, and Granny entered the tiny foyer, a captivated audience as the children's voices rose in song. They all offered hearty applause when the song ended.

"Come in, come in!" Patience said.

"Yes, I'll make hot chocolate," Adeline added. "Come in out of the cold, children."

When they stepped inside the foyer, a lone person at the rear of the crowd eased her way in behind the others. Florence Sutton. Granny took one look at her old friend and paled. She took a couple of steps backward.

Florence moved to the quilt hanging over the banister and fingered the square with the bluebonnets embroidered on it. "Oh, Myrtle Mae! You've been working on the Round Robin. I'm so glad.

I know how much you've always loved Texas bluebonnets in the springtime."

"Yes, well..." Granny's words trailed off. "Not a project I plan to finish anytime soon." She turned around and marched through the parlor, headed to the kitchen.

Florence's expression shifted from a smile to a frown.

Daniel excused himself to work on his flat tire. Pa offered to help him, but the young man insisted he could handle it on his own, now that his stomach and heart were full. Off he went, into the dark of night.

Patience joined Gilbert and the others in the parlor, where Ernest made an announcement.

"We have new puppies!"

The children all decided they needed to see the new pups. Violet, in particular, couldn't wait. Ernest led the way toward the front door.

When Granny entered the parlor with hot chocolate in hand, Florence and Gil were seated next to Pa on the sofa. She put the tray on the small table in front of them, then turned and walked straight back into the kitchen.

Florence took a cup of chocolate but barely had a sip before setting it down again. "I'm not feeling well, Gil. Could I wait in the car?"

"Of course. Will you be warm enough?"

"I will be fine." She shot a glance in the direction of the kitchen door.

Several minutes later the children returned, abuzz with excitement over what they'd seen. All but Ernest and Violet, who apparently could not be persuaded to leave the pups to join the others.

After the children drank their hot cocoa and wolfed down some of Granny Cochran's oatmeal cookies, Gil said it was time to move on.

"This was our last stop," he explained. "I need to get these kiddos home."

Just as he rose, they heard a noise in the foyer that sounded like the door opening. Had Ernest and Violet come inside after all, or was it Daniel, looking for help with the tire?

"Do you think Florence is coming back in?" Granny asked. She rose and looked as if she might head to the kitchen if that was the case.

"No," Gilbert said. "I suspect she's still in the car."

"But I heard someone open the door." Granny rose and walked to the foyer. A few minutes later, a cry rang out. "Oh no!"

Patience rose and raced to her grandmother's side. "What is it, Granny? Are you unwell?"

"I'm in perfect health." Granny pointed at the banister. "But don't you see? Someone has stolen the Round Robin quilt!"

CHAPTER THREE

"Are you all right, Grandma?" Gilbert asked when he opened the door to his vehicle.

"Just take me home."

"But I need to drop off a couple of the children before—"

"Fine, but don't dillydally. I want to get home as soon as possible."

"I understand. But you're acting mighty strange."

"How do you expect me to act?" Her voice broke. "My best friend made me feel unwelcome in her home after I came to mend fences. I'm brokenhearted right now, Gil."

"I understand."

"Nothing felt right after seeing that quilt on the banister. It brought back far too many memories. I had just given it to Myrtle Mae the Sunday before that awful day for her to take her turn. I hadn't seen it since."

"Oh, I see. And you feel it belongs to you?"

"No. It belongs to all of us, and it reminded me of what things used to be like, when we all got along. But we didn't stitch those blocks together to see them wrapped around guns and knives, which is exactly what happened that day."

"Who used it for that?" he asked.

"Someone in the Cochran family."

"Surely you don't think Myrtle Mae Cochran wrapped guns and knives in that quilt with the intention of harming someone."

"I'm not saying she did it, just that whoever did was out of line. And I told her so. None of us have seen it since."

"Until tonight," he said.

"Until tonight," his grandmother echoed. "And there it was on the banister, taunting me. So could you please take me home?"

"I'm just waiting on the children. I think Violet took them back to the barn to say good night to the pups."

"Go fetch them, Gil. I don't want to stay here one moment longer. I just want my own home, my own bed."

"I understand." He opened the car door and got out, then took several long strides in the dark toward the barn. His thoughts were firmly affixed to the pain his grandmother was in right now. This rift between friends ran deeper than he realized, and clearly that quilt played a role, strange as it might seem to him.

Guilt wriggled its way down his spine as he thought about the lawsuit he had helped file. No doubt it was the straw that broke the camel's back.

Thank goodness Violet came sprinting toward him, leading the pack of youngsters. "We're coming, Gil!"

"Grandma is ready to go," he explained.

"All right." She took hold of his hand. "You should see the pups—they're so sweet. Do you think Mama will let me have one?"

He wanted to say, "Not when she hears it's a Cochran pup" but didn't. Instead, he simply said, "Let's ask her. Maybe."

"I hope so. I've already picked one, a little spotted one."

"Spotted one? But Goldie is..."

"I know. She's a golden retriever. But there's a precious little spotted pup who doesn't fit in."

He understood that feeling.

The children squeezed themselves into the car, and Violet was all abuzz with chatter about the dogs. Unfortunately, his grandmother wasn't feeling as chatty.

"Sweet girl, I know you're excited, but Grandma just needs some peace and quiet right now."

"Are you upset?" Violet asked.

"I'm fine," she said.

Still, if her gruff tone was any indication, she was anything but.

"Granny, are you all right?" Patience chose her words carefully, knowing perfectly well her grandmother was upset.

"No, I'm not all right." Granny paced the foyer. "The quilt was right there, hanging over the railing."

"Are you certain?" Adeline asked. "Maybe you moved it but don't remember?"

"Of course I'm certain. I'm as certain as I'm standing here, it was on this railing before they arrived. Don't you remember seeing it?"

"Yes, I remember," she said.

"I never thought Florence capable of this." Granny pinched her eyes shut and then opened them again. "But now I see the reason she came—not to encourage me, not to make amends—but to steal the quilt that she feels belongs to her."

"You think Florence stole the quilt?" Patience asked.

"Well, of course. It's as plain as the nose on my face. She couldn't even stick around for a few minutes. When she disappeared, the quilt left with her. It's the logical conclusion."

Patience's father didn't seem convinced. "Ma, I don't think Florence would do such a thing."

"She's always been your best friend," Adeline reminded her. "Right?"

"Was," Granny said. "But no more. Florence and her crew were angry that I took longer than they thought I should to stitch my bluebonnet. But it was my turn to have it. Was it my fault I happened to have it in my possession on the day the fight broke out?"

"I think she was upset that it ended up being used to wrap weapons," Patience reminded her. "That's the main thing."

"We didn't plan on using them," her father explained. "And no harm came of it."

Patience agreed, though she would rather there had been no weapons that day at all.

"That quilt was supposed to bring us together. It only tore us further apart." Granny eased her way up the stairs, and Patience heard her mutter, "I knew I should've left it in the cedar chest."

Adeline disappeared into the parlor with Ernest, who was wanting more hot chocolate. Patience stood in the foyer with her father, hoping they could make sense of all this.

"It's just too much, Pa." She fought the temptation to sigh. "I'm so sad that the quilt was stolen."

"Maybe it wasn't," he said. "I've been worried about your grandmother for some time now. She's getting more and more—"

"Forgetful." Patience nodded. She had noticed. "First the pie. Now the quilt?"

"I'm not altogether sure the pie was really stolen," he said. "Though I would never tell her that."

"Are you thinking she misplaced it somewhere around the house?" Patience asked.

"Who knows? Maybe it will turn up in the linen closet. With the quilt." He paced the foyer, and she could read the sadness in his expression. "But before we blame it on her forgetfulness, let's piece this together. I need to finish my coffee before it gets cold, so let's discuss this in the other room."

"All right." She followed him into the parlor, where they found Adeline and Ernest deep in conversation about the puppies.

Her father eased his way into his favorite chair. "First, are we absolutely sure the quilt was on the banister when the carolers arrived?"

"It was," Patience said. "I remember specifically, because Florence said how glad she was that Granny was finishing her square."

"I suppose she is the most logical person to suspect," Pa said. "She's a Sutton, after all."

"But, Pa, Florence hasn't stolen anything before," Patience said. "What makes you think she—"

"I'm not saying I believe it, but these are strange and unusual times we are living in. Trust no one, especially those Suttons. They are capable of far more than we know, if last summer was any indicator."

"My goodness." Patience now felt the need to sit. She eased her way down onto the sofa. Should she remind Pa that the Cochrans had behaved poorly last summer as well? Did he only see one side in this?

"Then there's that reporter." Pa took a sip of his coffee and leaned back in his chair.

"Daniel?" Adeline looked flabbergasted by this notion. "Whyever would you suspect him?"

"We don't know him," Pa responded. "And he disappeared right after the carolers sang. He didn't even ask for my help with his flat tire. How did he manage to change it alone in the dark?"

"That's right!" Patience paused to think it through. "It must be him. We told him the story of the Round Robin quilt, so he knows its value. He also knows how it was used in the disagreement last summer."

Her father's brow furrowed. "You don't suppose he's stolen it so he can write about it for that newspaper of his, do you?"

Patience shifted her gaze to Adeline, who shrugged and said, "What did I do?"

What, indeed? She had gushed on and on with stories about the quilt, and all in front of that reporter. The idea that he would take advantage of them upset Patience.

Apparently, Pa was upset by the idea as well. "I find it odd that a total stranger shows up at our door and then a quilt goes missing just after. He clearly took an interest in it."

With a wave of her hand, Adeline dismissed this idea. "I think that's just silly. Why on earth would he need to steal it to write about it? I think one of the children took the quilt."

"But why would they do that?" Patience asked.

"You know how children are. Maybe they carried it off to the barn to cover up the puppies."

"I'll go check." Ernest rose. "If there's a quilt on the pups, I'll bring it back. I want to go check on the little runt anyway. But I want to take some more warm milk out for Goldie. Is that all right?"

"Of course." Patience and Pa spoke in unison.

Ernest walked into the kitchen. A few minutes later, they heard him leave through the back door.

The sound of the door reminded Patience of something that had happened earlier.

"We heard someone come in the front door while we were all in the parlor, remember?"

"That's right. Granny went to check on whoever came in when we heard it. That's when she discovered the quilt was gone," Adeline said.

A shiver ran up Patience's spine. "Do you think it's possible someone entered the house and walked off with it?"

"Are you referring to that drifter?" Adeline asked.

"Perhaps?" She shrugged. "Daniel did say he saw him walking down the road near our house just before he arrived, remember?"

Adeline nodded. "That makes a lot more sense than suspecting Daniel. If the drifter was willing to steal a pie, maybe he—"

"Broke into a house to steal a blanket?" Pa shook his head. "Where's the sense in that?"

"Well, it is cold outside," Adeline said.

"But how would a total stranger know there was a quilt draped over the banister just inside the door?" Patience asked. "What's his motivation, other than the cold?"

"Maybe he peeked through the window and saw it?" Adeline suggested. "Or maybe he's not a drifter. Maybe he's someone here to further divide the town. Could be he knows all about the quilt and is working for the Suttons to snatch it back."

That idea gave Patience the chills.

"And you were worried about crime rates in Houston!" Adeline's eyes bugged. "I come all the way here to Cut and Shoot to find out you've got looters and robbers as well."

"I would hardly call a missing quilt a robbery, Adeline," Patience said.

"I still wonder if Ma just misplaced it," Pa said. "Her memory is really failing her lately. I've been very concerned."

"It gives me the willies to think a stranger might've come in the front door while we were all in the parlor," Adeline said.

"If you're right—if there's any chance the drifter is out there, I'd better go fetch Ernest." Pa walked to the coatrack and pulled down his winter coat.

But by the time he got his hat and scarf in place, a noise sounded from the kitchen and Ernest's voice rang out in song. "'Joy to the world, the Lord is come.'"

"Sounds like he's back, Pa."

Ernest burst through the door from the kitchen to the parlor and plopped down onto the sofa. "It's freezing out there!"

"And you went out without a coat!" Patience scolded. "What were you thinking?"

"I was thinking I should take some warm milk to Goldie and check on the runt, of course."

"And look for the quilt?"

"There's no quilt on the pups. I did pack some straw around them to keep them warm."

Pa sighed. "I'm sure it's around here someplace. Let's look for it, shall we? Before bed, I mean."

They spent the next several minutes doing just that. Unfortunately, their search turned up nothing.

Pa finally headed to bed, and Ernest followed behind him up the stairs to his room. Patience and Adeline walked into the kitchen to tidy up. It wasn't like Granny to leave a mess behind, but there were sticky mugs in the sink as well as the empty platter that once held her oatmeal cookies.

Patience got right to work washing the dishes, then passed them off to her cousin to dry.

A couple of minutes into their work, Adeline started giggling.

"What's so funny?" Patience asked.

"Oh, sorry. I was just thinking about those stories Daniel told us. He's so funny. And handsome."

"My goodness. You have a one-track mind."

"So do you, Patience. You're not fooling me."

She lifted her hands from the soapy water and gave her cousin a curious look. "What do you mean by that?"

"You're completely smitten with Gilbert Sutton—feud or no feud. Sparks were flying between you two the whole time he was here."

"You're misreading the situation." She turned quickly to avoid letting her cousin see the heat that had risen to her cheeks at the mention of Gil's name.

"Be honest with yourself, Patience. You're in love with him."

"I...I'm not. That's just silly."

"Then prove it. Come with me to Houston. Let me introduce you to some city fellas for a change."

"I—I can't."

"Because you're not willing to leave Gil behind." Adeline set a dry mug on the countertop.

"No, because Pa needs my help with Ernest. And Granny..." Her words drifted off. "Well, you can see what kind of shape she's in. Someone has to stick around to help. Ever since Mama passed, I..." She let her voice trail to silence.

"I know, you feel responsible. You're the woman of the house."

"Yes," Patience agreed. "That's it, exactly."

"Not everything has to fall to you just because you're a female, Patience. You deserve a life too."

"I have a life."

"Yes, but have you ever traveled? I can take you places you've never seen!"

"Like?"

"Dublin."

"Ireland?" Patience's mouth fell open.

"No, Dublin, Texas. My girlfriends and I drove all the way up there to taste that new fizzy drink that's all the rage. Dr Pepper."

"I've never been to Dublin. But how is the fizzy drink?"

"Medicinal!" Adeline laughed. "It sure gave me a lift!"

Patience needed something to give her a lift right now, but not a fizzy drink. They needed to find her grandmother's quilt, and soon. Before more fuel was added to the Cut and Shoot feud.

"How did it go, Son?" Gil's mother greeted him with a worried expression etched on her face as soon as he arrived home.

"Mostly fine," he said. "But we had a bit of an incident at the end."

"Let me guess. At the Cochrans' house?"

"Yes."

"Where's your grandmother?" His mama peered out the door.

"She and Violet are in the car still talking about puppies. The Cochrans' dog just gave birth today. Brace yourself. I think Grandma is helping Violet come up with a way to ask you for one of them."

"Oh no." Mama's eyes widened. "Your father will never go for that. Remember the rabbit we took in last spring?"

"Boy, do I ever."

"Your father isn't an animal lover, Son. So I'm afraid the pup will not be coming here. And do I need to remind you that it's a Cochran animal? Your father most assuredly won't allow that, trust me."

Grandma made her way inside with Violet trailing behind her and still carrying on about the puppies.

"You should've seen them, Mama!" Violet said. "So tiny and cute! And their little eyes are sealed shut. They won't open for a week. But they should be open in time for Christmas."

"That's nice," their mother responded.

"Well, I'm going to bed." Violet skipped up the steps.

"I'm worn out myself," Grandma said. "But I would love something warm to drink. I wasn't feeling up to hot chocolate over at . . ." She couldn't finish the sentence, but the words "the Cochrans'" hung in the air between them all.

"Let me get that for you, Mother Sutton," Gil's mother said as she took a few steps toward the kitchen.

"No, if you don't mind, I'll just fetch it myself. Might do me good to spend a few minutes alone, if you don't mind."

"I don't mind a bit, as long as you're all right."

"Just fine and dandy."

Gil wasn't so sure about that, but his grandmother disappeared into the kitchen before he could say so. He turned to his mother with a shrug. "She's been acting funny ever since we left the Cochrans' place." He looked around. "Where's Pa?"

"He went to bed early. He's got another one of those headaches of his."

"What does the doc say?"

"That he's got to take it easy. Try not to let the stresses of life get him worked up. But for your father, that's—"

"Impossible."

"Yes." His mother sat down in her favorite armchair. "Which is exactly why I'm glad he's already in bed and not here to ask questions about the caroling tonight. The whole thing upset him."

"That we went?"

She released a lingering sigh. "I guess. Though he always loved caroling in years past, so I think he's torn about how this awful situation will end. We can't keep going like this. The town is too deeply divided to come together on even the simplest of things. Shopping on certain days of the week. Caroling in smaller numbers to avoid being around those you don't like. It's so depressing."

"Agreed." Still, he didn't know how to fix it.

A noise sounded from the kitchen. Sounded like his grandmother had opened the back door for some reason.

"Why is she going outside?" Gil's mother asked.

"I have no idea, but I'll find out." Gil rose and walked into the kitchen. Sure enough, Grandma Sutton was nowhere to be found. He peered through the window and strained to see her but could not under the shadows of night. He stepped out onto the back stoop and called her name.

"I'm here, Gil." She came hobbling his way, shivering as she approached.

"What in the world are you doing out here, Grandma?"

"I left my scarf in the Walkaround."

"I would have gotten it for you."

She stepped inside and slung the scarf around her neck. "I'm surely capable of fetching my own scarf. When I reach the point where I am not, I'll let you know. In the meantime, as I said before, I needed a few minutes to myself to collect my thoughts. I don't often get that around here."

Well, now. He felt good and truly told off.

His grandmother walked into the kitchen just as the teakettle on the stove began to whistle. She reached for a cup with one hand and the kettle with the other and said, "Just in time."

Still, he couldn't help but think that something about her behavior tonight seemed mighty peculiar.

CHAPTER FOUR

Patience awoke earlier than usual on Sunday morning. Out of the corner of her eye, she caught a glimpse of Adeline in bed next to her, sleeping soundly. She eased her way out from under the covers, shivering when her feet hit the floor.

After reaching for her robe, she slipped on her house shoes and padded down the stairs. Her fingers trailed the banister where she had last seen the Round Robin quilt. Hopefully it would turn up today. Granny had probably tucked it away in some obscure place and forgotten about it. Things like that seemed to be happening a lot lately.

In the meantime, she would get some coffee brewing and start on the bacon. Granny would be relieved not to have to do that.

Patience wrapped the robe tighter around herself and made her way into the kitchen, where she found her grandmother fully dressed and pulling out the cast-iron skillet.

"Granny, you're up early."

"Couldn't sleep." Granny placed the skillet on the stove and walked to the icebox.

"Still fretting over the quilt?"

She nodded, and moisture filled her eyes.

"Maybe it's just been misplaced," Patience suggested.

"Maybe."

"I saw it on the stair railing, like you said. But maybe you moved it and simply don't remember? I do things like that all the time."

"That's what I'm worried about, actually. I checked the cedar chest, just to make sure, but it's not there. I even looked on every bed, thinking maybe someone had taken it to sleep with. But it's not here, Patience. It's truly gone for good. And I'm sure I know who took it. We can't deny the obvious when it's staring us in the face."

Patience walked to the counter to the bin that held the coffee grounds. She filled the percolator, then added water and placed it on the stove next to the skillet.

"Granny, surely you don't really believe that Florence Sutton is capable of thievery."

"She wanted that quilt. She as much as told me so." Granny cut thick slices of bacon and placed them in the skillet, where they began to sizzle.

"But you've known Florence since you were children. You know her better than anyone. You can't truly believe she's capable of such a thing."

"I didn't think that any of the folks in this town were capable of wrongdoing until last summer. That awful day changed me. It's made me doubt everyone and everything."

"But Granny—"

"What kind of world do we live in, where people don't get along? What sort of town are we leaving behind for our children and grandchildren? That's what I want to know."

"Things will settle down. And the children are already leading the way. You heard them singing last night, Granny, their voices all blended in harmony. They're willing to work together. We should be too." She sniffed the air as the delicious aroma of bacon permeated the room.

"As soon as I get that quilt back from Florence, I'll think about it." Her grandmother dropped another thick slab of bacon into the hot pan. "In the meantime, I'm going to call the sheriff."

"And tell him that a quilt is missing? Do you really think he would care about such a thing?"

"I told him about the pie."

"I'm sure he blamed that on the sawmill workers. He'll probably do the same with the quilt."

"We'll see." Granny walked to the cupboard and retrieved a basket. She folded back the cloth in the basket, then turned to face Patience, eyes wide. "Patience, where are the biscuits?"

"What biscuits?"

"The ones left over from dinner last night. I wrapped them up and put them in this basket so I wouldn't have to bake again this morning. Someone has taken them." She held up the basket to prove her point. Sure enough, it was as empty as could be.

"I'm sorry, I have no recollection of biscuits, Granny. But I was pretty distracted last night."

"I know for a fact we had five biscuits left over, just enough for breakfast. I was planning to make gravy from the bacon fat, but there's no reason to do so if there are no biscuits."

Patience hardly knew what to say. Maybe Pa was right. Maybe Granny's memory was in worse shape than they realized.

"We have bread, Granny. I'll make toast. It will be perfect with the bacon and the gravy too."

"What sort of thieves do we have lurking about, to steal our food and my quilt?"

Did Granny really think the quilt belonged to her? Sure sounded like it.

"First my pie, now my biscuits." Granny paused, and her eyes took on a faraway look. "This makes me wonder if that drifter is still afoot. He is a food thief, after all."

"You think he came into our house and stole your biscuits? And the quilt?" Patience sliced the bread and reached for the butter. "Granny, he would have to be Houdini not to get caught. I can't imagine he came into the house."

"Well, I can." Granny waggled her finger at Patience. "He was here, on the property, yesterday afternoon. The foreman shooed him away, remember? He asked about a job."

"Did Pa offer to hire him?" Patience asked.

"I did not." Her father's voice sounded from the back door, where he stomped his boots on the mat to clean them off before stepping inside. "Ma, are you saying the drifter has been inside our house?"

"The biscuits are missing, Son." She held up the basket to show him. "I placed five in this basket after dinner last night. And now they're missing."

"I'm making toast." Patience continued to spread butter on the bread. "We'll have a good breakfast, all the same."

"And we're of the opinion that the drifter somehow managed to accomplish this?" her father asked.

"Jeb said he was lurking around, asking about work."

Pa shrugged. "He never came to me personally, so all I have to go on is what Jeb told me. I only saw the fella from a distance, and he skedaddled quick when I headed his way."

"So you chased him off?" Patience asked.

"No, I would have spoken to the man. If he needed work—or something to eat—I would have considered it. But right now, he's looking and acting more like a vagrant and less like a potential employee. His behavior—leaving as quickly as he did—leads me to believe he didn't really want to work at all."

"A vagrant...and a thief," Granny said.

Adeline entered the kitchen dressed in a frilly pink robe with excessive embroidery. "Another thief?"

"The biscuits are missing!" Granny held up the basket again, but it slipped out of her hand and hit the floor.

Adeline stared at it, clearly confused. "Well, surely you don't think Florence Sutton stole those too!"

After breakfast they loaded up in the wagon to ride to church. They arrived early, as was often the case, and Pa headed over to meet with the menfolk while Granny scurried off to talk to her friends, no doubt about the missing quilt.

The rustic, wood-framed Community House hadn't changed much over the years. Indeed, it seemed as if it remained every bit the same as Patience had always known it to be from her childhood. She loved this little building. Stepping inside brought a rush of warmth to her soul, and so many blissful memories washed over her. She saw herself as a pesky little girl once more, whispering to her friends in the rear pew. Ill-tempered pigtails had adorned her head back then. These days, she wore her auburn hair twisted up in a chignon.

But goodness, what precious, simple times she had known as a child in this blessed place. To think that this very building was now the reason for so much division. She couldn't bear it.

Patience swallowed hard, determined not to think about that right now. Instead, she hoped to answer the question about what the reporter happened to be doing standing in the middle of the meeting hall.

Adeline noticed him too. She jabbed Patience in the ribs with her elbow. "Patience, look who's here!" Her excited cousin pointed to where the young reporter stood visiting with Pastor Everson. She turned back to Patience, eyes wide. "How do I look? Is my hair all right?" She pinched her cheeks.

Before Patience could answer, Adeline made a beeline across the room to Daniel's side. Less than a minute later, she had fully engaged him in conversation. The pastor quickly moved on to another parishioner.

Patience decided she'd better join in the conversation to keep Adeline from making a silly goose of herself. And she might just take this opportunity to question Daniel about the missing quilt. Surely she could do so in a way that did not sound accusatory, though she secretly wondered if he had absconded with it to use in some story he might be cooking up.

He seemed more interested in asking questions about the Community House. He swept the room with his gaze. "So, this is where the infamous brouhaha took place."

"Brouhaha?" Adeline's laughter trilled across the room, garnering the attention of many nearby. "What a word. I love it."

"The scandal, if you prefer," he said.

"I do not prefer a scandal, unless it has something to do with the latest fashions from Paris or New York," Adeline said.

"I meant the big split took place here in this building." He gestured to the small area with its rustic wood floors and planked seating. "I pictured it differently. This church building is nothing like the ones I've visited in Conroe."

"It's a country church," Patience responded. "And doubles as a schoolhouse."

"It's nothing like my church in Houston either," Adeline agreed. "Back home, we're all stained glass and steeples."

"I think it's very homey," Patience argued. "And many wonderful things have happened in this room, so I'm happy with it as it is."

"A few not-so-wonderful things too." Daniel glanced toward the door. "So, when does the Sutton clan have their church meeting?"

"As soon as we Cochrans finish. That has been our arrangement for some time now," Patience explained. "But it's not just the Suttons. Nearly half the town attends their service. The other half attends ours."

"Remind me again what happened that day?" He pulled out a tablet and pencil.

Oh, no. He wasn't getting any more information out of them. "I'm sorry, but church is about to begin." Patience shut her lips firmly.

"Service isn't starting for fifteen minutes," Adeline said. "We have plenty of time."

Patience fought the temptation to sigh aloud. On the other hand, if this reporter wanted a story about what happened that horrible day, she would give him the real one—from her point of view, anyway. At least he would have his facts straight.

"Back in July, the folks in town were divided in opinion about the use of this building." She gestured to the humble meetinghouse room. "We had an understanding, I guess you could say, that any denomination could use the building with the exception of two that were believed to be…"

"Unacceptable?"

"Yes. And a certain pastor belonging to one of the two asked to use the building."

"What group was he with?" Daniel looked up from his tablet.

"The Apostolics," she said. "Anyway, I believe the discord came more as a result of the specific pastor in question than the group itself. There was a rumor that Pastor Stamps had, shall we say, a history."

"This is the most exciting part." Adeline rested her hand on her heart, her eyes widening, and she whispered, "They said the man frequented saloons."

"Yes, and I believe there was dancing involved in his story," Patience added.

"Heavens, no. Not *that.*" Daniel's lips curled up in a smile. "Dancing?"

"Anyway, half the townspeople believed the man had no right to use the building. And the other half—"

"Wait." Daniel raised his hand. "Which side was your family on?"

Patience straightened her shoulders. "We believed that the rumors were just that. Rumors. We thought it only fair to give the man a chance. Others who were not so charitable—"

"You're referring to the congregation that meets after yours."

"Yes. On the big day, well..."

"Oh, I know what happened that day." Daniel stopped writing and looked her in the eye. "Stamps was locked out."

"Yes." She glanced her father's direction, then looked back at Daniel. "We were locked out of our own meetinghouse."

"And half the town was very angry about that," he said. "Do I have that right?"

"Isn't it all so silly?" Adeline rolled her eyes. "I don't know why they can't just get along."

"Anyway..." Patience lowered her voice as the pastor happened by once more. "Both sides showed up armed with guns and knives."

"And I believe your side had them wrapped in quilts like the Round Robin your grandmother is working on."

"Yes..." She paused as he mentioned the Round Robin. "No one was harmed that day, and we ended up gathering under a tree to hear Pastor Stamps preach."

"The old tree-stump church meeting, then?" He smiled. "I've heard of those."

"Yes. But a rift grew up between the families that has had lasting consequences."

Before she could say anything else, the pastor took his place at the front of the room and called the congregation to their seats. Adeline invited Daniel to join them, and before Patience could dispute the idea, the man was tightly pressed into the spot between them. Adeline didn't seem to mind one little bit, but the whole thing felt awkward to Patience, what with Pa and Granny both shooting glances her way from their places on her left.

She did her best to focus on the pastor's message. He was spending the entire month of December addressing the nativity, and today he was focusing on "no room at the inn."

Her heart twisted as she thought about Mary and Joseph struggling to find a place to rest on the night baby Jesus was born.

"We need to make room in our hearts for the Savior," Pastor Everson said as he concluded. "And room for others too. Even those we don't always agree with."

Oh my. Granny wouldn't be happy about that last statement, now would she?

Gilbert pulled up in front of the meetinghouse with his family members in tow. They arrived just as the morning congregation poured out of the building. His parents refused to budge from the car until the crowd cleared. He knew the process would take a few minutes, but he didn't let that stop him from getting out.

His grandmother and Violet joined him on the church lawn, and they watched as the Cochrans headed down the front steps of the meetinghouse toward their wagon.

"Who's that fella?" His grandmother pointed at Daniel Jennings.

"I saw him at the Cochrans' last night." Violet looked a bit swoony. "I think he looks like a hero from a storybook. So handsome."

"Hardly a hero," Gilbert said. "I know him. He's a bit of a troublemaker back in Conroe."

"How so?" his grandmother asked.

"He cozies up to people to get stories for the paper. Salacious stories. I don't trust him at all."

"You should tell Adeline," Violet said. "Because she seems to be very chatty with him."

Yes, she did. And Patience appeared to be at ease around him too. So did her grandmother, who walked up just then and joined her granddaughters in conversation with him.

His own grandmother took one look at Myrtle Mae Cochran and headed straight back to the car.

"Grandma, where are you going?" he called out.

"I'll just wait in the car until after she's gone. Then I'll come inside."

Gilbert shook his head and walked in the direction of the Cochran clan. After a moment he managed to get Patience's attention.

"Gil?" She took a few steps in his direction and gave him a curious look. "You're early for church."

"Just by a few minutes." He kept his voice low. "But I'm glad I caught you. I wanted to mention something, just so you're aware."

"What's that?" Her brow wrinkled in confusion.

"You might want to tell your cousin to steer clear of Daniel Jennings."

"What? Why?"

"I'm just saying, you might tell Adeline not to get too close to that one. Where there's smoke, there's—"

"As if I could tell Adeline anything. You know her nearly as well as I do from all the summers we spent together as children. Has she ever *once* done anything I've asked her to do?"

He paused to think about it, then responded with a quiet, "No."

"Well then, what makes you think anything has changed?"

"She's a beautiful young woman. I'm just afraid—"

"Yes, she's very pretty." Patience seemed a bit put off as she spoke the words. "That's sure and certain."

"Just ask her to be careful, Patience. He has a reputation. That's all. And be careful what you tell him. I've known him to twist stories around and then put the twisted version in print."

Her eyes widened, and she looked a bit concerned by this revelation. Just as quickly, she seemed to take a different stance. "I'm a big girl, Gil. I can take care of myself."

She might be. But that didn't stop him from wanting to protect her with everything inside of him.

"You left in a hurry last night," she said.

"Yes, well, I had no choice," he responded. "You can't begin to imagine how upset my grandmother was when we left your place. I could hardly get a word out of her."

"She's not the only one who was upset. Granny went straight up to her room. She was so upset that the quilt is missing."

"The quilt is missing?"

"Yes, and Granny is beside herself."

He paused to think this through. As if they needed more trouble.

"I hate that the quilt has brought further division, but you have to understand how high emotions have been since that awful day,"

Patience said. "I have to believe the missing quilt is some sort of a statement that the feud isn't over."

"Someone stole the quilt to keep the feud alive?" That didn't seem reasonable to him.

Still, from the determined look on Patience's face, he could tell it seemed reasonable to her. And right now, all that mattered was making sure she knew he wasn't the enemy.

CHAPTER FIVE

On Monday morning Patience awoke to frost on the windows. She bounded from bed and peered through the glass, trying to see past it.

"Look, Adeline! There's frost on the windowpanes. Do you think we'll have a white Christmas this year?"

"In Texas?" Her cousin burrowed under the covers, shivering. "Never! And besides, Christmas is still more than a week away. Knowing Texas, it'll probably be ninety degrees by then."

"True." Texas weather did change on a dime. "We've got to get downstairs to help Granny with breakfast. It's Monday, and she always feeds the crew a big breakfast on Monday mornings."

"But I don't want to cook. I'm on holiday." Adeline pulled the covers over her head.

"Holiday?"

"Yes," she said from underneath the blanket. "I'm visiting my cousin in the far-off nether regions of Cut and Shoot, Texas, far from modern civilization. I deserve a break."

Funny words, coming from a girl who had scarcely done so much as a daily chore in all her life.

Patience pulled the covers back and convinced her cousin to climb out of bed and get dressed for the day. A few minutes later, they were both in the kitchen with Granny, making a hearty breakfast for the men—eggs, deer sausage, gravy, and biscuits. Lots and lots of biscuits.

The men started pouring in around seven thirty. Jeb arrived first. As foreman, he prided himself on punctuality. The other four workers arrived shortly thereafter, all of them starving, apparently. They settled in around the kitchen table, and Pa prayed, then they made quick work of eating their breakfast and swallowing down cup after cup of hot coffee, which Patience replenished every time the percolator emptied.

"Have you seen anything unusual around the place this morning?" her father asked Jeb as they wrapped up their meal.

"Like what?"

"Anything out of place? Anything missing?"

"Other than the pie that went missing on Saturday?" Jeb shook his head. "Not that I've noticed. But then again, I just got here. Haven't paid much attention."

"Just keep an eye out, if you don't mind," Pa said.

"So if that drifter shows back up, what should I tell him?" Jeb shoveled down a mouthful of eggs.

"Meaning, if he asks about a job?" Patience's father paused and appeared to be thinking. "Tell him to knock on my door and ask me himself. I'm willing to hear him out."

"But you're not really gonna hire him, are you?" one of the young men asked. "We don't know anything about him. And he might be the one stealing our food."

"I was really looking forward to a good apple pie," Jeb said. "Real shame."

Pa's gaze shot to Granny, and Patience imagined what he might be thinking. No doubt he had drawn the conclusion that Granny's pie was probably misplaced in the house somewhere instead of stolen by a stranger. Patience wasn't so sure.

"I'm baking more pies today, Clarence." Granny turned and flashed a smile at the young man. "Never you worry. Just look for an apple pie and a chess pie."

The men got excited by this prospect.

"I'll come fetch 'em, myself," Jeb said. "Just in case that fella's lurking around here."

Patience shivered at the idea that a stranger might be hovering nearby.

"I'm not opposed to hiring, if he's seriously looking for a job," Pa said. "Could be that's why he was here the other day. Poor fella probably needs a warm meal."

"Maybe." Jeb shrugged. "But he gave me a bad feeling, like he was up to something. I don't trust him since that pie went missing. Losing three of our workers last summer was bad enough, but now we're battling thieves to boot."

Patience knew that wasn't the only problem the mill was facing. Sales were down. Pa had told her as much. And with Jimmy headed to Dallas, they'd soon be shy one more worker as well. Pa really needed the extra help.

After they finished breakfast, the men went to work. Jeb paused at the back door with something else on his mind.

"Oh, that newspaper fella stopped by the mill on Saturday afternoon, asking some questions."

"Questions?" Patience asked. "About what?"

"About what happened last summer." He reached into his coat pocket and came out with a pair of gloves, which he pulled on.

"We met him that same evening," Pa said. "He told us he had a flat tire."

"I saw the car parked out on the road. Don't recall a flat tire. But he was loaded with questions about what happened. Wanted details about what split the town."

"He's five months late, asking questions about that story," Pa said. "Makes me wonder what he's really up to."

Patience couldn't help but wonder herself. "He asked me a bunch of questions yesterday in church," she said.

"I'd be careful around him," Jeb said as he put his hat on and took a step toward the back door. "Something about the fella doesn't ring true to me."

"Maybe he knows something we don't." These words came from Granny, who was working to clear the breakfast table of its dirty dishes.

"What do you mean, Granny?" Adeline rose to help her.

"I'm just saying, maybe there's something brewing on the Sutton side that we don't know about yet."

"Like what?" Patience asked.

Granny shrugged. "Who knows with that lot."

"Maybe another lawsuit?" Jeb suggested. "I heard Gilbert Sutton is back in town. Same time as that reporter. Just a coincidence, or more, maybe?"

"You think Gil—er, Gilbert—is here to file another lawsuit?" Patience stammered.

"Could be." Jeb shrugged.

"Impossible," Patience countered. "They couldn't be working together. Gil warned me to steer clear of that fella. He doesn't care for him. Why would he do that, if they were in cahoots?"

"To draw attention away from himself?" Jeb suggested.

Such a notion had never occurred to Patience. Was it possible she didn't know Gilbert Sutton as well as she thought she did?

Gilbert was none too pleased to see Daniel Jennings at his house on Monday afternoon. And when the pesky fella started asking questions about the town split, Gil fought the temptation to respond. Still, the man would not let it go.

"I hear there's more legal trouble coming," Daniel said. "You and your uncle have more filings on the way, right?"

"Where did you hear that?"

"I have my sources."

"Well, your sources are wrong," Gilbert said. "Nothing new has been filed."

"You're saying there's not an addendum to the lawsuit against the Cochrans and their crew? Because I heard otherwise."

"I'd like to know who you heard that from, first of all, and then I'd like you to leave the legal wrangling to the lawyers."

"Because we all know how trustworthy *they* are." Daniel laughed and glanced down at the notepad in his hand. "So, can I come in for a few minutes and ask a couple more questions? It won't take long, but I believe you can shed some light on some of the things I'll be covering in my article."

"You cannot come in. I won't be discussing any of this with you. This isn't a situation to be handled in the papers, especially with aspects of the suit still pending."

"Don't you think the people have a right to know?"

"The people of Conroe?" Gil asked. "That's ten miles from here. Why would they bother?"

"They've got money here, that's why. Conroe sustains some of your industries, like that sawmill of yours."

"Not my mill."

"Like that sawmill of the Cochrans. Most of their lumber is sold to folks in Conroe and beyond. So, if they're up to no good, then the people buying from them have a right to know. We could shut that mill down in a hurry if folks knew the truth about the family."

So that was what this was about. Did he really want to deepen the pain in Cut and Shoot by turning folks in nearby towns against them? Wasn't it bad enough folks here had turned on each other?

"What makes you say the Cochrans are up to no good?" These words came from Gilbert's mother, who appeared in the doorway behind him. "What do you know that we don't?"

"He knows nothing, Ma," Gil said. "He's blowing smoke. He's hoping we'll give him fuel to add to a nonexistent story. That's how these things work. If you tell a lie and build on it, folks begin to think it's the truth."

"Wrong, sir." Daniel closed his notepad. "You can talk to me . . . or not. But that won't change the fact that there's a bigger story brewing here. I have it on good authority that the town of Cut and Shoot is still as divided as ever."

"And you want to do what you can to ensure the problem gets worse and not better?" Daniel's mother asked. "Because it sounds to me like that's what you're up to here."

"Of course not. Just in it for the story." He stuck his pencil behind his ear and turned back toward his car. "If you change your mind, you know where to find me."

"I have no idea where to find you," Gilbert said. "Unless you're headed home to Conroe."

"Nope." Daniel strode to his vehicle. "I'm headed over to the Cochrans'. Last time I showed up, they invited me to dinner. Those rubes are pretty much eating out of my hand."

Okay, that was enough. Gilbert lunged forward, ready to give the man a punch to the gut. But his mother grabbed his arm and muttered, "It's not worth it, Gil."

In that moment, he wasn't so sure. Patience Cochran was worth it, and it was about time he made sure she knew that.

CHAPTER SIX

Granny finished up her pies just after lunchtime and sent Patience and Adeline to deliver them to the workers. The wind blew with such force that Patience very nearly dropped the chess pie as she crossed the expansive yard that led to the mill. She managed to hold on to it, but the sudden burst of wind whistling through the pines certainly made it difficult.

The men were thrilled to have such a treat and dove right in, a couple of them skipping the plates and using their hands to scoop up slices.

"My gracious." Adeline looked shocked by such behavior. "I'm trying to picture Mama's face if she saw such a thing."

"It's a sign that they love Granny's pies," Patience explained.

"Clearly. But what a way to prove it!"

Patience didn't know whether to be insulted by her cousin's constant remarks about how rustic life was in Cut and Shoot or to ignore them. For the moment, she chose to ignore them. Adeline had a good heart, though her attitude was a bit snobbish at times.

On the way back to the house, they stopped off at the barn to check on Goldie and the pups. They were the cutest things—five golden in color and one spotted pup, who appeared to be the runt.

Patience dropped to her knees next to the puppies and picked the spotted one up, tracing her finger along the top of the little one's head. He looked frail, and Patience wondered if Goldie was feeding him. Maybe she had pushed him aside. Sometimes things like that happened. Or maybe the other pups were just stronger and forced their way to the milk, leaving this baby to fend for himself.

"When will their eyes open?" Adeline asked as she knelt down next to Patience.

"It usually takes about a week."

"Oh, good. I'll still be here when it happens."

Patience's heart warmed. "I'm so glad you're staying for Christmas."

"And I'm glad Mama and Papa are driving up on Christmas Eve. It will be wonderful to have everyone together again."

"Yes, I miss Aunt Caroline and Uncle David."

To Patience's surprise, Adeline gave a heavy sigh.

"Are you troubled about something?" Patience nuzzled the tiny runt and gave it a wee kiss on the top of its head before setting it back down next to Goldie, who seemed more than a little anxious about having her brood disturbed.

"To be honest, I scarcely see Mama and Papa. He's always at work, and she's always off volunteering at this event or that. You're lucky to be so close to your family, Patience." Adeline clamped a hand over her mouth, then pulled it away. "I'm so sorry. I'm being insensitive. At least I have my mama."

"I understood your point. No offense taken, Adeline. And for the record, I'm glad you're part of our family. It's so good to have you here. Sometimes it helps to have a girl my age around. Seems like I'm surrounded by menfolk most of the time."

"What a happy problem." Adeline quirked her brows and laughed.

A creaking sound from the rafters caught their attention, and the wind whistled through the cracks in the barn's walls.

"My goodness, the wind is really kicking up, isn't it?" Adeline pulled her shawl tighter. "Should we put more straw over the pups to keep them warm?"

"Yes." Patience made quick work of doing just that.

After tending to the pups, they headed back out into the wind, and Patience turned her sights toward the house.

"Oh, Patience, look!" Adeline pointed at the Cadillac in the driveway. "We have a visitor." She turned to face her. "How do I look? Is my hair a mess?"

Her hair was a bit of a mess, truth be told, but what did it matter? In weather like this, no one would mind such a thing.

Daniel didn't seem to notice them. He got out of his car and walked to the front door of the house. Patience willed her elevated heart rate to calm itself down as she and Adeline approached him. Something about Daniel made her uneasy.

"My goodness, he's something to behold, is he not?" Adeline whispered.

"Yes, he's something," Patience agreed.

Granny answered Daniel's knock just as they arrived.

"Well, for goodness' sake," she said. "Why are you knocking, girls? Come on in out of that wind."

"Oh, we weren't—"

"I was the one knocking, ma'am." Daniel smiled brightly. "Hope you don't mind that I've come back for a visit."

"As long as you're not here to steal my pies, I don't mind a bit. But if you are here to steal my pies, I've got a frying pan I'll take to your head."

"I've never stolen a pie in my life and don't plan to start anytime soon."

He might not have stolen any pies, but Patience still wondered if he had stolen the quilt to use in an article for the paper.

Granny ushered them all inside and before long had offered him a slice of pie. Chess, to be precise. They all gathered around the kitchen table with cups of hot coffee and warm pie. Only then did Daniel reveal the reason for his visit.

"Ladies, I stopped by hoping for your help."

"Help with what?" Patience asked.

"I'm researching the town and need the assistance of folks who live here."

"Why?" Granny asked.

"For an article I'm writing, of course. I'm sorry, I thought I made that clear the other evening at dinner."

"Yes, but what sort of article?" Patience asked.

"About the history of the place...and the present, certainly. About the people. And the businesses."

"What do you need from us?" Adeline asked. "I'm willing to help."

No doubt she was.

"I was hoping you would show me around the area."

"In your Cadillac?" Adeline's eyes grew large.

"Of course."

"My daddy would be so jealous." A dreamy look came over Adeline. "He just loves the new Cadillac. Can I ride up front with you?"

"But of course, my fair lady!" He offered an exaggerated bow, as if she were royalty.

"We're not going, Addy." Patience hoped her words didn't come across as demanding, though she delivered them with a firmness she usually didn't use.

Adeline turned her way, her lips turning down in a pout. "Whyever not?"

"We are decorating for Christmas today, remember?"

"Yes, don't you dare think about leaving, you two." Granny gave them a stern look. "We've had this planned for days."

"We won't, Granny," Patience said. "We're going to stay and help."

Adeline didn't look happy about that, but she remained silent.

Their grandmother huffed off into the parlor, saying she needed to find the box of ornaments.

"Is she all right?" Daniel asked.

"She's been in such a mood." Adeline took a sip of her coffee. "For days now."

"Someone stole her Round Robin quilt on Saturday night," Patience explained. "She hasn't been herself ever since."

"That beautiful quilt has gone missing?" Daniel's glance shifted to the floor, then back up again. "Who would do such a thing? The Suttons, you think?"

"Granny suspects Florence, of course," Adeline said. "But we have other suspects as well."

"Suspects, eh?" Something about his shifty gaze seemed very suspicious indeed. He rose and said he needed to leave.

"Are you sure you can't stay and help us with the tree?" Adeline asked. "Maybe we could go for a little ride with you after that?"

"We can't leave, Adeline," Patience said again. "On the day we put up the tree we always pop corn and make cocoa and sing Christmas songs. It's a wonderful family day. Ernest looks forward to it. He and Pa will be here any minute now with the tree, and we'll get started."

"I don't want to interrupt family time," Daniel said. "I've already overstayed my welcome. I'll be on my way. Maybe I'll head back to the Suttons'."

"To the Suttons'?" Adeline asked.

"Yep. Had a very interesting visit with Gilbert Sutton before coming here. Now there's a man with some stories."

"What kind of stories?" Patience asked.

"Maybe you'd better ask him yourself. I can't say. But why do those Suttons seem so intent on shutting down your father's mill?"

"Shutting down my father's mill?" Patience stared at him. "Did they say that?"

"It's not my business. I'm just a reporter. I've got to hear all sides, of course."

Patience felt her temper rising. What in the world had Gil told this fellow? She followed him out to the porch and was happy to see the wind had died down. He donned his hat and then headed to his car. She couldn't resist the temptation to follow him. As he got into the driver's seat she said, "Daniel, I would rather you come out and tell me what you know. If Gil said something—"

"Nope." He shook his head. "I would hate to come between friends. What kind of man would I be if I did that?"

What kind, indeed? She drew a deep breath as she remembered Gil's words of warning about Daniel. Was he fabricating all of this? Did he mean to deepen the divide between the Cochrans and Suttons?

She walked alongside the car as he made his way slowly down the driveway.

"You ladies have a lovely day. You hear, now?" When he reached the road he turned to the left, the direction of the Suttons' place.

Adeline joined her at the end of the lane, looking none too happy. "And you thought I was a big flirt."

"Whatever do you mean?"

"You were practically leaning inside his car."

Patience's breath caught in her throat. "I was doing no such thing."

"You were flirting with him, Patience. Admit it."

"Flirting?" Her dander rose at such a notion. Daniel was a handsome man—no doubt about that—but he was hardly the sort to catch her eye, especially knowing he could not be trusted. Yes, he was well put together, but she preferred a man who didn't pay as much attention to his appearance or his fancy car. She most assuredly was not interested in him, especially now.

"Daniel fancies me," Adeline said. "And if you don't mind, I think it would be only right for you to back away so I stand a better chance."

"This is the silliest conversation we've ever had. I'm not interested in Daniel Jennings. I'm not sure I trust him."

"Whyever not?"

"Something about him doesn't ring true. I'm convinced he's just here for a story."

"I can't believe you're so suspicious of someone who's just doing his job. Or are you saying all of that to throw me off track?"

"I refuse to say another word in response because this is all too ridiculous."

"Fine, then. I'm ridiculous." Adeline turned and marched toward the house. "You go right on calling names. See if I care."

"I wasn't calling you names," Patience called after her. But her cousin was too far away to hear.

She would have to mend fences with her later. Right now, something else—or, rather, someone else—caught her eye.

The drifter. Hobbling down the road. The one who had stolen Granny's pie. Or, at least, the one Granny had accused of stealing her pie. For sure it was the same man Patience had seen in town on Saturday.

A feeling of sympathy filled her as she saw how bedraggled the poor old fella seemed. From the looks of things, he hadn't visited a barber in years. She had never seen a beard that long on a man before. And all that dirty hair hanging down under his cap? What sort of man wore his hair long like that?

There was something very unsettling about him. She paused, deep in thought as she pondered it. He had a familiar look to him.

She watched for a moment until he rounded the curve in the road and disappeared from view, then Patience turned toward the house. She arrived to find Pa and Ernest dragging a freshly cut tree through the back door. They pulled it through the kitchen and into the parlor, where Granny waited with the box of ornaments.

"Where's Adeline?" Patience asked.

Granny looked up from the box. "She just stormed up the stairs. Seems plenty upset about something. Didn't say what, only that she didn't feel like putting up a tree today."

"That's just silly. She's got to come down and join us."

"I wouldn't press her," Granny said. "Leave her be, honey. Sometimes people just need time and space."

Patience plopped onto the sofa, her thoughts in a whirl. "I just can't believe Adeline isn't speaking to me. It's ridiculous. It wasn't twenty-four hours ago she said that she couldn't understand people who kicked up a fuss and then refused to forgive one another."

"Folks tend to get riled up and hold others in unforgiveness, that's for sure." These words came from Pa as he hefted the tree into position.

"But she's my best friend. My cousin. It goes against nature to stop speaking to someone you've known and loved for so long."

"How well I understand." Granny's voice was quiet. "That's my dilemma, exactly."

"I can't imagine how you've borne it. It's only been a few minutes, and I'm already exhausted with it all."

"Imagine going six months." Granny clucked her tongue. "Six months without so much as an encouraging word from the person you depended on most for support, and all during one of the toughest seasons of your life."

"Toughest seasons?" These words came from Pa. "Because of the feud, you mean?"

Tears sprang to Granny's eyes. "Not just that."

"What else could you mean, Ma?" Patience's father shot a glance in his mother's direction. "Other than the feud, there hasn't been much going on."

"Oh yes, there has. You all probably think I don't notice, but I do. My memory is failing me. It's slipping away."

"Oh, Granny." Patience rested her hand on her grandmother's.

"But even so, I know I haven't misplaced that quilt. I know you all think that, but I did not, I assure you."

"We don't—" Patience didn't get to finish her sentence before Granny interrupted.

"I put it on the banister. It was there... and then it wasn't. And for the record, I took that pie out to the workers and set it on the picnic table for Jeb, just like I said. I didn't misplace that either. Though I have misplaced a few things in recent weeks, I'll admit. I lost my favorite locket. And I found the Christmas tablecloth in the icebox the other day."

"I'm sorry, Granny," Patience said.

"I wouldn't worry too much about all of that," Pa chimed in. "I'm always misplacing things."

"Me too," Ernest said. "The other day I lost my rain boots, but then I found them in the hallway."

"I left them there after I washed them off," Patience said. "They were muddy."

"I just don't want to lose my memories." Her grandmother grew silent. "They're all I have."

"You have us," Adeline's voice sounded from the doorway. She took a couple of tentative steps into the parlor. "You have us,

Granny. Not just your memories but your family—right here, right now."

She walked over and embraced Granny. Patience's heart flooded with relief that her cousin seemed to have come to her senses.

"I do, child." Granny smiled. "And I'd like to go on remembering all of you. And Grady too." Sadness filled her eyes as she mentioned their grandfather's name. "He left me at such a young age. But I've done the best I could to keep his memories alive."

"Tell us stories about him, Granny," Adeline suggested. "Maybe it will help to do that."

And so, she did. Granny filled their ears with tall tales about Pa's pa and their grandpa as they worked to trim the tree. The man who had won her heart by serenading her as she gazed down from her bedroom window. The man who had taught her to stop and smell the roses. He would—she felt sure—have been able to mend fences in their little town, had he still been here. She felt his loss keenly, even after all these years.

Patience thought once again about Gilbert. He had never serenaded her, but he always brought a smile to her face. And he had, for sure, taught her to stop and smell the roses. More than she cared to admit, he captivated her thoughts and her imagination, and all the more as she had spent time with him over the past couple of days. Would those feelings ever abate, or were they meant to carry on?

Perhaps only time would tell. But for now, just one thing mattered—Adeline and Granny were both smiling once again. It really was a Christmas miracle.

CHAPTER SEVEN

On Tuesday morning, Violet begged to go see the puppies. Gilbert didn't blame her. With school on holiday break, there was little to do during the day, particularly with the town so divided. She couldn't play with the neighborhood children, as she had so often done in years past. Half of them weren't speaking to the Suttons.

Not that the Cochrans were on the right side of the argument—at least to his family's way of thinking—but at least Ernest was still willing to play with Violet. And how could he disappoint his sister? Violet seemed particularly anxious about going to see that tiny spotted pup, so he relented and agreed to take her to the Cochrans' place just after breakfast. Hopefully Patience would be agreeable to the visit.

As they prepared to leave, he went in search of his gray coat. It was a bit frayed on the elbows, but on a day like today, with the temperatures dipping, he needed the warmth it offered. He searched the house, came up empty, and decided to look in his closet one more time.

"What are you looking for, Gil?" Violet asked she hovered in the doorway of his room.

"My gray coat."

Her nose wrinkled. "Don't wear that one. Wear the dark blue one instead. The new one."

"The blue one?" Why would Violet care about his wardrobe?

"Yes, it brings out the color of your eyes." She batted her eye-lashes playfully.

He frowned at her. "Since when do you care about the color of my eyes?"

"I don't." She pulled her gloves on. "But I have it on good author-ity that Patience does."

"Patience cares about the color of my eyes?" Well, this was a revelation.

Violet nodded. "Ernest said he overheard her talking to Adeline about your eyes and what a pretty shade of blue they are. So wear the blue jacket. According to my fashion magazines, blue is all the rage this season. Don't you want to be fashionable?"

This was an interesting twist, to be sure. Since when did his lit-tle sister read fashion magazines?

He reached for the blue jacket, if for no other reason than to keep Violet from making a bigger deal of the issue.

Thank goodness she was distracted by something else entirely. All the way to the Cochrans', Violet carried on and on about the pups. She brought with her a large basket filled with food items—and heaven only knew what else. All for the pups.

"Ernest and I will take such good care of them," she said. "Wait and see. They'll grow up to be big and strong."

"You do realize those puppies are far too young to eat that food," he argued.

"But Goldie's not."

"Goldie gets the best table scraps in town. Have you tasted Myrtle Mae Cochran's cooking?"

Violet's gaze shifted to the window and then back to him. "I have, but Goldie needs extra nutrition right now, since she's eating for a crew."

"You're a sweet girl, Violet." He smiled at her. "I'm proud of you for caring so much for animals like you do. I've never known you to be so attached to pups before."

"I just love them." A blissful look came over her. "I sure hope Mama and Daddy will let me bring one home in a few weeks. I've got my heart set on the little spotted one. Please put in a good word for me."

He hated to tell her that they would not allow it. Mama had been firm on that account, especially with the pup coming from the Cochran household and all. But, judging from the hopeful smile on her face, Violet had every reason to believe they would, so he didn't say anything. He would not dash her childish dreams. Right now, they brought hope, and every child needed that, especially at Christmastime.

They arrived at the Cochrans' to find the mill workers loading up a truck with fresh-cut lumber. The heady scent of pine overpowered him as he climbed out of his car. It brought with it so many memories of his childhood, the hours his family had spent at the Cochran home, visiting, sharing meals, laughing...talking.

Before the big split. Now, the scent of pine made him feel oddly reminiscent, and a little somber.

Before he could make it to the door, Adeline appeared on the porch. Ernest joined her seconds later. He came bounding down the steps to greet Violet, who sprang from the vehicle, a girl on a mission. Patience was the last to arrive, just after her grandmother.

Myrtle Mae took one look at him and promptly turned around and walked back into the house.

Talk about making a fella feel welcome.

Ernest and Violet made a beeline for the barn, and Gilbert took a couple of tentative steps toward Patience and Adeline.

"I heard the car coming up the drive." Adeline's nose wrinkled, and he could read the disappointment in her expression. "I thought maybe you were Daniel. But, clearly, you are not." She shrugged and then disappeared into the house.

"Don't leave on my account," he wanted to holler. Instead, he turned to face Patience. "She's interested in Daniel?"

"It would appear so."

"I could tell you stories about him by way of warning."

"Please don't." She put up her hand. "I've already cautioned Adeline, but she will not be swayed."

"All right, then. I won't. But I still say she needs to move with great caution where he is concerned."

"Agreed."

He walked up the steps and joined her on the porch. "I hope you don't mind that we stopped by. I know I'm probably not supposed to be here, but Violet just wouldn't let me be. She was fit to be tied over those pups."

"You're always welcome here, Gil," she said. "But I must ask you a question before we continue."

"What's that?"

"Daniel told me that you want to see my pa's mill shut down. Is that why you filed the lawsuit? To try to shut down our family business?"

"What?" He couldn't have been more shocked. "He told you that I wanted that?"

"Yes."

He reached for her hand, but she pulled it away. "Patience, I promise you, I've never said that. He implied in an earlier conversation with me that he would like to see that happen. Or, rather, that the buyers in Conroe might stop purchasing from your pa if they thought there was trouble brewing in Cut and Shoot."

"You didn't put him up to it?"

"Not at all. I want nothing more for your family than for business to thrive and do well for generations to come. You know me far better than that. I don't care how great the divide in this town, I care very much about you and your family. I always have, and I always will."

She seemed to soften a bit. "All right. I believe you."

"All the more reason to watch out for Daniel. He's really up to tricks, apparently."

"Oh, trust me, I will," she said. "Now, back to what you were saying about Violet and the puppies."

A wave of relief washed over him when he saw that Patience was no longer upset with him. "Violet is acting like a mother hen. She brought half of her belongings to care for those pups."

"Like what?" Patience asked.

"Food, I think?" He shrugged. "Who knows what else. Maybe she knitted sweaters for them. The child seems to be obsessed. She's in love with the little spotted one."

"Oh dear," Patience said. "I was thinking of keeping that one for myself."

"Please don't tell her." He didn't add the words, "Not that my parents will let her have it, anyway."

An awkward silence grew up between them. For a moment, he thought she might be miffed at him again. Her gaze shifted to the door, then back to him.

"I'm sorry if I seem out of sorts. It's been a particularly hard morning," she admitted. "I've been upset over what Daniel said, of course, but I'm also worried about Granny."

"I did notice she's been acting odd. Is she ill?"

"Not physically." Patience shot a glance at the front door, as if expecting her grandmother to materialize.

This certainly raised several questions. "What do you mean?"

"Do you want to take a little walk to see the puppies? I'll fill you in."

"Sure." He led the way to the yard and then walked alongside her in the direction of the barn.

"Granny is struggling with her memory again this morning," Patience said after a few moments of awkward silence. "She called me Caroline."

"Adeline's mother?"

"Yes." Patience stopped walking and gazed at him. "It was so odd. I hardly knew what to do."

"Maybe it was just a slip of the tongue?" Gilbert suggested. "I've called folks by the wrong name. And heaven knows my mama used to do it when I was a boy, especially when I was in trouble."

"Right, but this was different. For a minute there, she really seemed to think that I was her Caroline. And I got the sense she didn't remember we were living in 1912. Her thoughts shifted back to a different era, when Aunt Caroline was the age I am now." Worry lines creased Patience's brow. "I told Pa about it. We've been really worried about her. Last week she was very upset because she couldn't remember how to make her special chili—a dish she's made hundreds of times in the last forty years."

"That is concerning," Gilbert agreed.

"We are concerned. And I hate that this is happening when she's lost her dearest friend. Your grandmother meant everything to her, from the time they were girls in school. It's just heartbreaking that they don't speak now."

"I hate that too." He paused and noticed she was looking into his eyes. Then down at his jacket. Then into his eyes again. Oh my. Maybe Violet was right. "For the record," he finally managed after gathering his wits about him, "my grandmother was hoping to make peace by coming the other evening. Clearly, that didn't happen."

"Really?" Patience seemed intrigued by this. "Well, if there's any good news at all to come from Granny's memory loss, it's that she might not remember to be angry for much longer. If she can't remember it's 1912, then maybe she'll forget what happened."

"A blessing in disguise?" he offered.

"Maybe," Patience responded. "To be honest, I was tickled that your granny came the other night. It was a brave move."

"She really was hoping to mend fences," he said. "She wasn't here for the caroling. She's definitely not a singer. Have you ever heard Florence Sutton sing?"

"I confess, I have." Patience bit her lip to keep from laughing.

"Then you know she didn't come to sing harmony. She came to make harmony. I suspect, if the opportunity had presented itself, she would have made steps in that direction. And for the record, Violet and Ernest wanted the same result."

"I know. I'm so grateful they still speak. It was good of you to bring them caroling, so they had some semblance of normalcy this Christmas. Otherwise, I'm afraid this season would be a total wash for them."

"Yes, to have all the children together like that, acting like nothing was wrong, was a reminder of how things used to be."

"In their minds, nothing is wrong," Patience said. "They still love each other, just as they always have."

"Yes, for many of us, those feelings haven't changed."

Oh my. Had he really just said his feelings of love hadn't changed?

Patience smiled at him. "Well then, maybe you were right to come." She took a step toward the barn and slipped in a mud puddle.

Gilbert reached to take her arm to keep her from falling. "Careful there," he said. "I've got you."

"Yes, I see that." Her cheeks flushed pink.

He didn't let go of her arm as they stepped around the mud puddle together.

She gazed into his eyes once more, this time not looking away. "Can you help me figure out who took the quilt, Gil? If we can just get that settled, maybe we can make some progress toward reconciling our grandmothers."

"Sure, but how can I help?" He held tight to her arm and led her away from the slippery mud.

"First—and please don't take this the wrong way—will you make absolutely sure your grandmother doesn't have it?"

"My grandmother?" Was she serious?

"Yes." Patience sighed. "Granny is convinced she took it the other night. If we can rule that out, we can move on to other suspects."

"Suspects?" Well, this was a shocking turn of events. "My grandmother is a *suspect*?"

Patience hardly knew how to respond to his question. Maybe the word *suspect* was a bit too strong, all things considered. "In Granny's mind, yes," she said after a moment of thinking through her response. "But we have to consider that your grandmother may have taken it because she thought Granny wouldn't give it back to the other women. It belongs to all of them, after all."

Gil looked absolutely flabbergasted by this suggestion. "But my grandmother rode back to the house with me. I would have noticed if she had the quilt. I would have seen her carry it out to the car."

Patience hated to remind him of this, but she had no choice. "No, if you recall, she went out to the car ahead of you. So you didn't walk out together."

His tightened expression softened a bit. "Oh, that's right."

"And that's about the time the quilt went missing."

"I can't believe such a thing is even being suggested. She was empty-handed when I saw her. I found her in the back seat, ready to go home."

"Nothing strange happened when you got home? She didn't carry anything in?"

"No." He paused and appeared to be thinking. "Actually, now that you mention it, after we got home she disappeared outside for a few minutes to fetch her scarf from the car."

Patience hesitated, then said gently, "Do you think there's any chance she hid the quilt away in the car and then brought it into the house to hide? Maybe it's tucked away someplace in her room?"

"I can't imagine it. I've never known her to steal a thing. But I will look, I promise."

"Yes, please do. It will ease my mind. And once we rule out that possibility, maybe then we can figure out who really did take it."

"But who else could it be?" He paused for a moment and then snapped to attention. "I know. It had to be Daniel Jennings."

"Yes. He does seem to be the most likely prospect. He was here for a story, and I have wondered if, perhaps, he would stoop that low."

"I think he would. The Daniel Jennings who writes sensational headlines in the *Tribune* would do just about anything to nab a story."

"Even stealing?" she asked.

"He's renowned for his over-the-top headlines. I think he came here to drum up another one. You have to admit—he had the opportunity. I can see that he might have done this to stir things up even more."

"What kind of headlines?"

"Well, there was the time he accused the mayor of stealing money from the county funds. That one almost ended up in court. I know, because the mayor asked our firm to represent him. But we managed to talk him out of it because it would have been damaging to his political career. And there are a lot of other stories Daniel has cooked up. Many of them based on falsehoods. Hence, my earlier comment about protecting Adeline."

"I understand, and thank you for that."

"You're welcome. I don't want to see her hurt. And since we know he lied to you about my feelings regarding the mill, we already know that he would stoop pretty low."

"Good point."

They stopped outside the barn door, neither of them saying anything for a couple of minutes. Patience's thoughts were tightly wound around the events that had taken place on Saturday, before the quilt went missing.

"I've been wondering about that drifter," she said after a moment.

"The stranger in town?" Gil seemed perplexed by this idea. "You think he came into your house and stole a quilt?"

"It doesn't sound as likely, I know. Especially with so many people around on Saturday evening. But he had already stolen from us once, earlier that same day."

"What did he steal?"

"One of Granny's apple pies. She took it out to the picnic table for the mill workers, and it disappeared. Jeb said he saw the man hanging around at the same time it went missing."

"Well, we have to admit, your granny's pies are worth stealing." He paused. "But don't tell my grandmother I said that, all right? She's convinced hers are better."

"No one makes a better pie than my granny," Patience agreed.

"Maybe Goldie stole it?"

"I thought of that. But Goldie hasn't done anything like that since she was a pup."

"Well, to quote my little sister, she's eating for a crew now. So maybe she saw that pie and couldn't help herself."

"Then where is the pie dish?"

He frowned. "Hmm. Good point. We'll have to look for it in the barn."

"Good idea."

In the quiet that followed her comment, Patience could hear Violet and Ernest talking inside. She couldn't help but think about how sweet they sounded as they laughed and carried on about the puppies. The town of Cut and Shoot had a lot to learn from its children, didn't it?

She paused to glance over at Gil and realized his gaze had never left her face. A strange fluttering in her heart caught her off guard when some of the old emotions swept over her once again.

She did her best to push them away as he led her through the barn door.

Only then did she realize her arm was still linked through his.

CHAPTER EIGHT

On Wednesday morning, Gilbert did a little snooping around the house for the missing quilt. Maybe his grandmother had really brought it home after all. While she worked on breakfast in the kitchen, he slipped into her room with the excuse of straightening her lopsided curtain rod.

After straightening the rod, a quick perusal of the room turned up nothing. Then he checked the coat closet, the closet under the stairs, and even the barn. Nothing. She had plenty of quilts but not that one.

He finally ventured back to the kitchen and realized she was baking his favorite oatmeal cookies. He swiped one and took a big bite, then spoke around it.

"Grandma, can I ask a question?"

"Of course, son. But swallow first, please."

He did. "On the night of the Christmas caroling, when we got home, you returned to the car for something."

"Yes, that's right."

"What were you looking for?"

She turned away from her cookie project, and he could read the confusion in her expression. "Why, my scarf, of course. I thought I told you that already." She looked at him closely. "Since you visited with Patience yesterday, you've been a little distracted."

"Have I?"

"Yes. I daresay you're so smitten you can't even remember from one minute to the next what's happening around you." She smiled and appeared to go to a far-off place. "That's all right, son. I was the same way when I met your grandpa. I never could think straight after spending time with him. That's what love will do to you, I suppose."

"Love?"

"Well, of course, Gil." She walked to him and rested her hand on his arm. "We've all known it, from the time you and Patience were in school. I think you were both twelve or thirteen when Myrtle Mae and I had our first conversation about what a perfect match you would make. So I'm happy to see that you're making strides with the Cochrans, even if they're not yet ready to speak to me."

"I don't think Patience feels anything for me except friendship." He paused. "If even that, now that I've helped file the lawsuit against her family."

"Oh, she feels more. She's just caught in the middle—loving her family, and yet caring about you." His grandmother turned back to her cookies, which she scooped by the spoonful onto the baking sheet. "You and Patience keep right on seeing one another, even if you have to sneak off under the guise of tending to those pups of hers. And promise me this."

"What?"

She stopped working and gave him a warm smile. "That no matter how tense things get between us old folks, you won't let our silliness get in the way of something God has clearly ordained."

"Ordained?" Sounded so...official.

And yet, so accurate.

Friday morning Patience slipped out to the barn to see the pups. Adeline wouldn't budge from her spot in the bedroom where she had taken up camp reading fashion magazines. Such things didn't really appeal to Patience, who preferred her calico to frills and lace.

Adeline had argued that Christmas was coming and they needed to look their best, but with the guest list including only family, Patience didn't see the point in dressing to impress anyone. No, she would rather spend her time focused on her family. And maybe—just maybe—she could sneak in another visit with Gilbert.

Patience pulled back the barn door and immediately heard the scurrying of something overhead in the loft. Oh dear. Pa would be upset to hear they had squirrels nesting up there. Again. Maybe she should climb up to take a peek.

From her spot in the corner, Goldie began to whimper. Patience headed straight for her and gave her a large ham bone, which she had brought to pacify the new mama. Then she gave the pups a quick glance. Looked like the little spotted one was starting to perk up a bit. She had even gotten a little plump around the middle, like the others.

"Good job, Goldie." Patience patted her on the head. "You take good care of those babies."

She noticed several items to the side of their pen—things Violet must have brought from home. Her heart swelled with tenderness toward the little girl when she saw a teddy bear, some soft cloth dolls, and even a tin with cookies inside. Goldie wouldn't be going hungry anytime soon.

Patience spent a few minutes thinking about how precious the children were and how well they got along in spite of the rift between the parents and grandparents. Oh, that the rest of the town could have the heart of a child right now.

She rose and happened to glance down.

And that's when she saw Granny's pie dish, the one from the missing apple pie.

"Goldie!" She scolded the pup and wagged her finger at her. "So you're the one who stole that pie?"

Still, she could hardly be mad at the dog for being hungry. And Granny did make a terrific apple pie, after all.

Patience carried the pie dish to the house. When she arrived in the kitchen, she showed it to Granny.

"Oh, did Jeb give that back to you?" Granny asked.

"No, this is the dish from the missing pie."

"Missing pie?" Granny looked confused.

Patience didn't say anything else, but she took the dirty pie dish to the sink and began scrubbing it. After she dried it with the dish towel and put it away, she turned and saw that Granny was sitting at the table and making a list.

"I need to pick up a few things in town," Granny said as she folded the piece of paper and slipped it into her purse. "Would you please go with me?"

Patience agreed most willingly and recruited Adeline also. With Christmas just a few days away and Adeline's parents coming into town soon, they needed to be prepared.

The weather was warmer than usual, so they decided to walk instead of taking the wagon. Patience decided the sunlight would do her grandmother good.

Overhead the branches of the pine trees were barren and stark, but the sun peeked through them, casting lovely shimmers of light onto the lane below.

A car passed by, and Adeline stopped walking to give it a closer look. "Well, pooh. I was hoping it was Daniel."

"I hope he's gone back to Conroe, frankly," Patience said.

Adeline frowned as they continued walking again. "He can't have. He would have told me. I'm sure of it."

Patience didn't know why her cousin felt so sure. She changed the subject and chatted about the weather and their upcoming Christmas plans all the way into town.

"Look! Both sides of the street are decorated!" Granny placed a hand on her chest. "The Suttons did their part. Oh, I'm so glad."

Patience felt the glow of hope wash over her as she took it all in. Maybe they would see a Christmas miracle after all. Perhaps it had already begun.

When they walked into the mercantile, Granny reached into her pocket. "Now where's my list?" She looked at Patience. "Oh, yes. I remember now. I gave it to you, Patience."

"No, Granny. You didn't."

Her grandmother's expression tightened. "I most certainly did. Why would you say such a thing? I need my list, Patience. Please give it to me." She extended her hand in anticipation.

Patience froze in place, unsure of what to say. She had watched Granny tuck the slip of paper into her own purse. Why would she accuse Patience of taking it?

Adeline cleared her throat. "Tell you what, Granny. Let me peek inside your bag and see if Patience put it in there."

"Now, why would she do that?" Granny asked.

"Probably to keep it safe." Adeline took Granny's small bag and scoured through it, coming out with the slip of paper. "Here we are, safe and sound."

"Well, thank you for that, honey." Granny patted Adeline's arm. "Though I still don't know what Patience was doing in my purse. Back in my day, folks didn't do things like that."

Patience sighed and returned to the task at hand. "Could I see your list, Granny? We can divide it up. I'll fetch a few items and meet you at the register when I'm done."

"Sure, honey." Granny tore the paper in half and handed the bottom portion to Patience. "We should probably hurry up and get what we need. A storm is coming."

"But it's bright and sunny out, Granny." Adeline pointed to the window, where streams of sunlight poured in. "Don't you remember?"

"Oh, I know it's sunny at the moment." Granny rubbed her hip. "But my rheumatism is acting up. So I can tell you, a storm is on the way."

Well, that changed everything. One thing Patience knew for sure—Granny's mind might be going, but her hip was never wrong.

She glanced down at the grocery list, ready to get a move on, but a noise across the room caught her attention.

Granny let out a gasp. "Oh no!"

"What is it?"

"The Suttons just came in. They're not supposed to be here today. It's Friday. Friday is our day. And look! Gertrude Caldwell is here too. And Norma Jo Brighton. Did they know I was going to be here?"

"Here we go again." Adeline rolled her eyes. "It's all so silly."

"Silly or not, I told you a storm was brewing." Granny rubbed her hip again. "Just didn't realize it had nothing to do with the weather. Let's get our items and head home, girls."

Patience shot a look in the direction of the Sutton family and offered Gil a little shrug when he waved. She got busy gathering the items on her list, and he sidled up next to her.

"What are we buying?" he whispered.

"Preparing for Christmas dinner. Adeline's parents are coming," she whispered back. "But we shouldn't be speaking, Gil."

"We spoke at your house the other day."

"That was different. We were alone."

He paused and gave her a pensive look. "So it's all right for us to speak in certain places but not others? And we have to be alone?"

"Just not in front of our grandmothers or some of the other townspeople, that's all. You know how they are."

"Yes, I do. But I have a hankering to speak to you, so I might just have to pay you a visit later on. To check on the pups, of course."

"Of course."

Concern filled his eyes. "Hey, I wanted to let you know that I heard from my uncle."

"Not about that ridiculous lawsuit, I hope."

"No. It's about Daniel Jennings. He's back in Conroe and bragging about a big story he's about to break."

"Oh no." She lowered her voice even further. "About the quilt?"

He shrugged. "No idea. I just know my uncle said he was told it would be in the Sunday edition."

"Leave it to Daniel Jennings to ruin a perfectly good Sunday."

"What about Daniel?" Adeline stepped into place beside them.

"He's back in Conroe, stirring up trouble," Gilbert said.

Adeline's bright smile faded. "He's really gone?"

"Yes." Gilbert nodded. "Writing an article to make us all look ridiculous, no doubt."

"It's a shame he didn't stick around long enough to see Main Street all decked out," Patience said. "Then he would have seen that we really can come together when we try. Just the sight of it gives me such hope."

"Does it, now?" Gilbert quirked a brow. "Well, I'm awfully glad to hear that." An impish grin turned up the corners of his lips, and he started whistling a merry tune as he headed to the opposite side of the store.

"Do you think he had something to do with the decorating?" Adeline asked.

"Oh, no doubt about it." Patience gave him an admiring glance.

"I knew it!" Adeline pointed at Patience. "I said you were smitten with Gilbert Sutton. Your cheeks are red!"

"Don't be silly, Adeline. It's just from being in the sun, is all." Patience couldn't help but sneak another peek at Gilbert as he slipped a couple of chocolate bars into his grandmother's basket.

She finished shopping and met up with Granny at the register to pay for their merchandise. The shopkeeper greeted them and made small talk as he rang up their purchases. Granny paid him, and Adeline reached for the basket just as Florence Sutton stepped into line behind them with Gertrude Caldwell next to her.

The minute Granny saw them, her expression tightened. "Let's get out of here, girls."

"Don't leave on our account." Florence's eyes brimmed with moisture. "We can come back later."

"Why are you here at all?" Granny turned to face her. "It's Friday. You know perfectly well the Suttons agreed to shop on Saturday."

"I had no choice, Myrtle Mae. I have company coming for dinner tonight and need some things."

"Oh?" Granny almost looked interested.

"Friends from church. Gertrude and Fred, Maggie and Jasper. A few others."

The sadness in Granny's eyes was evident, and Patience didn't blame her. Just a few months ago, she would have been on the guest list. This party of Florence's was just another reminder of how divided their little town really was, decorated street or not.

"Well, I hope you have a lovely time." Granny took the basket from Adeline. "Be sure to show off that quilt to your guests."

"Quilt?" Florence looked perplexed. "What are you talking about?"

"The Round Robin quilt, of course." Granny shifted the basket to her other arm. "The one you took from our house the other night."

"Wh-what?"

"You can stop pretending now." Granny's voice rose, her tone angry. "You saw that quilt on the banister, and you just couldn't help yourself. You had to have it. So you snuck it out to Gil's car and took it home."

"I did no such thing!"

By now, several of the other ladies had gathered around, most of them on the Sutton side of things. Florence still seemed genuinely befuddled by Granny's accusation.

"You did." Granny balled her fist and planted it on her hip. "You wanted that quilt from the get-go. You said as much that horrible day last summer."

"I didn't want to see our hard work caught up in the fray of what was happening, Myrtle Mae. So, yes. I asked for the quilt back. But I certainly never took it from your banister last Saturday. I would never do anything like that." Her eyes filled with tears. "I came that night hoping to put all of this behind us."

"You're accusing your good friend of thievery?" Gertrude asked.

"You of all people should know better than that," Norma Jo added. "Florence is a godly woman. She would never steal a thing."

"I...I wouldn't. I didn't!" The poor woman erupted into tears. In that moment, Patience realized how wrong she had been, suspecting Florence in the first place. Clearly, this sweet woman hadn't taken the Round Robin quilt.

Gilbert did his best to calm his grandmother, but she seemed inconsolable. Gertrude and Norma Jo gathered around her as Granny headed to the door, muttering under her breath. Adeline followed behind, still down in the dumps after the news about Daniel leaving. Patience brought up the rear, feeling sick inside, watching all of this take place.

Granny was right about one thing. There was definitely a storm brewing—both inside the store and out. As soon as they stepped outside, the hovering gray clouds hung heavy over them. It was surprising how fast things could change.

"We've got to hurry." She took the basket of groceries from her grandmother. "Before it starts pouring."

They took a few steps in complete silence, but then Granny froze in her tracks.

"What's wrong, Granny?" Adeline asked. "You look as if you've seen a ghost."

"It's that man." She pointed at the corner of the building, where the drifter disappeared around the side of the mercantile. "Do you think he's following us?"

"Surely not," Patience said.

Still, the idea that he might be sent a shiver down her spine.

CHAPTER NINE

Sunday morning's church service should have been one of the most enjoyable of the year for Patience. After all, the annual Christmas service was usually festive and bright, filled with Christmas hymns and greetings all around. But today a heaviness hung in the air over Cut and Shoot.

By now, everyone had heard about the confrontation between Granny and Florence at the mercantile, and folks were whispering about it. A handful of them, who were convinced Florence had really absconded with the Round Robin quilt, were ready to storm the gates to take it back from the Suttons' house. But Patience felt sure it wasn't there. And what good would it do to further upset Florence? The poor woman genuinely appeared to be making attempts to mend fences. Now if only the Cochran side would do the same, perhaps all would be well.

Even Pastor Everson seemed a bit distracted as he rose to deliver the Christmas message. He started by sharing the parable of the sheep and the goats, reading from the twenty-fifth chapter of Matthew.

"'For I was an hungred, and ye gave me meat: I was thirsty, and ye gave me drink: I was a stranger, and ye took me in: Naked, and ye clothed me: I was sick, and ye visited me: I was in prison, and ye came unto me.'"

For a moment, Patience couldn't seem to understand what any of this had to do with Christmas. Then Pastor Everson tied the message back to his sermons from the prior two weeks, about Mary and Joseph and the innkeeper.

"Have you ever paused to think how the story of the Christchild would have been different had the innkeeper not taken in Mary and Joseph? Have you pondered the notion that there would have been no stable filled with hay, no place for the baby to lay his head?"

Patience had not given that any thought, to be honest.

"The Bible says that when you care for the needs of others with unashamed generosity, it is as if you're doing the same for Jesus Himself. Every act of kindness toward others is an act of kindness and love for Him. So feed the hungry. Give drink to the thirsty. Welcome the stranger. Clothe the naked. Care for the sick. And visit those who are oppressed. This Christmas, may we all strive to be sheep, not goats."

Patience thought about his words as they sang the final hymn. And the image of those pesky goats stayed with her as the service concluded. Had the townspeople been treating one another with unashamed generosity? Not since last summer. Since then, the well of kindness had dried up and taken generosity with it.

And though her friends and family members inside the walls of this meetinghouse greeted one another with Christmas wellwishes, she couldn't get past the nagging feeling that they needed to reach out to the others in town. Hopefully, some sort of truce could be called before Adeline's parents arrived on Christmas Eve. It would be a somber Christmas indeed if they had to greet their guests feeling the weight of bitterness against their one-time friends.

After the service ended, several of the men gathered for a meeting. Patience had no doubt it was related to the goings-on between Florence and Granny. After the men parted ways, she approached her father, who stood at the back of the meetinghouse with a furrowed brow.

"What's going on, Pa?" She lowered her voice, concerned about being overheard. "Why does everyone look so down in the dumps? Surely it's not just because of Granny and Florence."

"No, it's not just that. Something else has happened." He reached inside his coat and took out a folded newspaper, which he handed to her. "I was going to wait until later to show you this, but I guess now's the time."

"Show me what?"

"That newspaper fella went and did it."

Her breath caught in her throat. "Wrote an article about us?"

"Yep. And I wouldn't say he's painted any of us in a good light, so brace yourself."

Patience scanned the headline: QUILTING GUILD TRIES TO STITCH UP BROKEN RELATIONSHIPS IN CUT AND SHOOT. That didn't sound too bad.

Adeline joined them and saw the paper in her hand. "Oh, the *Tribune*! Did Daniel publish his article yet?"

"It would appear so." She pointed to the large print at the top of the page.

"Well, judging from the headline, it's a positive take, anyway," Adeline said. "All of that stuff about stitching up relationships sounds lovely."

"Keep reading." Pa reached for his hat and walked toward the wagon. "But do me a favor and hide that paper when you're done. I don't want your grandmother to see it. She's already upset enough this morning about that run-in at the mercantile."

"Florence was trying to be kind, Pa. I was there and saw the whole thing."

"Me too," Adeline chimed in. "Florence said she wanted to make peace. She was trying to be a sheep, and Granny responded like a, well..." She stopped short of saying the word.

"Oh, I know. I heard all about it from some of the others who were there. Many of them would like to put the events of last summer behind us and move on. But after reading this article, I'm afraid that will be more difficult than ever."

"Oh dear," Patience said, with a strong feeling of foreboding.

"Just hide the paper once you've read it," he said. "Please don't let your grandmother know about it."

"Don't let me know about what?" Granny appeared in the open doorway of the meetinghouse.

Patience was tempted to tuck the paper away, but her grandmother saw it and snatched it from her hand. She scanned the title and smiled. "Why, this article is all about our quilt. Who wrote it?"

"That young man who came to dinner last Saturday night before the carolers arrived," Patience told her. "Remember?"

"Gilbert?" Tiny creases formed between her eyes. "Is that right?"

"No, Granny. Daniel Jennings. Dark hair. Beautiful brown eyes." Adeline was positively glowing. "He was driving a Cadillac."

Granny smiled at her. "I'm pretty sure I would have remembered a Cadillac in my driveway."

"Well, he didn't actually pull into the driveway," Adeline explained. "He had a flat tire out on the road."

"I'm starting to think that whole flat tire story was a ruse," Patience said. "Maybe he was just trying to work his way into our house that night to weasel information out of us for his story."

"That's a strong accusation, Patience," Adeline said. "With no foundation at all."

"Yes, and Gilbert has always been such a nice young man," Granny said. "It doesn't sound like him to do something underhanded like that. Though those Suttons are capable of far more devious behavior than I suspected, now that I think of it."

"We're not talking about Gil— Oh, never mind." Patience gave up.

"Now, let's read this article and see what glowing things Gil has to say about the quilt."

"You know what I say about the paper, Granny." Patience took it and tucked it under her arm. "It's nothing but tittle-tattle. We need to keep our minds and hearts pure."

"Tittle-tattle?"

"Yes. Now, what did you say you were making for lunch? Didn't you need my help with something?"

"I've got a wonderful pot roast in the oven. Can you help me peel potatoes to go with it?"

"I would be happy to do that." She managed to turn the conversation to food, but her thoughts were still firmly affixed to that article.

Gilbert paced the outside of the meetinghouse, deep in thought. Everyone in town was abuzz with the news about the article that had just come out. He had no doubt in his mind that Daniel Jennings had deliberately written the hit piece to make the whole town look bad, particularly the Cochran side. His mention of the mill could not have been coincidental. But why was he so intent on it shutting down? There had to be more to that story.

Daniel's description of the quilt was very through and accurate. He must have taken it, to be able to describe it in such detail. Either that, or he had given it more than a passing glance on the night it went missing. Something about this whole thing just didn't ring true.

Gilbert watched out of the corner of his eye as Patience and her family passed by on the way to their wagon. Patience shot him a quick glance, and he could read the pain in her expression. In all likelihood, she had read the article too.

He signaled for her to join him, and she met him behind a large wagon.

"I'm nervous about being seen speaking to you," Patience said. "Tensions are so high right now. No telling what one of our folks would say to you."

He took hold of her hand and gave it a squeeze. "Therein lies the problem. Even those of us who want to keep the peace are caught in the crossfires."

"Like that story about how you want to see the mill shut down?"

"I think Daniel made that up to cause trouble. I'm telling you, that's what he does—he puts on a friendly face and wins the confidence of people, then starts twisting stories to pull them into a web. It's some sort of strange gift he has, to manipulate people."

"Well, he's not going to manipulate me," Patience said decidedly.

"Did you read the article?" Gilbert asked.

She shook her head. "No, but I saw the title."

"It's not good, but I promise I had nothing to do with it. He tries to make it look as if we want to see your pa's mill shut down, but like I told you, that's not true, and I'm happy to tell your father that."

"Let me read it." She pulled out the paper and skimmed it, her eyes growing wide. "Oh, Gil, this is awful."

"I know. But it's all based on hearsay and lies."

"Riddled with untruths. How could we have ever trusted that man?"

"I didn't."

"Well, Adeline sure did. Just goes to show you that a handsome face does not a gentleman make." She folded the paper. "We must figure out a way to expose him so that folks in Conroe don't stop buying their lumber from my pa. This article could devastate his business."

"Oh, I've been thinking of ways all morning," he said. "But trust me when I say that God might not approve of half of them." In fact, Gilbert was pretty sure the Almighty wouldn't approve of *any* of them.

CHAPTER TEN

Just after lunch on Christmas Eve, Violet Sutton appeared at the Cochrans' front door in the middle of a rainstorm. Patience greeted her with a welcoming smile but noticed at once that the child did not look well. Her face was pale and drawn, and her red-rimmed eyes looked puffy.

"Violet, what are you doing out here in such awful weather? It's freezing, and you're soaking wet!"

"I, well..." Violet looked around. "Is Ernest home?"

"He is, but does your family know you're here?"

She shook her head. "No. Mama and Grandma are baking, and Daddy is upstairs wrapping Mama's presents."

"And Gil?"

"He went into Conroe today."

"Last-minute shopping?"

Violet coughed, then caught her breath. "I don't think so. He seemed upset about something."

"Strange. Did he drop you off on his way?"

"No." A fit of coughing erupted again. "I walked."

"All the way from your place? In this weather?" Right now, the child looked as if she might fall down.

"It was important. I needed to come see..." She gestured to the barn.

"Goldie and the pups? They're doing just fine. It's Christmas Eve. You should be home with your family, honey, especially if you're not feeling well."

"I—I—choo!" Violet sneezed.

Granny appeared in the foyer. She caught one look at the frail youngster and ushered her inside. "Come in here out of the cold, girl." Granny took hold of her hand and led her inside. "You're shivering."

"It's c-c-old."

Granny placed her hand on the youngster's forehead. "You're burning up!"

"Come up to my room, Violet," Patience said. "We'll get you out of those wet clothes."

"I'll bring up some hot tea," Granny said.

Patience led the way to her room, where she found Adeline sprawled out across the bed looking at magazines. The moment Adeline saw Violet, she sprang to her feet, worry lines creasing her brows.

"What have we here?"

"I think she's sick."

As if to prove her point, Violet went into a fit of coughing. Ernest appeared in the doorway, a concerned look on his face, but Adeline shooed him away and shut the door.

Patience helped Violet change into a warm nightgown, and Adeline gave her heavy socks to put on her feet. Violet curled up on Patience's bed, snuggled tightly under the covers. The youngster's trembling finally slowed, although Patience feared the fever might be behind the chills, not just the wet clothes she had been wearing.

"I think we should send for her parents, don't you?" Patience asked.

"Of course," Adeline responded. "Is your pa here?"

"He's tending to a broken machine in the mill, but..." She was pretty sure that Pa wouldn't be comfortable going to the Suttons' place. For that matter, she didn't know if they would be willing to come here either. Perhaps she should just take Violet home herself. Still, she hated to get out in this weather, much less take Violet out again. And driving Pa's work truck was tough enough, even on a clear day.

"Oh bother, this feud," Adeline said. "I'll go."

"She's not well enough to go back out in that storm, and I don't think it's a good idea for you to be driving in it either."

"I'm not worried about the weather. But someone needs to fetch the child's mother. Or the doctor. Her family has to know, Patience."

"Of course. I agree. I'm just trying to figure out how to best handle it without making the situation worse."

"I've told you, I don't mind a bit."

They stepped into the hallway, ready to head downstairs, but ran smack-dab into Ernest, who appeared to be pacing.

"Is she all right?" He gave them an imploring look.

"I don't know," Patience said. "It could be exposure to the cold and rain. Or it might be influenza. She's feverish."

"It's my fault."

"How could it be your fault? Did you ask her to come?"

"Not really, but I... we..."

"You're tending to the pups together. I know that, Ernest. But there was no need for her to come today."

"I know. I told you, it's all my fault." He took off down the stairs and out the front door, into the rain. With no coat. Foolish boy.

Before they could decide what needed to be done about Ernest, Granny brought up the tea. Unfortunately, they weren't able to rouse Violet to drink any. She lay curled up in the bed under the covers, alternating between coughing and shivering.

Adeline put on her coat and prepared to leave for the Suttons'. Patience walked her to the door, torn over whether or not she should go with her.

"I think you need to stay here with Violet," Adeline said. "I'll be fine. I'm not worried about any silly little town feud."

"Please let them know they are welcome here," Patience said. "I'll go out and warn Pa they're on the way. He'll probably stay put in the mill, if I know him."

"Better that than a shooting match between the Hatfields and McCoys." Adeline grabbed the truck keys from the hook near the door. "Now remind me how to get there."

Patience gave quick instructions, then Adeline opened the front door and they walked out onto the porch. Patience saw Ernest disappear inside the barn and shut the door behind him.

"Ernest is acting mighty strange," Adeline said. She put the truck keys in her pocket so she could button her coat.

"I think he's feeling guilty. No doubt he put Violet up to coming over today to care for the pups. They've been very diligent with Goldie and her babies."

"True. They're out in that barn more than they're in the house these days." Adeline continued to button her coat. "And look...the weather is clearing." She pointed to the sky. Sure enough, the sun was now peeking through, at least one tiny sliver of it. She reached into her pocket and pulled the keys back out. "Hopefully, I will return soon."

"Be safe, Adeline. And...thank you."

Moments later, her father's truck roared to life, and Adeline performed a very choppy job of backing out of the drive and into the street.

Patience turned toward the house and was almost to the door when the sound of tires screeching across their gravel drive caught her attention. Her heart flooded with relief when she saw Gil's Walkaround pulling up.

"Praise the Lord!" were the only words that came to mind.

Gil pulled up to the Cochrans' house, his heart racing. He prayed he would find Violet here. After the morning he'd had, the last thing he needed was a missing kid sister.

He bounded from the vehicle just as Patience headed his way. "Is Violet here?"

"Yes, she just arrived a few minutes ago, Gil." Patience reached to grip his hand. "And she's not well."

"Not well?" He followed Patience up the steps and into the foyer.

"She's not."

He took a shaky breath. "I left the house early this morning, so I missed everything. Mama did say that Violet was in quite a mood. Didn't want to get out of bed. Barely touched her breakfast or lunch. She disappeared on them while I was gone. I arrived home to find her missing."

"She's very ill. Feverish...and coughing."

"Oh no. I had no idea she was sick." He removed his gloves. "Can I see her?"

"She's up in my room, hopefully sleeping. We changed her out of her wet clothes and put her under the covers. Adeline just left to go fetch your ma and pa. We were worried about her."

"Thank you." He owed her a debt of gratitude. "No doubt she came to help with those puppies. She's been going on and on about that little spotted one. They were worried it might not live." He shrugged out of his damp coat and hung it on the coatrack.

"I guess, though I didn't realize the pup was that bad off. Ernest must have invited her over. He just took off for the barn, saying it was his fault."

"Poor kid."

"No telling what those two have been cooking up over the past few days," she said. "I was just headed out to the barn to check on Ernest. He's out there without a coat. I'm afraid he'll end up in the same condition as Violet if we're not careful."

Gil reached for his coat and slipped it back on, ready to help her. "I'm coming with you. We'll get Ernest inside, and then I'll check on Violet. No point in disturbing her if she's sleeping."

"All right," Patience said. "But I want to also go to the mill and tell Pa that your parents are on their way. He needs to know."

"Agreed. Do you think it's all right that I'm with you?" He wasn't sure how Mr. Cochran would respond to seeing him, all things considered.

"Yes. I say we do this...together."

"Agreed." He reached to squeeze her hand.

She donned her coat and shawl, then they went to the mill to fetch her father. He seemed more than a little concerned at the news that Violet was ill in their home.

He shot a glance Gil's way. "Your family will think we put her up to coming."

"Surely not," Gil responded. "They know how hardheaded Violet is."

"We can't worry about that right now, Pa," Patience said. "Gil is here, and we will tend to her until her parents arrive. Granny's inside with her. But I'm worried about Ernest too. He's in the barn, and he's got to be freezing out there. He has no coat on."

"What is that boy up to?" her father asked.

"Who knows? We're headed to fetch him now. You might want to go inside until Gil's family arrives. Granny seems mighty confused at all that's going on."

Mr. Cochran set his work aside, wiped his hands, and headed for the house.

Gil held tight to Patience's hand as they walked across the wet ground toward the barn. A sudden burst of wind caught her scarf and nearly whipped it off her neck. He caught it and settled it back in place, feeling more than a little protective of her.

Just as they got to the barn door, he heard noises coming from inside. Voices. Was Ernest talking to Goldie?

"Who is he talking to?" Patience paused and leaned in.

Just then he heard a terrible cough. Was Ernest sick as well? Gilbert swung the door open, and they stepped inside. A coughing fit that seemed to come from the rafters echoed across the barn.

Patience called out her brother's name, and seconds later Ernest came rushing down the ladder from the loft, looking healthy as a horse.

"Patience, you scared me." He took hold of her hand. "Let's go back to the house."

"Who were you talking to?" Gilbert asked.

"Me? Talking?" Ernest's gaze shifted up to the loft, then to the corner, where Goldie and the pups rested quietly." "No one."

"We heard you. And why were you coughing?" Patience asked. "Are you sick too?"

"Nope. Not at all. Come on." He tugged on her hand. "Goldie needs to rest."

Suddenly another fit of coughing split the air.

"See!" Patience bounded to the ladder.

"No, Patience! Don't!" Ernest tugged at her sleeve. "Don't go up there. You'll spoil everything."

"Spoil everything?" This made no sense at all to Patience.

"I'll go." Gilbert rushed up the ladder, and seconds later she heard his firm voice as he spoke to someone.

"Who is up there, Gil?" Patience called out.

"Someone who needed us," Ernest said. His gaze shifted to the barn floor. "We were just doing what Pastor Everson said we should do, Patience."

"The pastor told you to put someone in the loft?"

"He told us that the innkeeper took in Mary and Joseph when they needed him most. If not for the innkeeper, baby Jesus wouldn't have been born in the stable. He told us to make room in the inn of our heart for strangers, and that's what we did."

"What?"

"Only now you've spoiled it." Her brother turned away from her, muttering, "And now Pa's gonna be mad at me."

She gathered her skirts and ascended the ladder to the loft, where she found Gil kneeling over something.

Make that *someone*.

"Oh my goodness!" She stared down at the man who was frail and trembling under the quilt. The Round Robin quilt.

"Don't be mad, Patience. Please." Her brother's tearful words came from below. "We didn't know it was the Round Robin quilt until after we brought it out to Mr. Grady. Then we couldn't figure out how to get it back to the house without folks finding out what we'd done."

"Wait...Mr. Grady?"

The man's coughs filled the loft, and he hunched up under the quilt, as if he was in pain.

"He was just so cold!" Ernest appeared on the ladder behind her. "And sick. And we wanted to—"

"It's my fault," the man said in a shaky voice. "These children have been bringing me food and coffee and making sure I had what I need to get well. I tried to sneak off a couple of times, but they came after me and brought me back." Another round of coughing sounded.

Patience pulled the quilt over his trembling shoulders. "But why didn't you just come to the door and ask?"

"Because I..." He pushed the quilt away and tried to stand but could not. He fell back and whispered, "Because I knew Myrtle Mae would never let me through the door. How could she, after all I've done to her?"

CHAPTER ELEVEN

Gil jumped into action, realizing this man needed not just the warmth of the Cochran home but the comfort of his family as well. He flew into action, giving instructions. "Ernest, I'm going to need your help. We're going to get Mr. Grady down the ladder and into the house, out of the cold."

"But..." Patience's eyes widened. "I don't know, Gil. Pa might—"

"Might turn me out to the wolves," Grady mumbled. "I wouldn't blame him if he did."

"Or, he might make room in the inn." Ernest's eyes lit up. "I'll help you, Gilbert."

Gilbert gestured for Patience to grab the quilt. As he and Ernest worked together to help the man to his feet, she folded the quilt and slung it over her arm. Only then did he notice the man was wearing his gray coat, the one with the faded elbows. That explained Violet's sudden fascination with the blue one.

Brought out the color of his blue eyes, eh?

They would have a conversation about that.

Once she recovered, of course. No doubt she had picked up whatever illness this poor fella was struggling with. Hopefully, both of them would recover with good care. But first, to get this stranger inside, out of the cold.

Working together, Gil and Ernest managed to get the frail elderly man down the ladder. He shivered uncontrollably as Patience swung the barn door open.

"Put one arm over my shoulders," Gil instructed him. "And the other over Ernest's." He looked at the boy. "You up for this?"

"You betcha." Ernest nodded. "But promise you'll stick up for me, Gil. Pa's not gonna be happy."

Gilbert wasn't so sure about that. He had a sneaking suspicion this stranger might be just the ticket to melt the hearts of everyone in the Cochran family. Perhaps even everyone in the town.

They stepped outside the barn into the sunlight. Patience stared into the man's face, seeing him up close and in full view. In that moment, she saw it all. Clearly. Take away the beard and the silver hair, remove the grime and the dirty clothes, and this man was a dead ringer for her father. A much older version, of course, but a dead ringer.

She could hardly manage a word, but her heart rate accelerated as she draped the Round Robin quilt over his shoulders. Then she trudged along behind Gil and Ernest, who helped him hobble toward the house.

All the way there, her mind reeled. What would Pa say when he clamped eyes on his pa? What would Granny say? Patience still couldn't make sense of the particulars, but the name Grady now made sense. Grady Cochran was her grandfather. And, apparently, Granny's story about him "leaving her" wasn't quite what she had implied.

As they got to the driveway, a car pulled in. A fancy car. For a moment, her heart flip-flopped as fear gripped her. Had Daniel returned in search of more information to use in another article? No, on second glance she realized Adeline's parents had arrived.

Well, terrific. Talk about perfect timing. They got out of their car, and Uncle David moved swiftly in her direction. "Can I be of some help?" He slipped into Ernest's place and helped Gil get her grandfather up the front steps of the house.

Aunt Caroline came along behind them, worry lines creasing her forehead. "Who is that man, Patience? He looks familiar."

She shook her head, unwilling—or unable—to respond. Aunt Caroline was about to find out, but she wouldn't be the one to tell her.

Patience opened the front door and made way for the men to enter the house. Somehow in the process, the Round Robin quilt slipped from her grandfather's shoulders. Patience knelt down to pick it up, then slung it over the banister.

As they got him settled, Granny entered the room from the kitchen. She took one look at the man on the sofa and turned white as a sheet. She managed one shaky word, "G-Grady!" then clamped a hand over her mouth and sank into the armchair on the opposite side of the room.

"What in the world is happening?" Aunt Caroline pulled off her scarf and rushed to her mother's side. "You look as if you've seen a ghost, Mama."

"I—I have." Granny stared at the man.

Patience knelt beside her grandmother's chair and slipped an arm over her shoulder. "Are you all right, Granny?"

Pa entered the room, greeted his younger sister and brother-in-law, and then shifted his gaze to the sofa.

Patience looked on as her father took rapid steps toward the man. For a moment, he said nothing. Then, suddenly, he knelt down and threw his arms around the man's neck, embracing him. "Pa!"

"Pa?" Aunt Caroline echoed, her voice shrill. "*Pa?*"

Granny began to tremble violently.

More noise sounded at the front door. Seconds later Adeline burst through the foyer with Violet's parents in tow. Oh dear. More awkward timing. Adeline led Mr. and Mrs. Sutton up the stairs to see their daughter, then returned to the parlor to discover her parents had arrived.

Adeline greeted them, and then her gaze shifted to the man on the sofa.

"What's happening here?" She looked back and forth between her mother and Patience's father, who was now sitting by his pa on the sofa.

"He's our grandpa," Ernest said. "Merry Christmas!"

"Our…what?" Adeline's eyes bugged. "Oh, my stars."

Grandpa pulled off his hat and turned to face Granny with a quiet, "Myrtle Mae."

"Grady Cochran, you…you…" Granny erupted in tears. "I'm—I'm seeing things!"

"No, Ma, you're not." Patience's father spoke calmly. "It's really him. Pa's come home."

Grandpa extended his hand. "It's me, Myrtle Mae. Back from the grave. If you'll have me."

Aunt Caroline looked as if she might faint. Uncle David held tight to her. "You...you told us he passed away, Mama."

Grandpa looked wounded by this news. "You told them I died?"

"What was I going to tell them?" Granny finally managed. "That you left for Spindletop to make your fortune and never came home again?"

"I knew, Ma." Patience's father rose and took several steps in her direction. "I found the letters he sent to you years ago."

"What letters?" Granny looked more than a little confused.

Grandpa looked wounded that she didn't seem to remember. "I sent a dozen or more over the years, Myrtle Mae. On your birthday. At Christmastime. You never saw them?"

"I..." She looked genuinely perplexed by this news. "I don't remember any letters."

Pa walked over to the gun cabinet and unlocked it, then came out with a bundle of envelopes. "Ma, you stashed them right here. I found them years ago when I was looking for bullets."

"You hid my letters in the gun cabinet?"

Granny paused, and a moment later seemed to remember. "Oh my goodness. I hid those away so no one would see them."

"But I did," Pa said. "I found them and read every one."

"So you knew, Son." Grandpa's eyes filled with tears.

"I knew too." A quiet voice came from the doorway, and Patience turned to discover Florence Sutton standing there, holding the Round Robin quilt.

"I *knew* you took that quilt!" Granny rose and pointed an arthritic finger her way.

"No." Florence gripped it tightly. "I found it on the banister. Just now."

"Liar!" Granny's shrill voice rang out.

"No, she's right, Granny," Ernest said. "The quilt was in the barn this whole time. I took it there the night of the caroling."

A collective gasp went up from Granny, Pa, and the other adults in the room.

"Ernest Eugene Cochran!" Pa strode in his direction. "We sent you out to the barn that very night to look for it. But you came back empty-handed."

"Well, I . . . " He kicked at the floorboards with the toe of his boot. "I said I'd check to see if the quilt was with the pups. And it wasn't."

"But you knew all along—"

"That someone was cold and hungry." He gestured to the man on the sofa. His grandfather. "That's why I took more warm milk that night."

"And my breakfast biscuits." Granny crossed her arms and narrowed her eyes.

"Yes, all right. I took the biscuits too. And some dried jerky. And a couple of cookies. And some apples."

"And an apple pie?" Granny asked.

"You're the best pie maker in town, Myrtle Mae." Florence offered her a warm smile as she passed the quilt her way.

"Thank you." Granny spread the quilt over her knees and leaned back in the armchair.

"I daresay that apple pie saved my life." Grandpa licked his lips. "It was the first act of kindness anyone had shown me in some time."

Gilbert turned to Grandpa. "And I'm going to venture a guess that my kid sister gave you that coat."

"Sure did." He beamed. "Just enough to keep the chill away."

A frail voice sounded from the foot of the stairs. "You hardly wear it anyway, Gil." Violet stepped into the room, looking pale and drawn, swallowed by Patience's nightgown and robe. "And you look so much nicer in the blue one." Her gaze shifted to Patience. "Don't you agree, Patience? It brings out the color of his eyes."

Patience's cheeks blazed with heat. "I…well… I never noticed the color of his eyes before. What color are they anyway?"

"Of course you have," Adeline said with the wave of a hand. "I'm always having to hear about it. They are the color of bluebonnets in the spring."

Thank goodness, Mr. and Mrs. Sutton appeared behind Violet and scolded her for getting out of bed. The youngster crossed the room and took a seat on the sofa next to Grandpa, who offered her a warm smile.

At that point, everyone in the room started talking. Aunt Caroline wanted to go back to the part where Florence knew that her long-lost father was still alive when she did not. Pa was angry at Ernest for lying about the quilt. Granny was confused about the letters in the gun cabinet. Mrs. Sutton went on scolding Violet for getting out of bed, and Uncle David just looked bewildered.

So did Gilbert's father, who remained strangely quiet. Though he did shoot a troubled gaze in Pa's direction a time or two. Would the men end up in another fight, like that horrible day? Or could the Lord somehow grab hold of this chaotic situation and calm things down? Patience ushered up a silent prayer to that end.

CHAPTER TWELVE

While everyone around him was talking excitedly, Gilbert heard a pounding on the door. He rushed to open it and was stunned to find Gertrude Caldwell and Norma Jo Brighton as well as their husbands. Behind them came several from the Cochran side, including the shopkeeper, Mr. Pepperdine, and Pastor Everson. Before long over a dozen of the town's most vocal residents were crammed into the foyer. Gilbert prayed violence wouldn't break out.

Gertrude pushed her way into the parlor, and the others followed her.

Patience's grandmother looked their way and groaned. "Oh no. Now what?"

"We heard there was a fight," Gertrude said. "So we came at once."

"A fight?" Adeline's mother looked petrified at this announcement. "What have we stumbled into?"

Norma Jo waved her arms, clearly worked up. "You Cochrans kidnapped little Violet Sutton, and you're holding her captive in your home."

"No such thing," Gil said, hoping he could turn this situation around before it got out of hand.

"There's not an ounce of truth to that!" Patience chimed in.

"I'm not kidnapped," Violet said from her spot on the sofa next to Grady. "I'm right here. On purpose. And Mama and Daddy are here now. We're all fine."

This calmed the women down, but they seemed plenty confused. And then, just as quickly, Gertrude seemed to recognize Grady. Her mouth fell open as she stared at the frail man on the sofa.

"You're not seeing a ghost, Gertie," Gil's grandmother said from her spot near the kitchen door. "Grady's back."

Gertrude shook her finger at Grady. "How dare you leave our friend like that!"

Gil did a double-take. Did Gertrude just call Myrtle Mae Cochran her friend?

Norma Jo pointed to the Round Robin quilt spread over Granny's knees. "It was here all along! Why did you lie about the quilt being missing? To stir up more trouble?"

"I wasn't lying." Granny raised her voice. "I don't tell lies!"

"I'll tell you who's trying to stir up more trouble." These words came from Mr. Cochran. "You Suttons put that reporter up to that terrible story in the paper. I could lose the mill, thanks to all of you."

Oh no. Just when Gil thought things couldn't possibly get any worse.

"You think we were behind that article?" his father asked.

"Well, sure." At this point, the people in the room were divided into two very clear groups—Suttons and friends on one side of the room, and Cochrans on the other.

Gilbert would fix this, if it was the last thing he did.

"No!" He lifted his hand. "I drove to Conroe this morning and paid Daniel Jennings a visit. I now know why he wanted the mill shut down."

"And why is that?" Mr. Cochran turned his way.

"He's got a brother in the lumber business in Lufkin. Jennings has been trying to get the businesses in Conroe to buy from him. He came here to stir up trouble, hoping to convince folks not to buy from you."

"He thinks folks would prefer to go all the way to Lufkin for their lumber?" Patience's father asked. "Why would they go so far away when I've got the best pine in the state right here?"

"That's what I told him," Gilbert said. "We had words. I'll leave it at that."

Adeline cringed. "Please tell me you did not strike that handsome face."

"No, I didn't resort to violence," Gil responded. "I hit him with words instead. I threatened a lawsuit."

"Good for you!" Patience said.

"That's my boy!" his father chimed in.

Gilbert nodded. "Anyway, the long and short of it is, he will be retracting the story."

"Praise the Lord," Pastor Everson said.

"Yes, and amen!" Florence echoed, hands clutched to her chest.

Gilbert addressed the whole group. "And while I've got your undivided attention, I want everyone to drop those ridiculous lawsuits you've made us file. I'd like to see you all put an end to this nonsense once and for all."

Patience couldn't get over the fact that Gil—her Gil—had driven to Conroe to confront Daniel Jennings on her family's behalf. She owed him so much. She took a step in his direction, and he slipped his arm around her shoulders, drawing her close. Her heart fluttered. Then, just as quickly, it settled down as she gazed into those gorgeous eyes of his.

If only the townspeople would come together in a show of unity. Then things could get back to normal.

Unfortunately, Gertrude and Norma Jo didn't seem content to do that. Gertrude walked over to Granny and extended her hand. "Give me that quilt for safekeeping, Myrtle Mae. I think I should be the one to watch over it until a decision can be made about it."

"But I'm not done with my square," Granny argued.

Patience watched in shock as her grandmother rose and tossed the quilt onto the floor. Then she reached into her pocket and pulled out a pair of scissors.

A collective gasp went up.

"What are you doing, Myrtle Mae?" Florence asked.

"I've decided the only way to make everyone happy is to cut the quilt into pieces. Everyone can take their square. Then you folks on that side of the room can make your own quilt, and we can make ours."

"But . . ." Gertrude looked dumbfounded by this. "So much work went into piecing them together."

"Exactly." Granny eased her way down to the floor, rubbing her hip all the way.

Patience's heart quickened when she saw the tears in her grandmother's eyes. Years of work had gone into piecing together the friendships in this room, and nothing should have torn them asunder. And that, she supposed, was the point of this demonstration. But, from what she could tell, Granny was actually of a mind to start cutting.

With trembling hand her grandmother rested the blades of the scissors next to her square, the one she had worked so hard on.

"Wait. Stop!" Norma Jo put up her hand. "My pink peony is perfect next to your bluebonnets, Myrtle Mae. It just won't look the same elsewhere."

"Yes, and I added that purple iris to complement the peony," Gertrude added. "There was an order to all of this."

"There was, indeed," Florence said. "Do any of you know why I chose yellow daisies?"

Granny looked up from her spot on the floor. "You have daisies in your front garden every spring."

"No." Florence shook her head. "There's more to it than that. I chose the Gerbera daisy because it represents friendship. I had no way of knowing how deeply those friendships would be tested before this quilt was complete. The enemy has stolen the peace and joy from this town. But I refuse to let him continue to do so. Myrtle Mae, our friendship is something that has brought me tremendous joy over the years. I hope you know that."

Granny's eyes misted over. "Are you saying you think the quilt should remain in one piece?" she asked as she set the scissors aside.

"Yes." Florence reached down and snatched the scissors, then offered her friend a hand up. "We've got to put a stop to this nonsense once and for all, just like Gil said—not just the menfolk but the women too."

"Why did you come that night, if not to take the quilt?" Granny asked.

"I came to apologize, Myrtle Mae," Florence said. "Too much time has been stolen from us. I can't abide it anymore. It's…it's killing me!" She threw her arms around Granny's neck, and before long both women were a sobbing mess.

Overcome, Granny finally let go and eased her way down onto the sofa next to Grady, who reached to take her hand.

"You know me." Florence put her hands on her hips and stared intently at Granny. "And deep in your heart you know that I could never go to my grave with bad blood between us."

"Who-who's going to their grave?" Granny sniffled. "Why are you talking like that?"

"Because, Myrtle Mae, none of us knows the number of our days. I could walk out onto Main Street right now and get run down by an automobile."

"True." Granny seemed to lose herself to her thoughts. "I've seen the way some of those drivers tear through town, with no regard for others."

"We're safer in our buggies and wagons." A hint of a smile tipped up the edges of Florence's lips. She turned to address the whole room. "I say we pick up where we left off last summer, ladies. Finish up your bluebonnet square, Myrtle Mae, and we'll meet this week to start the binding and quilting process. We'll stitch friendships back together, one quilt block at a time."

This sounded like the perfect solution to Patience. And, thankfully, everyone in the room seemed to agree. They all began to speak at once, their voices blending in harmony, for the first time in months. She could hardly make out what anyone was saying, but what did it matter, since they all appeared to be on the same team?

In the midst of it all, Patience was grateful for one more thing: at the moment, no one was talking about her and Gil. She shot a quick glance his way and noticed for the first time that he happened to be wearing that new blue jacket.

The one that looked so nice with his eyes.

Love Lost and Found

by

Ruth Logan Herne

"A new baby is like the beginning of all things—wonder,
hope, a dream of possibilities."

—Eda J. LeShan

✐◦ CHAPTER ONE ◦✐

Cut and Shoot, Texas
Present Day

Cole Lafferty wasn't happy about being summoned out of the field and up to the house midday. Not with another storm predicted for lower Texas. He'd had enough with storms, with wind, with disabled fencing—

And now he had to stop in the middle of the final stretch.

The last thunderstorm had weakened two miles of fence, and the thought of rounding up three dozen prime horses held little appeal, but when Jim Lafferty put out the call, his sons were expected to listen. Both of them. Even when the oldest was about to turn thirty and the younger one was on the cusp of his veterinary degree at Texas A&M.

"I'll take over the fence." Brent was the future veterinarian, home for Thanksgiving weekend. He crossed the yard as Cole climbed out of his well-used pickup. Brent waggled the Jeep keys in his hand. "Where'd you leave off?"

Normally Cole would welcome the help, but his younger brother had worked hard to get to this point in his degree. Cole didn't want misplaced guilt or sympathy to pull Brent from his studies. "You've got finals coming up. Two days off for Thanksgiving doesn't mean you have to jump in and do hard labor." Brent had shared how tough this last push was. Cole didn't want to do anything to mess up his brother's goals and dreams. Not when Brent had taken time off two years ago when Cole had most needed an extra set of hands.

"I've got this, Cole." Brent motioned up the lane. "How much is left?"

"A quarter-mile plus. Not too bad. I got the roughest spots done. Started this end. Heading north."

"Got it." A few years ago, his brother would have made fun of him. He didn't do that much now. Not since—

"I've got what I need in the Jeep," Brent said. "I'm on it."

"Who's here?" Cole didn't mean to scowl at the berry-red SUV that had pulled right up to the front steps before Brent came to get him. On second thought, maybe he did mean to. He scowled a lot lately, it seemed.

"It's some fellow from Houston," Brent called back. He started the Jeep and headed out.

Cole sighed.

There were two ways to look at the major Texas city south of them. It was either a forty-minute drive or a lifetime away from Cut and Shoot, depending on perspective. Like the town's name suggested, Cut and Shoot wasn't your typical dot on the map. It was unique, and folks who called Cut and Shoot home liked it that way. They'd adopted the odd name after a town squabble over a century before, a squabble that had involved some of his ancestors and so many others. The name stuck, and sometimes it even fit. He'd been tempted to cut and shoot more than once since losing his little boy to a tragic accident two years before.

He'd felt drowned in sorrow then, and he was barely treading water now. So much for those who said the first year would be the hardest.

Why was someone from the city here to see them now? Developers had been buying up land in nearby Conroe, and some people said Cut and Shoot was next. Urban encroachment had hiked prices and population in Conroe. He repeatedly heard how the Lafferty family was sitting on a gold mine now—untapped land. These days, a half-acre building lot was going north of forty grand, and they owned eighty-three acres of woods, grazing land, and hay lots.

To cash in, they'd have to sell the ranch when they should be expanding it. Selling would break his heart.

What else was new?

Been there, done that. Still not repaired after over two years of anger, angst, longing, and grieving. When they'd buried Beau Michael Lafferty in the nearby cemetery, they'd buried Cole's heart and a big chunk of his soul with him. And yet—

Here he was. Waking. Breathing. Eating.

Not living. Well, technically, he was. But not in any way that mattered.

He sucked in a breath and went through the kitchen door. His mother would skin him alive if he tracked dirt into her front rooms, so he kicked off his boots. And even though he didn't like taking them off and tugging them back on, he did the same thing at his place, ten minutes up the road. Habit, he guessed. And not wanting to scrub floors.

He liked the city from a distance. He hadn't gone on to college like Brent. Instead, he'd worked, studied genetics, traits, and animal health online, and ended up with money in the bank and a wealth of knowledge he'd love to use to expand the ranch. Maybe someday his dad would see that the sense of that move outweighed the risk. Maybe someday he could tell him that he'd already made an offer to Cousin Lisa for her land. Land that had been in the Sutton/Cochran families for over seventy years. Time would tell.

Conroe was city enough for him. More than enough after two decades of suburban growth. He had everything he needed in a twenty-mile radius, and there was nothing, absolutely nothing, Houston could offer. So why did he need to see whoever was here? Was it a prospective buyer? On Thanksgiving weekend? That would be the only reason his dad would call him off a job.

He stepped through the curved arch separating the dining area from the living room.

Three people turned his way. His parents, Norrie and Jim Lafferty, and a stranger. An old man. Really old. Like maybe shouldn't-be-driving old. And in his arms, he held a baby, the really small kind that slept hard and woke harder. The kind he'd had once upon a time.

His throat closed, his palms went damp, and his heart did a solid *wump!* in his chest, sending an adrenaline rush through his system.

With effort, he took his eyes off the man on the love seat. He faced his father and clenched his hands, distinctly uncomfortable. "You needed me?"

"We do, Cole." It was his mother who spoke. "Mr. Smith has driven up from Houston to talk to you."

He turned toward the man. "Do I know you?" He sounded curt and didn't care.

"Come sit."

His mother again. His father looked almost as uncomfortable as Cole felt, but why?

"You don't know me, son," the old man began.

The baby started fussing right then. Its arms flailed up, and it let out a squeak and a grimace.

His heart beat harder. Faster.

"I'm here to do the bidding of a young woman."

"A young woman? What woman?"

"Her name is Mary Smith."

Mary Smith? If Cole was convinced of anything in this world, it was that whoever this man was talking about, her real name wasn't Mary Smith.

"Jane Doe wasn't available?" he quipped, then immediately regretted the retort.

"Mary has some difficulties," the elderly man continued. "She can't take care of little Libby here." He shifted the baby, and for a split second it almost looked like he might drop her. The baby's face screwed up into a tiny look of fury, then she passed gas and relaxed.

"Oh my." His mother's face got that look all women seemed to get over young of any kind. She wanted to hold the baby. Pace around the room with it—her—patting her back, comforting her, making her happy.

He wanted to run.

"I brought some stuff in this bag here. Mary wanted this done now. Needs it done now."

Cole frowned. "Needs what done?"

"Well, son, see, that's the thing. She's giving her baby to you. And your missus, though your mom explained that she's not around right now, and I'm sorry to hear that. Real sorry. Be that as it may, it like to broke young Mary's heart when she saw what happened to you folks a couple of years ago. She said she couldn't even imagine such a thing and here she was, with this perfect baby and no way to care for her—"

"How old is the baby?"

"Seven weeks plus a few days. Mary can't keep her. That's one thing we know. I'm nearing ninety myself. Our options, as you can see, are limited."

"People don't give away babies."

"Now that's true and not true, dependin' on circumstances, but in this case, it's a necessity. Mary could have gone ahead and gone to an agency, but, like I said. She saw your story and wanted you and your wife to adopt Libby. If you don't mind."

His breath caught. He stared at the old man, then his parents, then the baby. "You can't be serious." Something raw swelled inside him. Something raw and awful and painful rose up so tight and hard that he couldn't draw a deep breath, much less get words out.

"At my age, we take a whole lot of things serious, son. God and time top the list. Can you take her, please?" He reached out as if to pass the baby to him. Cole wouldn't have taken her except that the old man's arms trembled. Just a little, but enough. Enough to make him take the baby into his arms.

She gazed up, her eyes wide. He'd forgotten how big babies' eyes were. Big eyes tucked in a tiny, round face.

She studied him hard, and then she reached one little hand up. Straight to his face, as if she meant to do it, to the rough stubble on his cheek.

She smiled. It was a tiny smile of approval, most likely caused by gas, but it made him feel like he passed muster.

His heart shook, and he looked up again.

The elderly man sported a ragged beard that hadn't been tended in a very long time. He wore black-rimmed glasses. The lenses made his eyes look owlish. His long hair was thin and gray. His clothes were old, dirty, wrinkled, and worn.

He looked like any number of homeless men you'd see on Houston streets. Grease stains marked his baggy trousers, and his shirt didn't look much better, but both looked better than the side-split sneakers that had seen better days a long time ago.

"I gotta get on," the old man said.

"Wait. What? And leave her here?" Cole said the words while at the same time realizing he couldn't hand this newborn back to the old man.

"This is where her mama wants her to be. I don't argue with mamas. Learnt that lesson when I was young."

"Here." Cole snatched up a piece of paper and a pen from his mother's desk. "Write down the mother's contact information. So we can thank her."

His brain scoffed at his choice of words, but what else could he say? *Write things down so we can get this stolen child back where she belongs?*

Pretending he wanted to thank the mother seemed less confrontational.

The old man looked at him funny. Then he bent and wrote MARY SMITH in all caps. "There you go. That's all you'll get out of me."

Cole's father came forward. "How about your name, sir? What is your name?"

"My name is Ned. Ned Smith. The important thing is that your boy and his missus have been given a great gift." He moved toward the door and swung it open. "There's a note from Mary in the bag there, and we've talked with lawyers. They'll send papers along, make things nice and legal. But Libby here, she needed to be where she's going to be. And that's the truth of it."

He walked out the door, down the steps, and got into his car. Not one of the three Laffertys moved to stop him. Then he turned the car around and headed up the lane.

He left the baby here.

Cole couldn't wrap his head around that, but the baby chose that moment to fill her diaper, which brought him straight back to reality.

His mother lifted the denim bag. "There are diapers in here. And wipes. Hand me the baby, Cole. I'll change her."

He almost handed her over, but he'd changed his share of diapers. "I've got it. Can you lay down a towel or a blanket? Right before you call the police and tell them what just happened?"

"I'll get the blanket." His mother settled a cozy cotton throw onto the love seat cushion. "But I'm not calling the police."

"Of course we are. We just had a certifiably crazy man drop off a human child. A baby. One that doesn't belong to us." He couldn't believe he was saying those words. To his mother, no less. Of course they were calling the police. There was no other choice.

"I say we take time to breathe, find out a little more about the situation, and go from there," said his father.

Cole had settled the baby girl onto the blanket.

She was small. So small. He tried to remember if Beau had ever been this small. He must have been, but he'd been potty trained for nearly six months before—

He shoved the thought aside, completed the initial drill, and got the tiny girl all cleaned up.

Clumsy, but complete. By the time he was done, the baby smelled better, his father had disposed of the dirty diaper, and his mother had warmed a bottle she'd found in the bag next to a can of formula.

He tipped the baby back in his arm and touched the nipple to her cheek.

She turned, eager, and finished the four-ounce bottle in record time.

Then she burped, tucked her head against his heart, and fell sound asleep. And for the life of him, he couldn't put her down.

So what was he going to do when the authorities did get called and showed up with their retinue of social workers and interventionists?

He had no idea. He motioned to the bag. "Mom. Is there really a note?"

She removed a handful of things from the bag, then pulled out a piece of paper. "There is." She raised it and put her reading glasses on. "'Being unable to do so, I give permission for Cole and Carolee Lafferty to care for my child, Libby, from this day forward.'"

She flipped it over, looking for more, but found nothing. "That's it. It's signed 'Mary Smith.' It's dated. Today's date, Cole. And there's even a notary stamp, which means she had her identity and her wishes authorized."

Cole held Libby a little closer. "The guy said his name was Ned Smith. He must be a relative of this Mary Smith."

His mom shrugged. "Don't know. Seems likely. I'd say he'd have to be a great-grandfather or something, since he said he's almost ninety."

It made no sense.

None.

He couldn't keep this baby. He knew that.

But he couldn't put her in foster care either, not when the mother's wishes were so clear. The note bought them time to make decisions. He had every intention of making the most of it.

CHAPTER TWO

Carolee saw Cole's image on her cell screen, and her heart hit a hard stop. Real hard. She couldn't see Cole's face and not be reminded that she'd put that look of sorrow in his eyes. The grief that gripped a good man's heart was on her. She could have made different choices the day of the accident, but her stubborn nature made her pick up her preschool-aged son and get into that car.

Then the unthinkable happened. Beau was gone, Cole was heartbroken, and it was all on her.

She'd left, thinking that would be better. It wasn't. Being separated only made it harder to talk, and so she didn't talk with him.

She'd avoided it successfully for a long time, but the holidays were upon them.

She hated the holidays. Now, with their baby son gone, she dreaded any sense of celebration, because it was wrong. All wrong.

But maybe he was having a hard time too. Maybe his heart was torn like hers, with shredded ends that could never be put right again. She reached for the phone, then stopped.

What comfort could she give?

None.

Not then. Not now.

The phone went quiet eventually, but a few seconds later it chimed a voice mail.

Cole never left a message. He didn't like phones all that much and liked messages even less, so why a voice mail now?

She reached out to check the message as the phone rang again.

It was Cole again. But was it an accident? Or on purpose?

Either way, she had to answer it. They'd had an understanding back in the day, back when they were together. That if either of them called again immediately after an unanswered call, the other should consider it an emergency. He might have pocket-dialed her, but she couldn't be sure, and so she reached down and swiped the phone. "Cole. Hey. What's up?"

"I need help." He spoke quickly, as if short on time. "Brent is at school, my parents took off for places unknown, and I'm in over my head, Carolee. Can you come over? Like now? Right now? Because I'm so tired I can't see straight. I'd forgotten what functioning while brain-dead feels like."

He wasn't making sense, and Cole always made sense. He made sense of the worst possible situations because he was faith-filled and pragmatic and believed in all kinds of things she'd pushed aside two long years ago. But she couldn't ignore the pleading note in his voice.

She swallowed hard. "I'll come right over. Are you at the ranch?"

"Our place." The home they'd shared until last year, a fateful ten-minute drive from the main house on the ranch.

The lump in her throat thickened. The cozy Craftsman house was her version of a Norman Rockwell painting, Texas style. "Okay."

It wasn't their place any longer, even though they were still married. It was *his* place. She kept peeking at real estate ads, wondering if he'd listed it yet, but that hadn't happened. And then she'd torment herself by wondering if he hadn't listed it because he was dating someone who would eventually share the little house with him. Those musings did no good, of course. They only made her chest go tight and her heart sink further.

The temps hadn't fallen yet. The seventy-plus-degree Thanksgiving weekend would soon shift downward into a cool wet stretch that was common December weather in South Texas. Maybe cool enough to ward off any more thunderstorms. The cooling ocean had pushed them out of hurricane season at last. She always breathed a sigh of relief when they chalked off another year damage-free, but it was a risk you took to live in lower Texas.

She drove out of Conroe. The streets weren't busy yet. People were either at church or getting ready to go to church, so the business districts stood oddly vacant.

But Cole wasn't at church.

The timing told her that, because usually he'd be in the middle right pew of Caney Creek Community right now. He liked the music at the later service better but had attended the early service because cleaning up midday meant losing valuable time on the ranch. Regret stabbed her as she drove south.

Why hadn't she gotten Beau up and ready to go to church with his daddy all those times Cole had gone alone? She'd taken Sundays as her sleep-in day after working all week, which meant she very rarely headed to church with Beau. More often, she'd have a second and third cup of coffee on the back deck, watching nature do its thing.

Now her lack of discipline shamed her.

Cole hadn't faulted her. He'd loved her, understood her. More than anyone, ever.

But she should have gotten out of bed and gone to church as a family. Now that chance was gone.

She averted her eyes when she passed the cemetery.

She stopped by often. She'd planted flowers in the fall, and they'd done all right. Summer flowers dried up in the heady heat of a South Texas day, and there was no way to keep things watered properly. But Beau's gravesite was flanked with bright-toned pansies now. Pansies did well here this time of year. And Beau had loved the pansies at the farmer's market, so it fit.

She pulled around the last bend of the lane and pulled up next to Cole's truck. She didn't stop to think. If she did, she'd turn the car around and head right back to Conroe. So she refused to speculate why she was here.

She climbed out of the car and moved forward.

Ring the bell? Don't ring the bell? Knock? She raised her hand to do just that when the door swung open. "Don't knock, Lee. For all that's good and holy in this world, I implore you. Don't knock. Don't talk loud. Make as little noise as you possibly can."

He looked so bad she wanted to comfort him and take care of him, but she pushed those feelings away with both hands. "Are you sick?"

To her surprise, he shook his head. "Can't sleep. Partially her fault. Partially mine." He pressed his hands to his face, as if trying to gather thoughts or words. Maybe both. "I need to sleep, and I'm afraid that if I do, she'll wake up."

At that moment, she heard a baby cry.

A baby.

She knew Cole's family, and they shared the same friends. No one in that circle had a newborn baby, which meant what?

She had no idea, but she recognized the sharp pierce to her heart. She'd shied away from babies for a long time now, and with good reason.

Cole brought his hands back down. "She's awake. And I'm going to be holding her or feeding her and fall asleep or I'll put her down and fall asleep and I won't hear her when she wakes up and my parents went out of town, which is—"

She didn't need to know his opinion of his parents' vacation life. She needed to know one thing and one thing only. "Whose baby is it, Cole?"

"Ours."

She whirled around. "What?"

The baby's cries were growing more insistent. Cole met her gaze, then turned and walked toward the first bedroom in the small home. The spare room they both used as an office. Not Beau's room. "It's a long story. But yes, Lee. She's ours. She was pretty much put on our doorstep Friday afternoon, and that means I haven't slept since I crawled out of the sack Friday morning."

The accuracy of his words showed in his face, his shoulders, and the hollows beneath his eyes.

"I called you Saturday to tell you, but your phone went straight to voice mail. It wasn't the kind of message I wanted to leave."

Her phone. She'd dropped it and broken it midweek and had to get a new one. She'd seen the missed call once her info had been downloaded from the cloud. She'd ignored it.

The office looked the same except a portable playpen had been added. The one they used for Beau when he was tiny. The one they'd tucked away when he outgrew it so that baby number two would have one ready and waiting, but she couldn't think of that now. Didn't dare think of all that now. She leaned in and lifted the little girl. "She's wet."

"That seems to be her status quo. My mom dropped off a bunch of diapers yesterday, but she didn't get the kind we used with Beau, so everything keeps getting soaked."

There was a soft blanket padding the wide-bottomed chair they'd tucked in this room. She set the angry baby down there. "Are there more clothes?"

"Just these gown things. Three of them."

"One to wear, two to wash. It gets you through the day most times."

"And these two little blankets. And three bottles, the half-size ones. We didn't use them much with Beau."

Because she'd nursed him. Almost greedily, in fact, because she rarely let Cole feed his own son a bottle. Only after Beau was gone did she look back at what a foolish wife she'd been, and that only added to her self-loathing. "Is there a bottle ready?"

He nodded and moved toward their kitchen.

His kitchen, she corrected herself quickly.

But when she finished changing the baby and had her wrapped in a soft cotton receiving blanket, she moved to the front room like she'd done so many times before.

The rocking chair was still there, facing the fireplace, like it had been since they discovered they were expecting nearly five years before. She sat down in the rocker, and when Cole handed her the warmed-up bottle, their fingers met. Their eyes did too, and for just a moment she was in a place where love surrounded them. Then he blinked, and she came back to reality. "So. Whose child is she? For real this time."

"Mary Smith's."

She frowned. "Don't mess with me, Cole."

"I'm not." He settled into a corner of the couch, leaned back, and pulled a sofa pillow to his chest. "Some old guy showed up on Friday, and he had little Libby here with him."

"That's her name?"

"According to him. I like it. It's a nice name for a little cowgirl, don't you think?"

"So some old guy just brings a baby to you."

Cole yawned, then yawned again. "He said that Mary Smith saw our story and found herself in a circumstance that didn't allow her to keep her baby, so she asked him to bring Libby to us. There was even a handwritten note spelling it all out. Signed by Mary Smith, as unbelievable as it is. I thought we should call the police ASAP and hand her over, but my parents were of a different mindset. Mom mentioned how tough things could be on Mary Smith if we went all legal on her, and you know Mom has a soft spot where motherhood is concerned. Thirty-plus years of working as a labor-and-delivery nurse will do that to you."

Carolee sputtered as the tiny girl eagerly worked on emptying the bottle. "That's utterly ridiculous. And impossible. People don't just hand babies out like pamphlets. There are processes. You remember when Rachel and Nate from church adopted their kids. They went through a long process to get approved and then picked by the birth mothers."

"Well, it seems our birth mother skipped a few steps."

"Cole, I—"

He yawned again, then shifted his position and tucked his head onto the pillow, against the arm of the sofa.

His eyes drifted shut. He sighed softly, and she'd have to be blind not to see his level of exhaustion.

She wasn't blind. Or unfeeling.

In fact, watching him doze off while she held this beautiful baby girl in her arms pushed so many buttons that for a moment—a brief moment—she longed to relax into the scene and just breathe.

It was impossible. She knew it. He knew it too. So would anyone with half a brain. But for that post-Thanksgiving moment, the setting brought up all the old thoughts and feelings that had filled this room for years. Love. Family. Peace. Longing. And a dash of faith thrown in.

She couldn't let herself get attached. She knew that.

But he needed sleep desperately, and he hadn't called any of the women who seemed bent on dropping off cakes or cookies or casseroles after she'd moved out.

She'd heard about them. People loved to talk, and in a small town like Cut and Shoot, they talked a lot. That was part of the reason she'd gone up the road to Conroe.

Out of sight, out of mind.

And yet, clearly not, because when her estranged husband needed help, he didn't call someone else.

He called her.

And for that moment, it felt like she was right where she belonged.

CHAPTER THREE

Cole didn't want to wake up.

Lost in a dream that made everything right, his brain relaxed into the soft movement of feet on the floor and the slow croon that Carolee used to get Beau to sleep. It worked almost all the time for her, and almost never for him. But that didn't matter, because—

Reality smacked him upside the head as he woke up.

Beau was gone.

His wife was gone too, separated from him. But it was her voice, the sound of her feet, walking, pacing, rocking a baby to sleep.

And when he forced his eyes open, it all came rushing back. But today was different because Carolee was really there, in their living room, walking with a tiny baby.

Not Beau.

Libby.

He squeezed his eyes shut. And when he opened them again, it didn't all disappear like it had so many times before. Too many times to count. Seeing his estranged wife there, in their home, with a baby in her arms, was simply too right to ever be wrong.

She didn't believe that. She blamed herself for the crash that robbed them of their beautiful boy, despite so many facts to dispute her guilt. The concept that accidents happen didn't work with Carolee. She knew she'd had choices. She could have stayed at the ranch that day, but she wanted to get home and weather the storm in their house, where Beau's things were. To her that meant that if she'd made another choice, Beau would still be alive. She couldn't get around that.

"You're awake."

"Kind of." He rubbed his face and sat up. "How long was I out?"

"Three hours. Not long enough, from the looks of it."

"But enough to take the edge off," he replied. He stood and drew close to her. Partially to peek at the baby. Partially to savor the moment of them together again. "How's she doing?"

"Two diaper changes, and we're on the next bottle. One short nap. Very short."

"Catnaps." He moved toward the kitchen and brewed a quick cup of coffee as she settled into the rocker. "Want some?" He raised a mug, and she nodded.

"My mother said that some babies don't develop normal sleep patterns or napping patterns for years. That some take catnaps of twenty minutes and wake right up, ready to play for three hours before the next one. Beau wasn't like that."

He said it deliberately. For a long time, he'd tiptoed around Beau's existence because he avoided anything that put the shadowed desperation and grief on his wife's face, but the time for treading lightly was over. Mostly, anyway.

She took a breath, then nodded gently, her chin resting on Libby's tiny head. "He slept hard, like his daddy. But when he woke up, he was ready to play all day."

"Yeah." He didn't hide the regret in his tone, but he didn't belabor it either. "So, we have to figure out what we're doing here, Lee." He'd given her that nickname when she'd gone off to San Antonio to get her Doctor of Physical Therapy degree, mostly because her pageant-loving mother insisted on everyone using Carolee's full name. Carolee Hobson Vance. He wasn't sure if her mom wanted Carolee to become an actress, a model, or a game-show host. A physical therapist hadn't even made the long list. Her mama saw Carolee going off to new lands, new ideas, new heights. Staying in Cut and Shoot and Conroe had been a bitter pill for Lee's limelight-loving mother to swallow.

"What *you're* doing," she replied. "As in call the police and report that someone has just given away a baby. They're going to want to know why you didn't call on Friday."

"I'm not calling."

She stared at him. "You have to, Cole."

"I don't," he drawled. "I'm not getting the law and social services involved in any of this at the moment. I have the note from the mother, asking for us to care for the baby temporarily. The old guy said the rest is coming, so I'm going to pray. Bide my time for a few days and see what's what. I want to find Libby's mother, figure out what this is all about, and make some sense of the situation. Once the law's involved, we lose all control."

"Not we." She spoke firmly, but he noticed how closely she snuggled the baby. "You. I have a job to go back to. So do you. I'm pretty sure the ranch isn't going to run itself."

"Dad will help. Mom too. But you are specifically named in this letter from Mary Smith—"

"I can't be."

"You are," he assured her.

"This is a legal matter, Cole."

It was, and Texas ranchers weren't strangers to the machinations of government, permits, and rules. Even in a freedom-loving state like theirs, rules were meant to be followed, but as long as Mary Smith was the baby's mother, they had permission. For now, at least. "Don't you think we can do this?"

"I don't think we have a choice. She's not ours, Cole. She's not our business."

"Except her mom picked us. I don't see that being any different than hiring a babysitter. People leave kids in other people's care all the time, Lee, and it's not as if we're bad people." He grinned. "At least you're not."

She didn't smile, but her frown relaxed. He set her coffee on the small table nearby. "Knowing a woman did that means something to me. It reminds me of when that cat brought her kitten to the farmer's wife. You know, in that story you used to read to Beau."

She'd read him the James Herriot story again and again because Beau loved animals. He loved cats, and one of Cole's regrets was not letting him have one. If he could, he'd go back and change that, and Beau would have his cat. And a dog. And—

He'd missed some chances then. He was ready to make up for them now.

"That's not fair, Cole."

He squatted next to the glider. "What's not fair is to instantly go against the mother's wishes instead of checking things out."

"It's too much." She stood and handed him the baby. Then she turned toward the door, ignoring the coffee. "She's not ours, and I can't pretend she is. And I'm not about to play detective with you to find this child's mother. And what about the father, Cole? Have you thought about that? That somewhere, this baby has a father who might love her? Care about her? Want her?"

"All the more reason we tackle this together."

She stared at him with such hurt and sorrow that he almost caved. He met her gaze as he lifted the baby slightly. "She needs us. And I think we need her, Lee. At least to know we've done the best we can do for her."

"There are professionals who are trained to do this very thing. I don't know why that's such a bad option, Cole."

"Because it's not what her mother wanted," he said. "And above all else, with whatever is going on, I want to respect what she wanted. That means a lot to me."

Her eyes went wide, but then they filled with tears.

She stayed them by pressing her hands to her cheeks, and it hurt him because he could tell she'd had a lot of practice making that move. "I've got to go."

"Okay." He wanted to convince her to stay, to plead his case, but he knew his wife.

He was a jump-in-with-both-feet kind of guy, but she tested the water. She needed time.

And so, he stopped talking. He let her go. When she got to the door, she turned, and he could tell she wanted to say something. But she didn't. She slipped out the door, down the front steps, and got into her car without a backward glance.

Fifteen minutes later his phone rang. He swiped it quickly when her name came up. "Hey."

"You can't do this alone."

He fought back a sigh of relief. "Agreed. My mom said she can watch the baby through the day, but she's doing afternoon shift at the hospital for December. Per diem, that is."

"I can come by after work, but I won't be there until almost five."

"Dad and I can do the interim. Then I can take over at night."

"And sleep when?"

"When she naps."

"And if she doesn't?"

"We reconfigure. Mom's got more flexibility than she had when Beau was a newborn. She'll help."

"And how do you propose we find this mother? This Mary Smith?"

That was a question that had either too many answers or none. "I'm not sure, but they've got those ancestry sites all over the place. I say we send a sample of Libby's DNA off and see what we find. If she's related to anyone who's on a site, we'll hear, right?"

"That's actually a good idea."

He almost smiled. "So, I'll see you tomorrow afternoon?"

"No. Tonight. I'm going to grab some things and come back over. I'll sleep on the couch so we can tag-team feedings."

"You sure, Lee?" He didn't say that her offer made his heart beat faster. That the thought of her making steps toward him was the crux of every prayer he'd prayed for over a year. "I'd be lying to say I couldn't use the help, but if you do this, I take the couch. I sleep there most nights anyway."

Silence stretched between them.

"My way or the highway, Cole."

He wasn't about to argue over sleep-time details. "I'll take the room. You can have the couch."

"I'll see you at six. I'll bring supper."

"Bring it tomorrow when Hoppy's is open," he suggested. "I've got pulled pork in the freezer. Let's do that tonight." She loved his pulled pork. Would that offer push too many buttons?

She didn't hesitate, and that loosened the vise around his heart a little more. "I'll get some good rolls for toasting. Do you want mac salad?"

Carolee's mac salad was the stuff dreams were made of. "Yes, ma'am."

"See you later."

He put down the phone.

Libby was still sleeping.

He yawned and stretched, then cleaned the two used bottles, fixed fresh formula, and washed the wet sleeping gown.

They'd packed away Beau's things before Carolee had walked out.

He didn't know if packing them away was right or wrong, but that's how it was when you had no experience with death. You faked it. Pretended. Got through the days.

He checked on Libby and, somehow, seeing her there, tucked in and sound asleep, brought hope back to his heart. Something that had been missing for far too long.

He took the gift of time to open his laptop and check out ancestry sites. He didn't know which to choose, so he bookmarked all three and ordered kits to arrive by Tuesday. By the time Carolee parked her car alongside his truck, the pork was warmed and the baby was fed. When she came through the front door, he hit the remote for country radio.

Christmas music came on instead.

His hand stopped, midair.

Carolee had avoided Christmas since their loss. Christmas lights, Christmas music, church services, festivals. She'd sidestepped all of it because it simply hurt too much. He reached to switch it off. He didn't want to turn an uplifting moment into a downhill slope, but she raised her hand. "Leave it, Cole."

Winsome notes of "Greensleeves" filled the air as strings and flutes stretched out poignant notes of old. "It's all right?"

She'd stopped inside the door. Now she closed it behind her, glanced toward the sleeping baby, then him.

Her expression went soft. She glanced from Libby to him again, then moved into the room. In one hand, she had a dish. In the other, she tugged a carry-on-sized roller bag. She handed him the macaroni salad and parked the bag. "In light of our current situation, I think 'What Child is This?' is perfect."

They tag-teamed the night.

At least they pretended to tag-team. He woke up when it was her turn, and he was pretty sure she did the same as he fed the hungry baby somewhere between four and dawn. She pretended to stay asleep, but he hadn't shared five years of life with her and not learned her habits.

But she didn't look tired in the morning. She looked beautiful.

He didn't tell her that, because he didn't want to undercut any inroads they may have made the day before. His brain cautioned PATIENCE in all-caps letters, but his heart felt differently. His heart longed to welcome her back, beg her to try again, but he'd learned a tough lesson the past year—forcing someone to stay doesn't work.

But if they returned on their own, that was a whole other matter.

"Your mom's okay with coming over today?" she asked as she slipped a sweater over her blouse.

"I'm taking Libby to their place. Mom's got what she needs there, and I thought that would be easier for her."

Carolee paused. Her hand was on the doorknob, and it stayed right there.

Then she turned the knob and slipped out the door. "See you later."

"All right."

She didn't look at him or the baby. She kept herself distant purposely, and he knew he should be doing the same. But he couldn't.

And when they take this baby away? When someone realizes what the old man has done and tracks her down, how are you going to handle that?

Badly.

He knew that. He'd known it from the beginning, but a man didn't turn his back on a needy calf or colt. He didn't languish in bed when there were chores waiting, and he never took the care of children lightly, because they were the most precious gifts of all.

He knew he was in for a wake-up call.

But he was doing the right thing. He had to keep believing that. He hoped their investigation would turn up some answers, even knowing he wouldn't be able to pretend he would like what he found. But that was a problem for another day.

When he packed Libby into her car seat, she let him know just how displeased she was with him all the way to the ranch house. But when he unbuckled her in his mother's living room, the baby looked up at him and smiled. Not one of those pretend smiles either. A real one, even though she was a little young for that. "Mom, look."

His mother peered over his arm. "Oh, that little sweetums knows how to wrap you around her itty-bitty finger, doesn't she?"

His mother reached for the baby. "Hand her over. Your dad's got a buyer coming in from the Hill Country. A dude ranch there looking for new paints. Breeding stock."

Buyers with cash in hand were always a welcome thing. And the Texas Hill Country was famous for its wide selection of dude ranches. Some were strictly recreational while others combined the agribusiness of recreation with a full-on ranching operation. Savvy ranchers liked to bring in new, clean lines. Like theirs.

"I'll go meet Dad. Call me if anything comes up, okay?"

"Will do."

She didn't roll her eyes at him like she would have before they lost Beau. Back then she would tease them sometimes about being new parents, about worrying too much.

She wasn't comfortable with that now, not after what happened. And she would never be comfortable with it again.

Chapter Four

He called her two hours later, prior to the buyer showing up.

And then he showed up at the house around lunchtime, even though he had two PB&J sandwiches tucked in his bags. He'd left his thermal coffee mug at the barn, but he filled a disposable to-go cup at the house, and that worked while he pretended he wasn't checking on Libby.

At two thirty he stopped himself from calling his mother again.

It wasn't easy, but he did it. At two forty-five, his phone rang with an unknown number. "Lafferty Ranch. Cole speaking."

"It's Ned Smith, Mr. Lafferty. Calling about Libby."

A slipknot tightened around his heart. "The Ned Smith that delivered a baby girl to my house a few days ago? That Ned Smith?"

"It's me. How's she doing? How are y'all doing?"

"She's fine. We're fine. I've been waiting for this call, expecting someone would be coming by for her soon."

"That won't happen," Ned replied. "But we did get the paperwork in the post to you just now. I sent it overnight so we don't waste time. It's got signatures and lawyers and even a copy of the petition to the courts to approve the whole business, the voluntary relinquishment stuff. I double-checked."

So he double-checked, did he? How reassuring.

"Just wanted you to be on the watch is all."

Cole supposed he should appreciate that. "All's good here."

"I'm glad to hear it. Mary will be too. This means a lot to her."

"Mr. Smith, tell me the truth. Is there really a Mary Smith? Does she exist?"

"Well, that baby came from somewhere, didn't she?" Ned sounded abrupt, but then he sighed. "She exists. Her life's taken some turns, but if I can help her get this settled so she can get on with things, I'll do it. No one can fault a mama looking out for her baby, now can they?"

"No, they can't. But what's to stop this woman from showing up out of nowhere in a few weeks, months, or even years, to take her baby back? I've done my homework. That kind of thing happens all the time. And I can tell you straight up that my wife and I can't handle that kind of thing. It's probably best to—"

"That won't happen, son." Ned's voice went soft. "It can't happen, and that's all I can say right now. I promised privacy, and I mean to keep my word. It's..."

He went quiet. Cole thought he'd hung up, but the seconds were still ticking away on his phone. What was the old man doing? And then, a little softer, Ned said, "Goodbye for now."

He broke the connection.

Cole called his cousin Jeremy, who was with local law enforcement. Jeremy was good at following rules, but he was family, and Cole was willing to take a chance. "I got a call just now. I know you can't trace the call and tell me anything about the person—"

"Why do I sense there's a 'but' coming?" groused Jeremy.

"I just need to know if it's a burner. That's all."

"A crew of well-fed monkeys could find that out with the right phone app."

"For real?"

"Yup. And breaking no laws. Won't give you legal info. But it will tell you what you're dealing with. Kind of."

He thanked Jeremy, disconnected, then searched for the tracing app, and when it had installed, he typed Ned Smith's number into it.

Just as he'd suspected.

Ned Smith was savvy enough to use a burner phone.

Houston was the biggest city in Texas and the fourth largest in the country. So how was he supposed to find one old man or one young woman in a city of over two million when they were using probably false names and burner phones?

His phone pinged a text.

Your scheduled delivery from ABC ANCESTRY will be delivered tomorrow between 9 AM and 12 PM.

They'd have the kits tomorrow.

Sure, it would take a few weeks to get results, but they had things under control for the moment. Maybe he and Carolee could do some legwork in the meantime.

Sure enough, when he got back to the house at half-past supper, Carolee handed him a printout.

"What's this?" He stared down at the list of names. Then the light dawned. "Birth announcements."

"All the ones posted in the Houston papers for October." She pointed to the first list. "We're figuring that Libby is about seven to eight weeks old, right?"

"That's what he said. Seven-and-a-half weeks old on Friday, so eight weeks now."

"Then let's look back eight weeks. Even nine weeks and see who's had a baby that's listed here with just a mother's name. Or no name."

He'd forgotten that newspapers did this.

They'd listed Beau in the local papers. "Infant son of Cole and Carolee Lafferty." Then the date and his weight. Where he was born. His grandparents' names.

He'd thought it funny then, that births were listed.

Now he was grateful.

He'd gone by The Hoppy Kitchen to get food because Carolee had picked Libby up from his parents' house and brought her back here.

He wondered how that would go because she had to pass the accident scene. The storm had come onshore as a Category One hurricane. Lots of people thought "no big deal" when they heard that status.

It ended up being a huge deal. The storm moved inland with tropical-storm-force winds and a glut of rain. Then it hit a slow-moving low-pressure system and stalled. The combination funneled copious amounts of Gulf rain into lower Texas and took out a section of road that had been undermined from past gully washers. Carolee had no warning when she happened on it and lost control of the car.

If only the weakened culverts had been noticed sooner. If they had—

He wrestled his thoughts to the ground. "Should we eat first?"

"Eat during," she shot back. "I haven't been to Hoppy's in a long time, and Miss Libby could start stirring at any moment. This is a treat. Fish for me. Burger for you?"

"You know it." They used to stop by the popular little dive when it first opened. It was one of the hidden gems in Conroe, and he'd stayed away for over a year. Seemed like she'd done the same.

They sat side by side at the table's end with the printouts in front of them. She set a pink highlighter between them, and they scanned the first two sheets between bites.

Nothing fit. There was nothing to highlight.

They studied the next page.

Still nothing. By page three, the birth dates were later in October. Libby's birthday couldn't be that late. Not if she was really eight weeks old.

"Do you think it could have been as early as September, Lee?"

She pushed half of her fries his way like she'd always done. The three pieces of fish were her main meal. "The last week, maybe? If she was born in Houston. The Houston area," she corrected herself. "And if they listed it. But there's the question," she mused as she reached for another fry. "If this was an unplanned baby, would you list it in the papers? They used to publish all of them, from the hospital records. It's different now. Parents submit the announcements themselves."

"So these aren't all the births."

"No. But I thought it was worth—" She stopped talking abruptly. She'd lifted the last sheet, the one with announcements late in the month of October. Too late for Libby. But then she set the paper down in front of him. "Number four," she said. "Lindsey Liberty, born October fifth, six pounds, twelve ounces. Beloved."

"No mother's or father's name."

"No," she agreed. She highlighted the entry with the bright pink marker. "That middle name. Liberty. Do you think that's where Libby comes from?"

"It could be. But why not just call her Lindsey?"

"I guess they wanted to make it harder to trace her birth. And this listing was done weeks later than most babies born on that date. We're four pages in."

"An afterthought?" he asked, but that seemed weird.

Carolee sighed. "Or maybe her mama just wanted to do what all mamas do? Brag about her baby. Announce their presence. Notice how most of them have parents listed, at least one. Most have both. Not this one."

"And a lot with grandparents' names too."

"If this is Libby's announcement, someone didn't want it flagged or noticed or recognized. And that's understandable if you're going to give the baby away."

"And yet it's here," he noted. "If it's hers."

The baby stirred.

"Countdown." Carolee began to eat fast, and she was right. When a newborn got down to business, time was of the essence. "She likes the swing."

Cole was surprised. "She does?"

"Yes. Your mother got down the swing she used for Beau. Libby liked it."

"Beau loved that thing." Their son had lulled many an hour away with the soothing click of the back-and-forth motion. It had been a steady presence in the house for several months.

"He did. Should we get his out?"

He knew what she was asking. Not just should they, but could they? Could they get out a piece of infant equipment they'd gotten for their lost child and use it for this abandoned little girl? "If it gives us more sleeping time, the answer is yes." He didn't stop to think about it too much.

Apparently, neither did she. "Can you get it down while I put stuff away?"

"Yes, ma'am." He pulled a stepladder over to the storage access above the bedroom wing. Five minutes later he'd brought down the swing. He hesitated for several long seconds, then began to move the stepladder out of the way.

"Cole?" She called to him from around the corner as the baby began to peep a little louder.

He loved hearing her voice here, in their home. He had to work to keep his tone normal. "Yeah?"

"There's a bin up there."

He knew that. He'd seen it.

She poked her head around the corner as she dried her hands. "It's clear with a blue top."

"The one marked 'newborn'?"

She breathed deep and nodded. "Having those onesies and T-shirts down here will make this a lot easier. Until someone realizes what's happened and comes to pick her up."

"I'll get it. And the old man called me today."

"He what?" She came around the corner quickly. "And you're just telling me this? Way to bury the lede."

"He said they shipped the legal papers to us."

She stood there, holding the dish towel and the plate she'd been drying.

"He asked after the baby, and I said she was fine, and he said he'd sent out the papers he'd talked about. Signed and dated. Including the petition to the judge to approve their voluntary termination of rights."

Her eyes had gone round. She frowned, then seemed to shake herself. "Those were his words?"

"Yes. Well, I prettied them up a little, but yes. That's what he said."

He read the look in her eyes. Disbelief. Surprise. And a hint of wonder mixed with a strong dash of doubt. "We'll see when they get here. In the meantime, maybe we can figure out who placed that ad for Lindsey Liberty."

"Can't hurt to try." She stared up at him for long seconds before posing a question. "He actually said he'd sent the papers?"

He was halfway up the ladder to retrieve the plastic tote. "His words."

"Oh my."

He heard the hint of hope in her voice, and it took work to ignore it because he'd felt the same way when Ned Smith—or whatever his name was—spoke to him earlier. As if maybe, somehow, this was real.

Except it couldn't be.

Libby stirred in earnest this time. He heard the fridge open and close as Carolee took out a bottle, and then the sound of water running meant she was warming it under a steady stream.

And she was humming. Humming the same Christmas song that was on the radio when he flicked on the country station that had morphed to holiday music for the next five weeks.

What child is this, who, laid to rest, on Mary's lap is sleeping?

The question of the hour.

What child was this? Whose baby? And why was her birth mother intent on giving her away or, more specifically, giving her to them?

And why did the very thought of that drive both fear and joy straight into his heart?

Chapter Five

Fed Ex and UPS arrived at the ranch house within ten minutes of each other the next morning.

One dropped off two of the three ancestry kits.

The other delivered an overnighted, legal-sized envelope marked *Documents*. He had to sign for that one, and when he gripped the pen, his hand shook slightly. He firmed his hold on the pen, scribbled a signature, and took the envelope.

He called Carolee right away. "The tests are here. Do you want me to wait and do them with you tonight? Or get them done and back in the mail before the post office closes?"

"Don't wait. The longer we wait, the more of a chance we'll lose our hearts to this precious baby."

"I think the ship's sailed on that."

She sighed, but it wasn't an all-sad sigh. It was a sigh of agreement. "True words. Can you and your mom get them shipped out?"

"Looks pretty simple. We're on it. And Lee?"

"Yes?"

"The papers are here. I'm going to wait to read them until tonight, when you and I are back at the house."

"It's surreal, Cole."

"I know."

"And I know I shouldn't get attached, but how does a normal person not get attached to a baby?"

"I can't imagine it."

"Me either. Gotta go. I have an appointment with an unsuccessful rock climber's knee in ten."

"You take care of that. I've got this."

"You always do, Cole."

He didn't refute the words, but he knew better. He knew how bad the last two years had been. How hard it was to get up and take a breath. To see another long day of nothing good in front of him.

"See you later."

He joined his father in the north pasture, then returned to the ranch house midday. He drank fresh coffee, and he and his mother procured samples from a less-than-cooperative baby.

"This is easy when they're teething and drooling a mile a minute," noted his mother. "Not so much now."

In the end they were successful. He took the samples to the post office and paid for overnight delivery.

Then he went back to work.

He and his father had reconfigured a section of fence that morning. A tough job for someone alone, made much easier with the two of them working together. They'd adjusted the outer perimeter so the horses could get to fresh water unless there was a freeze. That didn't happen often, but the assurance of readily available water for nearly forty horses was significant.

They had eight mares ready to foal in January and seven more in February. They'd kept wooded areas in several pastures. The small sections of forested ground offered natural shade and comfort during the long hot months of a Texas summer. Cole motioned toward the first area of segregated mares. "I'd like to get the creep feeder rebuilt before Christmas. That way if foals start dropping in early January, we'll be ready."

"We've got six weeks yet. Give or take. There's no hurry."

Cole paused and looked closer at his father, who wasn't looking back at him.

He was looking off, toward the paddock, and when the sun came out from behind a bank of clouds, his father's pallor stuck out. Beneath the gray stubble of a ten-day beard, his father's skin tone had no luster. More concerning was his lack of ambition, because if "Don't Wait" had a poster child, it was Jim Lafferty. "You feeling all right? You look a little pale."

His father frowned. "I'm fine. I think the creep feeder's okay for another year. Or at least until January." He half barked the reply, and then paused. When he spoke, it was in a quieter tone. "We need to figure out stuff with that baby one way or another. The feed bin'll wait."

The creep feeder was a sectioned-off area so that young horses could get their fill as they grew. Their need for nutrition was crucial, and greedy mares were known to overeat. The creep feeder allowed the small horses to duck under a rail to get to the food and kept the always-hungry mamas to the outer marker.

His father was right about one thing. They needed to prioritize whatever was going on with Libby. Something in his father's expression made him drop the subject.

Jim Lafferty was an old-school rancher.

That meant he was stubborn, hardworking, and crotchety about things he couldn't control, like the weather.

Cole was like him in many ways, but his mother had curbed the crotchety side from the day he announced he wanted to stay and work the ranch with his dad. She'd sat him down and given him a stern warning about attitude. She let him know that grumpy farmers and/or ranchers aren't fun.

But his father's tone and pallor seemed to be more than a bad morning or troubling circumstances. It looked like the problem was physical. Other than a few bouts of flu over the years, his dad hadn't missed a day on the ranch. Cole pushed the unwelcome thoughts aside. One thing at a time. "I'm going to head up and take Libby back to my place. I want to check out whatever those papers are when Carolee gets there."

"Don't be fooled, Son. Or foolish."

While his dad took his SUV north, Cole drove south to the ranch house. He kicked off his boots and found his mother rocking the baby in the living room. "I keep reminding myself not to get used to this." He stroked Libby's head. "That it's a temporary repose."

"And if it's not?"

He frowned and perched on the arm of his father's chair. It was the only place he dared sit in work clothes. "That's not something I can afford to consider."

"But what if it's real?"

Why would she say that? He sighed. "It's not, of course. People don't simply give babies away. If someone wanted to give a baby up, they'd contact an adoption agency and go through them, Mom."

"Maybe Mary Smith wanted more say in where her baby goes."

"She said she saw our story." Cole frowned. "That was two years ago. And she remembered it? It seems unlikely. It makes no sense. A one-paragraph mention in a Houston paper of a traffic fatality is something you read and feel bad about for a day or two. Not something that you remember for two years."

His mother paused the rocker. For a few seconds, she seemed to consider his words, then she shrugged. "I suppose you're right. Maybe I'm clutching at straws. Call me an optimist, but I'm not assuming the worst here."

"Then you're the only one who isn't." He spoke kindly, but he was firm. "I don't want anyone's heart crushed over this situation, but I'm also unwilling to hand her over to the authorities and get caught in the system. I'm going to head home with her so Lee and I can go over the papers that Ned sent. My first question is, how does one sign a legal relinquishment document with an alias? Unless Mary Smith is her real name. And we want to see what we can track down about the birth announcement."

His mother had stood up with the baby. She'd draped the receiving blanket on the back of the chair but turned to him, startled. "Birth announcement?"

"One that went into the *Herald* in late October."

"But if Libby's two months old—"

He nodded. "We almost missed it because of that, but it was put in late. There was a very short announcement of a baby named Lindsey Liberty. Born October fifth. No mother or father listed, just one word after her weight." He drew a breath and reached for Libby. "Beloved."

"Oh my."

"I don't know if it's her or not, and I don't know what it means." He crossed to the table and began tucking Libby into the car seat.

The newborn let him know what she thought of that at the top of her lungs. He leaned in, kissed her little cheeks, and said, "Hey, missy. I've lassoed my share of calves and colts so's I could do right by them. A mite like you hasn't got a prayer of convincin' me otherwise. Consider yourself trapped."

"Nice drawl, cowboy." His mother looped an arm around him, then reached up and kissed Cole's cheek. "Whatever happens, I want you and Carolee to be happy. That's my Christmas wish. And my daily prayer as well."

"All I know is that before little Miss Libby rolled into town, nothing got my wife to cross that line in the sand she drew last year. But I never stopped praying and reaching out now and again. It's like working a stubborn fishing hole. And if it was God who sent this baby to tempt my Carolee back to where she belongs, I'll be ever grateful. No matter what happens," he added. He lifted the seat and rocked it gently, hoping to calm the baby down. Nope. "Maybe being around Libby will break down that wall of guilt. Working around horses and cattle all my life, I know that accidents happen. They just do."

"But Carolee had a Bubble Wrap mother," his mom replied. "Carolee is tough, but if you've never had to deal with tragedy or loss, that first time can be a crusher."

He'd never considered that while they were dating. They were too busy falling in love. And although they talked about the dangers of horses and wrangling and tractors, hills, and trees, she'd never experienced anything like that. She'd lived a pageant-and-protected suburban life until that fateful day.

If he'd been here, he'd have been driving, but he and his father were moving the herd to higher ground when they saw the water rising. And no one—not them, not the town, not the highway department, knew that the culvert was compromised beneath the asphalt, until the whole thing gave way.

Libby thought little of his seat-rocking efforts. She squalled, angry at being in lockdown.

He headed toward the door. "Sooner I get her over to my place, the sooner she's in a swing. Thanks for grabbing more bottles, Mom. And formula. I didn't know you had time to get over to Conroe."

"Happy to help," she told him. "And that pot of chicken stew is for you guys. I've got one here for me and Dad."

He wanted to ask about his father, but the baby's shrieks made conversation impossible. "Appreciate it."

By the time he got home, the temperature had dropped ten degrees. A storm front was moving in. Nothing major. Just dank chill with misty rain and heavier showers predicted later. December weather.

He started a small fire because he knew Carolee loved them. He put out two bowls and the last two rolls from the bread drawer.

Libby had dozed off in the swing. She liked her pacifier, which meant it was Cole's new BFF, so when Carolee came in just after five, the house was warm, and the table was set. Not fancy, but done. She eyed the baby in the swing. "Sound asleep."

"Peaceful. Unlike her ride home. Our little friend does not like being strapped down or tethered. And she's not afraid to let me know it. You hungry?"

"You said the papers came?"

He got her drift. "Papers first." He'd set the flat-rate envelope on the counter. He brought it over to the table and laid it down. "Coffee?"

"Desperately. I skipped my afternoon cup to talk to a high school senior who messed her elbow up just before the big playoff volleyball game. She's dealing with a lot of questions about why her, why now, and what if."

"And you know what that feels like." Cole spoke softly.

She didn't deny it. "Yes. So I can understand her, but I can't change anything for her, and that's frustrating. I don't know what to say to her."

"You can pray for her."

She made a face of disparagement. But then she sighed. "I know. I know it should be my first go-to, but it's not, because I keep thinking that God could have changed things if He wanted to. Even though I know that's not how it works intellectually, it's all I can think of. So then I just get mad at Him and don't want to talk to Him."

"Trust me on this," he said. "God understands." He reached out and touched her cheek. "He knows, and He cares."

She froze, and then she smiled up at him.

And then, for just a moment, he cupped her cheek. "I'll get the coffee."

She nodded. And when he turned to cross the small but nicely laid-out kitchen, he felt her gaze follow him.

He wouldn't make too much of that. Yet.

But it felt wonderful, nonetheless.

I love him.

The realization hit home as Cole moved to get the coffee, but then, she'd always loved him.

That had never been an issue. Still wasn't. But if she couldn't forgive herself for stupid decision-making that led to the loss of their son, how could he forgive her?

He couldn't.

She knew that. No matter what he said, she understood her actions that day. She could have stayed at his mother's that afternoon. A warm, safe house with no dangers attached, but she was a stubborn first-time mother.

She recognized that now. With the help of an understanding therapist who wasn't afraid to let her talk and always had time to listen.

So why hadn't she wised up sooner? If she had—

"Here you go. Can you slice that open, please?" He set down the coffee and laid a sharp knife on top of the package. She slit the top and withdrew a clipped sheaf of papers.

But there, tucked on top, bound by the clip, was a smaller envelope. Addressed to them. She swallowed hard. Then she extracted it and handed it to Cole. "You read this."

He took it from her, lifted the flap, and removed the note. She didn't know what to expect. A heartfelt note, an explanation?

Her heart beat faster.

And then Cole made a face. A kind of cryptic and funny face, which meant it probably wasn't a heartfelt note. She raised a hand to see for herself, and he slid it over. "She's had her shots, it seems."

A shot record. Important, yes. But not what she expected when she saw the hand-addressed envelope. "The first ones. And this tells us what she still needs. That's good. Not what I was expecting to see, but good to know."

"I thought it was a letter." He stared down at the papers.

"Me too. An explanation."

"Clearly that would be too easy." He sounded grumpy.

She poked his arm. "She's offering up her child. The lack of a letter should be the least of our concerns."

"I hate when you're right. Tell the truth, though." He raised his mug and looked at her over the rim. "You thought it was going to answer questions too."

She met his gaze and admitted it. "I did. And it answered some questions. Just not the ones we were asking. Cole, look at this." She lifted the next section of documents. "These are actual relinquishment papers. Notarized. With a petition to the court to shift custody to us."

That was exactly what they were. In fairly simple English, the papers spelled out the intent of one DBA Mary E. Smith to relinquish all rights, claims, and hold on the infant child known as Libby Smith and that said custody should be given to Cole and Carolee Lafferty of Cut and Shoot, Texas.

"What's DBA?" asked Carolee.

"Doing business as," Cole replied. "I use it when I'm conducting business as Lafferty Equine. That's a DBA."

"So as long as this name represents her—the mother," she clarified, "it's okay to not use a real name?"

"A lot of business is done using DBAs. In this case, I think the judge would have to be aware of the actual identity to make sure it was legal, but yeah. Once the judge approves the transaction—"

"An odd and impersonal term for a baby exchange."

"And yet legal and concise. It says that in order to complete a full adoption, we need a home study. And there's a waiting period. But that there are no fees due, no fees needed except incurred court costs as designated by the state of Texas."

"No money?"

He met her gaze. "You thought there would be. Me too."

"I had a couple schools of thought," she admitted. "Total altruism was third on the list. I figured once these mysterious papers came, they'd have an exorbitant fee attached. A fishing expedition. Dangle the bait of a beautiful baby in front of us and see how much we'll pay to get back in the family business."

"I wondered that too. But the old man seemed so sincere and honest."

"Any good actor can pull that off," she replied. "And yet... There's no quid pro quo attached. So why is that, Cole? Why is Mary Smith giving her child to us?"

He shook his head as the baby began to stir. "I have no idea."

"Someone knows."

He started to stand but waited.

"Someone knows us or about us and more than some little article two years back, right? It's almost as if this person, or someone close to her, knows who we are."

"Lots of people know us, Lee."

"I know." Having spent well over a decade being in multiple pageants and dance troupes meant she knew a lot of people, and Lafferty Equine was renowned. Anyone with a love of horses knew the Lafferty name and what they'd done to breed clean and clear paint and quarter horse lines. Conroe and Cut and Shoot had been small towns twenty years ago. Cut and Shoot was still small even though they'd voted to rename themselves a "city" years ago. It was a quaint Western town, but Conroe had become more suburban as people moved north, away from congestion. "I know a lot of people, and the ranch is like a landmark to anyone who knows or loves your family, history, horses, or anything to do with the Lonestar State."

"Uncle Nathan was well-liked and well-respected."

"Yes." Cole's uncle had served the state as a member of Congress for a dozen years before an accident claimed his life while they were dating.

People had come out in droves to pay their respects to him, so why hadn't she realized what it would be like when they lost Beau? The outpouring of love and support after the accident had overwhelmed her. There had been a groundswell of people attending not just Beau's funeral, but lining the streets of Conroe and Cut and Shoot as the hearse carried his small body to a shaded plot in the local cemetery. "That narrows it down to roughly a few thousand people."

Carolee pored over the slim stack of papers. A separate paper clip, smaller than the original binder clip, segregated other forms. A sticky note marked the top copy. *Sign as indicated by X in presence of a notary.* Below that was a short sheet of legal instructions.

"How do we know what's legal or not?" she asked.

Cole sighed. "How do we know what's moral or not? What if you're right, and there's a father out there, wishing he could be a dad?"

"Except his signature is right here." She'd gone through the top papers, and there was a separate relinquishment form signed by someone doing business as John Patrick Smith.

"I'm going to have Joel look at these tomorrow."

Joel was an old friend. He'd gone to law school after undergrad and had joined his father's firm a few years back. They'd all been childhood friends. It seemed like a lifetime ago. "Can I come with?"

"Of course."

Libby squirmed again. She scrunched up her little face, let out a yelp, and by the overwrought expression, they knew exactly what she was doing. "Cleanup on aisle one," Cole quipped.

Carolee stood quickly. "I'm on it. I missed her today. A lot," she admitted as she paused the swing and extracted the baby.

She nuzzled the baby's neck, and when she stopped, Libby captured her heart with a smile. Even with a nasty diaper, she smiled up at Carolee as if certain that help was on the way.

It was.

The thought of losing her heart to this innocent baby should strike fear into her. Yesterday it had, but today, missing her all day—

All right, missing him too—

And coming home to food and a fire and a baby and legal papers that might actually be legit for reasons they couldn't imagine—

Made the ache in her heart a little less noticeable. That hadn't happened in a long while. For the moment, she intended to enjoy the thought of a new beginning. Or maybe it was a second chance. And maybe—just maybe—she'd be strong enough to make that leap of faith.

Chapter Six

The petition to the court was legitimate.

Joel Goodnight ran it by his father to double-check because he wasn't about to make a determination on his own. He said as much to Cole and Carolee the following week when they met in the law office's small conference room. "It's legit. The petition has been presented to the court and expedited."

"Sped up?" asked Cole. "Why?"

"No reason given. That doesn't mean there isn't a reason, but it might mean they aren't free to discuss it. Or choose not to. I just know it's been done. Now the question is, why is it being done?" He frowned. "I don't want to be the guy that rains on the parade, but does it make sense to you guys?"

"It does not." Cole exchanged a look with Carolee as he took the seat next to her. They'd left Libby with his mother so they could focus on the conversation. "We've turned up next to nothing. We found a birth announcement we thought might be related, but couldn't get any information on it, and you can't check for live births with the county unless you have a name. And we don't. Did your people find anything?"

"Nothing to solve the questions of who and why. But when my mother found out what we were looking into—"

"So much for lawyer/client privilege," remarked Carolee, but she smiled when she said it. Not much stayed quiet in Cut and Shoot.

"It's not like the whole town doesn't know that someone dropped a baby on your doorstep," said Joel frankly. "But my mother said she noticed a dark SUV going down a back lane at the ranch a few weeks ago. She figured it was someone to see you or your dad, but it was unusual because no one uses that access anymore. Not in a fancy rig like that. With tinted windows. A buyer, maybe?"

Cole frowned. "Did she say when?"

"She knows exactly when because she keeps copious notes on every client and prospective buyer and seller she works with," Joel assured them. His mother was one of the top real estate agents in the area. "I asked her, and she looked in her notes. She spotted the SUV using the back access on the Friday before Thanksgiving. Midafternoon."

Cole frowned. "Dad and I weren't there. We were meeting my brother for the game. We sold two prime colts to an Aggie alumnus. He sent us three tickets they couldn't use and put in an order for a pair of two-year-old mares come summer."

"Good guy to know." Joel sat forward and steepled his hands on the table between them.

"You said they came in the back way?" Cole thought about it. No one came onto the ranch that way. The service lane was just that, for ranch workers to gain access to the rear of the ranch. "And she's sure it was that day?"

"One hundred percent. That was the only time she was out that way showing properties. Was your mom home?"

Cole shrugged. "I don't know. She's doing per diem at the hospital and usually does the afternoon shift. I'd have to check with her. It was late when we got home, so I didn't see her."

"Who knew you were gone?"

A cold chill snaked up Cole's spine. There hadn't been a lot of stock theft in recent years, but there was enough to make a wise man keep good fences and an accurate count. "A lot of people. Dad was so excited about going to the game that he mentioned it about a hundred times. Minimum."

"Horse rustlers?" Carolee put a hand on Cole's. "I know the Higbys had a pair go missing last year. Their grandson was so upset about it. Who'd think that in this day and age people would go around stealing horses?"

"I don't know the intent," Joel replied. "But Mom was sure of what she saw. It didn't mean anything to her at the time because she knows you and your dad are up in that area sometimes. But if you weren't, and your mother was gone, why was some high-end SUV checking out the upper pastures?"

Cole didn't know. And nothing was missing. Yet. But horse thieves got away with their treachery because stock was often kept in rotating pastures, depending on the season. And they segregated the expectant mothers, so there were multiple grazing areas to keep safe.

Joel looked at them. Then he splayed his hands. "It's probably nothing."

"There's a lot of valuable stock up there." Cole stood. "I'm going to padlock a gate across that lane," he told them. "It's not foolproof. Someone could come in from up above, but it will make it harder to access the paddocks. Most people won't be foolish enough to try driving a fancy SUV through the ditch. And I'll do a head count. Just in case."

"Are you forgetting something, Cole?"

He looked at Carolee. She'd stood too. Then he looked at Joel. "Signing the papers."

He sank back down. Clenched his hands. Then he stood again. "I can't."

Carolee reached out and took his hand.

"I know how much this means to both of us," he told her. He covered her hand in both of his. "We've fallen in love with this baby girl. You have. I have. But I can't in good conscience simply take someone's child without knowing why they're doing this or what's behind the gesture. I get how people want privacy, but this isn't a calf or a colt we're talking about. It's a human baby, and I can't just say 'oh, all right, thanks so much, we're glad we've got your baby.'"

"At present, no laws are being broken," Joel told him. "Someone has asked for you to watch their child, and you've agreed by your actions if not by your signature. But what happens if the baby gets sick and needs medical care? You don't have the legal standing to authorize that. You don't have the legal standing to even set up standard doctor's appointments. I suggest we reach out to their counsel and ask for that permission to be extended immediately. It would give you some temporary coverage and keep Libby safe. That buys you a little time. And I'd like to ask for details about the mother." He frowned. "It might work, it might not, but there's no harm in asking, is there?"

Carolee glanced from Joel to Cole and back again. "Will that make her nervous?"

Joel shrugged. "The request may never get to her if counsel is acting on her behalf. I think it's worth a try."

Cole turned her way. "I know this is all very confusing."

She didn't disagree. "Sure is."

"And I know we've both fallen for this baby."

"Also agreed."

"So what do we do, Lee?" He looked to her for answers because a part of him wanted to sign the papers, grab an extra box of diapers, and keep the baby. But the part with a conscience fought the ease of that option.

"We find out more," she told him. "Somehow. Some way. Having Libby with us has been a game changer for me." She included Joel in her look. "It's opened my eyes to the thought of children needing help. Needing homes. And maybe even the thought of a future, and that's something I haven't considered in years. But I can't live with myself if we simply sign off on this as our good fortune if there's a mother out there maybe being forced to give up her child. That's not right, is it?"

Joel's dad walked into the conference room just then and cleared his throat. "It's done all the time," he said bluntly. "I apologize for being late. I was stuck on a conference call that should have ended before it began. Carolee." He took a seat opposite Carolee and leveled a steady look her way. "Lots of people give up rights to their children. That's the truth of it. And there are lots of people who have those rights taken away for good reason. That's the reality Joel and I live in. I'm not saying this to convince you two of anything, but to set the record straight. Sometimes we know the reasons why parents walk away. There are a lot of them." He ticked off his fingers as he continued. "Drugs. Embarrassment. New relationships. Mental illness. Selfishness. Physical illness. Change in status. Not everyone can juggle work and a child. And some people actually go into this process with clear, clean thoughts for their own, private reasons. That's how I assessed this one as I appraised these papers." He tapped the papers on the table as he spoke.

"They presented the baby in an unconventional manner," he continued, "but they followed through with legal documentation that's in order. A lot of people who submit relinquishment papers, especially for adoptions, request anonymity. It's less common today than it was forty years ago, but there are some who want or need a clean break. People that know it would be difficult or impossible to watch someone else raise their child without questioning decisions or wanting more input. There's a degree of wisdom to that. The unusual aspect of this particular relinquishment is how the mother chose a couple—an estranged couple, at that—"

Cole and Carolee exchanged a quick wince.

"—to raise their child. Why you? Why now? Why not someone who's been on an adoption registry for several years, waiting and hoping and praying to be picked?"

"Exactly why we can't sign the papers. Yet," added Cole. "Why us is the question of the day. And the fact that the baby was nearly eight weeks old when Ned brought her to us."

"Ned?"

"The old man who dropped her off. He used the name Ned Smith. Where was she for those first seven weeks? And what made the mother decide to move forward then, after she had a chance to bond with her baby? Wouldn't that make it much harder for her?"

"Or it gave her a chance to say goodbye," reasoned Joel.

"In either case, we need more information." Cole kept it simple. "We'll keep searching for answers, and you'll reach out and request medical power of attorney or whatever it is you lawyers call it."

"We'll do that right away," Joel assured them. "That way you don't have to worry about tracking anything down. Are you guys bringing the baby to Christmas on Main this weekend?"

The annual Conroe Christmas celebration was scheduled for the coming weekend. Cole made a face. "We talked about it."

"A lot these last few days," admitted Carolee. "It's such a wonderful event, and we're so lucky to have that here, but if we show up with a baby, that's just going to generate more talk."

"Probably no more than there already is," said Joel. "But whatever you decide, Saturday's weather is supposed to be nice and mild and no rain. That's when Liz and I are heading down with the twins. Why not meet us there? You know how people are with twins. Trust me, with our matched set, most people won't even notice you're alongside us."

Cole looked at Carolee.

She returned the look, then nodded. "About five o'clock?"

"Just in time to see the tree get lit up. And hear the best high school orchestras our county's got to offer."

The annual celebration had grown over the past several years. The whole town turned out for it. And one of the Baptist churches staged a living nativity using the church as an inn and an outbuilding as the stable. The nativity included Mary and Joseph, a requisite donkey from a neighboring farm, half a dozen sheep from another one, and a few ducks and chickens. Local people played the part of shepherds and angels, the innkeeper, and the Holy Family. Cole hadn't seen it yet, but he'd heard wonderful things about it. He stood again. "We'll see you Saturday then."

"I'll text you where we'll be. And we'll get that medical permission form."

"Thank you."

Cole and Carolee walked out of the building together. Cole motioned up the street. "Want coffee?"

She didn't hesitate. "Yes. And a chance to talk without interruption and without being overheard. Can we drink it in the car?"

"Sure can."

Ten minutes later they were parked outside Galavant's Café.

He'd kept his order simple.

So did she, even though she liked a loaded coffee. The more flavor, cream, and syrup, the better. He used to tease her about it all the time because she'd trade a meal for a fancy coffee.

She sipped the robust blend and sighed. "I'm ridiculously confused. And I'm right back to where we were last week. Who singled us out for the honor of raising this baby, and why? And I don't care if the paperwork and the petition seem legit to Joel and his dad, it still seems suspect to me. And I don't know what to do about that."

"It seems suspect because it is suspect. To us," Cole stressed. "Clearly not as suspect to Mr. Goodnight, and he's been doing family law for forty years. He's seen it all. I think for the moment we're okay going ahead like we've been doing," he went on. "As long as we get that medical permission form. But what then? What if we can't find out more, Lee?" He set his coffee down and faced her. "You know where I stand. I've loved you since we were fifteen years old, and that's never changed, but I don't want you to be coaxed back into our marriage because of Libby. Or coerced at the thought of an instant family. I want you to realize that you have nothing to feel guilty about. Nothing to hate yourself for. Because if you can't do that, I'm afraid those old feelings are going to crop up and swamp you when things go wrong." He took her hand. "My mom lost two babies," he said quietly.

Carolee's brows shifted up in surprise.

"One before I was born and one after. She was devastated. She rarely talked about it, because she was so mad and angry and disappointed, both at God and herself. She felt He and her body had betrayed her. Her words. Not mine. She said it took her a long time to accept the frailties of the human body and the grace of God. You know my mom. She's a tough character, but she said those losses brought her to her knees. And eventually back to faith."

"I can't make any promises, Cole."

He knew that because he knew her. Undeserved guilt had weighed heavy on her for a long time.

"I question my choices every single day. Every night. The whole thing haunts me. I feel happy when I'm with you and Libby, but I can't get that storm and the crash and the water out of my head. It's there every time I try to fall asleep and way too often when I wake up."

What could he say? This was a battle she'd been fighting for a long time.

He reached over and hugged her, despite the awkwardness of the car. "I want those feelings banished. Accidents happen to everyone. No one knew that culvert had gone bad, and we travel that stretch multiple times a day. I think of it all the time too," he admitted. "What if I'd gotten those horses moved earlier? Gotten back to my parents' place quicker? Would we have stayed there? Gone on? Or maybe stayed late enough to get the warning about the washout? I don't have answers to that, Lee. But I know one thing. That I was given the very best of life for a while. A short while. I hate that it was cut short, I hate that Beau is gone, but I take comfort that we had him. Even for a short while. That we had each other. And if I had to do it all over again, knowing what we'd be going through, knowing what would happen, I would do it. Because three years with our baby boy would still be better than a lifetime of never knowing him. And that's how I get through the day."

She was crying. Her tears wet his shirt, his collar, his chest.

And still he held her, even as Christmas lights began to blink on around them. He held her against his well-washed flannel and wished there was some form of osmosis that would make his faith her faith.

There wasn't, he knew that. But his prayer, every night and every day, was for her to forgive herself, because until that happened, there wasn't a chance of being successful together.

She pulled back finally.

He didn't have tissues in the car.

She had a clutch in her purse. She pulled them out, wiped her face, blew her nose, and frowned. "I don't know why you're so nice to me. So good to me. So—"

He leaned over and kissed her. The kind of kiss that sent a message all its own. And when he stopped kissing her, he leaned his forehead against hers. "That's why," he whispered. "Reason enough right there, Carolee Lafferty."

She batted her eyelashes against his, then against his cheek, giving him butterfly kisses the way she used to do to him—and to their son. "I want your strength, Cole."

"Mine to give. Yours to take. With a nice dose of faith on the side, Ms. Lafferty." He winked and drew back.

They'd said enough for now.

She'd made some steps forward. He recognized that, but he was wise enough to know the toughest steps were the last ones.

He'd make them as easy as he could and then—

The rest was up to her.

✄ Chapter Seven ✄

Carolee checked her reflection in the apartment mirror before she left to meet Cole and the baby late Saturday afternoon.

She looked good, if she did say so herself. The short peacoat was offset by a red-and-white striped scarf and red gloves. It wasn't cold by Yankee standards, but it was cool. Texas cool, anyway.

She added mascara and didn't have to worry about blush, because her cheeks were pink with anticipation.

She hadn't thought about looking attractive for a long time. Professional, yes. That was part of the job. But attractive hadn't made the short list until Cole put in a call for help two weeks ago.

She'd gone back to her apartment to get clean clothes. As she closed the door behind her, she realized something.

The apartment didn't feel right anymore. Being here. Living here.

The house felt right. Warm. Inviting. Cozy.

The house she'd shared with a beloved husband and a treasured son had been off-limits for a long time, and now it felt like home again.

It wasn't just Libby either. Or Cole. It was the combination of events that got her talking again. Thinking again. Even praying again.

She pushed those thoughts aside.

Grief had tumbled her over a rocky edge, and sure, rock walls could be climbed, but could they be conquered? Could she ever move forward with enough confidence to feel like she could be a wife and mother again? A good one?

She shoved those questions aside too.

Christmas lights surrounded her as she stepped out of the apartment. What began as a Main Street event had turned into a season of lights and music, carols and joy. Church bells rang out, playing carillon-style hymns like a bell choir on Sunday morning. The sounds and sights echoed around her, and for the first time in two years, she breathed in Christmas.

And it felt good.

She scanned the area for Cole's big black truck as she pulled into the lot a few minutes later, but didn't see it.

She climbed out and was about to call him when he pulled in. He parked a few spots down, and she walked over to meet him.

Her heart sped up, her cheeks went warm, and she had to tamp down both reactions. He hopped out as she tapped her watch and lifted a brow in question.

"Diaper emergency. A complete change of everything. And I do mean everything. Top to bottom," he added cheerfully as he swung open the back door of the extended cab. Then he paused and looked at her. Really looked. "Whoa."

She smiled, a little self-conscious.

"You look amazing. Absolutely amazing." He drawled the words nice and slow, which wasn't fair, because he knew the effect it had on her. He leaned down and planted a kiss on her lips. "Nice to see you, darlin'."

"You saw me ninety minutes ago," she reminded him as he unlatched the car seat. She took it from him as he withdrew the stroller. He set it down and snapped it open. But before she put Libby into the stroller, he withdrew something else.

The chest-worn baby carrier.

He held it up. "I was wondering if it might get too chilly for her in the stroller, even with the blankets and the fuzzy hat. And she's not a big fan of being strapped in. Would this work better?"

It would.

Beau had loved being tucked against their chests as a newborn. The body warmth and the rocking movement kept him safe, secure, and content.

For just a moment she hesitated. This wasn't just pushing an adorable baby in a stroller. This was mama-and-daddy comfort care. Intimate. And—

She set the infant seat down and lifted her chin and her arms. "Much better idea. Can you help me get it on?"

"Sure can." He fastened the support system, then tested the waistband. "Snug enough for you?"

"Snug enough to hold a baby twice her size."

He laughed and loosened it slightly. "Better?" He leaned forward from behind.

She looked back.

And then he kissed her again. But when Libby peeped from the seat, he broke the kiss. "Nice to see you, Mrs. Lafferty."

"Nice to be seen," she whispered.

He took Libby from the seat and helped lower her into the chest carrier.

It felt perfect.

It shouldn't. A part of her knew that, like she knew that this baby wasn't hers and wouldn't be staying. People didn't just give babies away. But sliding Libby into the carrier was a simple act of love. It felt marvelous.

He tucked the stroller away, refastened the car seat to the base, then shut the door. "Let's go check this out, ladies."

It was a wonderful festival. Booths lined both sides of the street, offset by festive storefronts. Piped-in Christmas music played at one end, and local high school musical groups filled the opposite end with everything from Christmas jazz to a cappella choirs, hour by hour. They'd missed the parade, but that was all right. Libby wouldn't know the difference, but when Cole peeked down, he whistled softly. "She's all eyes," he told Carolee. "The lights, maybe? Or the people? The colors? Whatever it is, this little one is all over it."

They met up with Joel and his family a few minutes later, and when they'd grabbed hot chocolate for the grown-ups, Joel spotted a break in Santa's line. "Let's head over before it gets crowded again," he suggested. "If I accomplish nothing else tonight, I want a picture of the girls with Santa."

The twins were nine months old. They weren't supposed to be identical, but Carolee couldn't tell them apart. She said that to Gwen, Joel's wife, as they walked toward the big tent holding Santa and his elves.

"Me either," Gwen said. "I cried for a week because I thought I was the worst mother ever, and then my mother used a permanent marker to put a tiny dot on Theresa's arm. No spot? Amelia. Spot? Theresa. She said she learned that trick from her mother because she could never tell my mother and her sister apart until they were almost five years old."

"I wonder if she felt guilty about it?" asked Carolee.

Gwen shook her head. "She didn't," she said. "She said she was too busy keeping two babies fed and dry to do a whole lot of what she refers to as 'self-reflective nonsense.'"

Then, realizing what she'd said and who she'd said it to, she put her hand over her mouth. "Oh Carolee, I'm sorry I said that. I didn't mean—"

"It's fine, Gwen. Really."

Usually, it wasn't fine. Usually, she'd go home and cry for a week when someone failed to recognize the frailty of her emotions, but she didn't feel that way now. Not at all. For the first time in two years, she was able to hear someone talk about their child without taking it personally.

Gwen was raising the twins by trying to keep things practical and light. Something Carolee hadn't been able to do with Beau. Was that because she'd been an only child with an overly doting mother? Or was it normal to go a little overboard with your first child, like those funny TV commercials showed?

Joel moved toward Santa.

The jolly fellow chuckled in a very Santa-like way as they brought the twins up to him. He held one in each arm while Joel and Gwen took a minimum of a dozen pics each. As they moved to take the babies off Santa's lap, Santa shifted his gaze to Carolee and Cole. "Your turn? We can make it a whole family shot if you want to leave the little one where she is."

Carolee shook her head. "We're good," she said.

"Ah." The man smiled and nodded in the kind of understanding way you'd expect from a Santa Claus actor. "All y'all have fun tonight, you hear? It's a good night for families."

"Sure is." Cole looped an arm around Carolee's shoulders. He planted a kiss on her head, then peeked down at Libby. "But maybe one shot with just Santa and Libby? What do you think, Lee? It might be the kind of thing her mama would like to see when we find her."

Put that way, the idea appealed. "I like that thought," she said. The concept of all of them with Santa was a pretense she couldn't embrace, but a baby's first Christmas shouldn't be ignored.

Cole took Libby out of the carrier and moved forward. He nestled Libby into Santa's arms. And then he exchanged a smile with Santa as he stepped back.

Joel and Carolee snapped pics with their phones. And when Carolee came forward to take the baby, Joel called her name just as she leaned in.

She turned.

So did Cole.

Joel snapped a picture of the four of them—Carolee on Santa's right and Cole on the left, with Libby still wide-eyed in the middle.

"Couldn't resist," he told them as they brought the baby to the sidewalk area. Traffic had been closed off, and people roamed the displays, the booths, the music, and the food. There was a coloring station for kids, a saucy Mrs. Claus reading "A Visit from St. Nicholas" to a delighted group of avid listeners, and Mrs. Van de Meer was selling her handmade wooden picture frames in various sizes.

Cole bought an eight-by-ten. When he showed it to her, Carolee questioned him with a look.

"We'll put the picture in this," he explained. "I think that's nicer than taping it on a wall, don't you?"

She smiled. "It is."

They made it through the displays and the carols and the joy. By the time they moseyed back to the truck after food and feeding three babies, things were growing quiet.

"We made it for Santa," declared Joel. "My two Christmas goals were pictures at the nativity over at the Baptist church and a picture with Santa. Now I've got everything I ever wanted." He grinned at Gwen. "Don't put anything under the tree for this good old boy. I've got it all." The minute the words were out of his mouth, a look of pain changed his expression. "Hey. Guys. I'm sorry, I didn't mean—"

"Don't worry about it, Joel." Carolee put a hand on his arm. "You two have so much to celebrate. And even though Libby isn't ours, when Santa asked us to bring her over, I—"

Cole stopped dead in the road. "He did, didn't he?"

Carolee frowned.

"He called her 'she,'" he exclaimed. "You can leave the baby where *she* is." He repeated the phrase word for word. "But no one would look at Libby and assume she's a girl tonight, right? She's in one of Beau's sleepers and a blue and white baby wrap. So how did he know she was a girl?"

"Lucky guess?" offered Joel. "After all, he had a fifty-fifty chance."

"Ned," replied Cole. "The man who brought Libby to us."

"That Santa didn't look like a decrepit old man," argued Carolee. "He was the most convincing Santa I've ever seen."

A festival organizer was riding by in a golf cart. Cole waved her down and asked about Santa.

"Halburt Cochran was going to do it like he's done the past two years," she replied.

Hal Cochran was one of the many people Cole could call cousin in the Cut and Shoot area. It harkened back to the days when the original Cochrans owned the lumber mill and the town squabbled over church and preaching and faith. It seemed that wood was in their blood, because Hal owned the Cochran mill now. "That plan went awry a couple of days ago, I heard," she continued. "Hal came down sick, or something happened out at the farm, so he gave Penny Meyers the name of an old friend. I'm so glad he was able to step in. He wouldn't take a lick of money either. Just said to put it to a good cause. He said families should have more of this kind of thing to do, and he was just glad he was available tonight. But also glad that Hal's suit was big enough for a generous pillow."

"We've got to pay Hal a visit," said Cole as the woman drove off.

"Not while he's sick," Carolee replied. "We'll check in with him in a couple of days, all right? You're sure that was Ned Smith?"

"I should have realized it then, but I didn't, because he was so convincing, but yes. The voice. The eyes. Kind of a different blue, you know?"

"Sky blue. And twinkly."

"Yes. But everything else threw me off."

"That's not a bad thing."

Cole turned toward Joel.

"It gave you guys a night out without worrying. And maybe he hoped you'd bring the baby tonight. Maybe he hoped to see how she was doing. Or maybe he was really just helping an old friend." Joel leaned closer and kept his voice low. "But now we know more. We wondered why they chose you, right? Well, if this guy has ties to the area, that's a big clue. Whoever he is, he's got friends here, and that means the answer might be right here in Cut and Shoot. Let me know what Hal says, all right?"

"I will," Cole assured him. "And guys?"

Joel and Gwen had started for their minivan. They turned back.

"Thanks for making tonight so normal."

Joel grinned. "Normal works."

It did, Carolee decided. She helped Cole get Libby into her car seat.

Libby lit up the night with a very loud protest.

Cole shut the door quickly. "And on that note... Meet you at home, okay?"

"Yeah. See you in a few." She climbed into her car and started the engine.

The festive celebration was ending, but the streets and businesses of Conroe were lit with joy, and as Carolee pulled out onto the street, a pinch of that joy stole right into her heart.

They'd figure out who Ned Smith was, but until then, she'd relish each moment of the current reality for the blessing it was. Not just for them but for a sorrowed mother someplace, doing something so difficult that words couldn't describe it. Carolee didn't know why, but she understood that there were only a few reasons a mother would give up her beloved child. And the first and foremost was the best reason ever.

Sacrificial love.

CHAPTER EIGHT

Cole's mother was stirring a big pot of beef stew the next morning. Extended family often stopped by on Sunday afternoons for food, football, conversation, and fun.

She stopped stirring and turned his way at the mention of Ned's relationship to Hal Cochran. "You really think last night's Santa was the man who brought Libby here?"

"I know it was," Cole told her. "I just didn't know it *then*."

"Well, I wouldn't say this around Grandpa Mike because it might hurt his feelings, but a lot of old men look alike." She winced when she made the allusion, as if she were insulting mankind in general. "And he was dressed in a Santa outfit, right? So that makes it even harder to see behind the glasses, the beard, and the wig."

"It was him," Cole told her. "I'm sure of it. He referred to Libby as a 'she,' even though she was dressed in blue because she made a mess of the little Christmas onesie we got her."

"You've been shopping for her?" She added an array of seasonings to the stew and picked up the wooden spoon again.

"Out of necessity, not expectation." He said it firmly, although when Carolee had walked in with a pair of Christmas outfits, his heart had done a spin roll in his chest, sensing the possibilities. "I can't imagine giving her back," he went on. "I push that thought away even though I understand the inevitability. Joel and his dad said the papers are all in order, but there's no way we can accept this—accept her—without knowing more."

"Lots of people know next to nothing when they adopt children." She set the spoon on the plate she'd set off to the side.

"They've generally been looking into adoption and working with professionals," he shot back. "That's different than having a baby dropped on your doorstep—"

"Living room." She folded her arms and met his gaze. "I don't know how or why this happened, Cole, but I do know one thing. You and Carolee have looked better the last two weeks than you have in a long time, and that's directly because of that baby. And some young woman's generosity. And as your mother, although I don't want to see you guys get hurt again, I love seeing you together and smiling. But I do agree," she added with a sigh. "I feel the same hesitancy you do. We need more information because . . . what if the baby is stolen?"

He made a face. "I'm pretty sure the news would be all over a stolen-baby story."

"Well, okay, not stolen, per se, but maybe *coerced* is a better word? You know, where the family doesn't allow the young mother to keep her child?"

"Um, hello. The fifties called and want their storyline back."

She disparaged him with a look. "You can scoff, but I know a lot of people who would be profoundly embarrassed by an unwed pregnancy. Not everyone is accepting of things like that."

He frowned because he knew a couple of people who fit that description. "Well, that thought just makes this whole thing worse." The memory of his conversation with Joel came to him, and he motioned north of the house. "Were you working the Friday before

Thanksgiving, Mom? Or were you here? I'm asking because Mrs. Goodnight saw a swanky SUV going up the back lane toward the east paddock, and Dad and I were gone that day. Whoever it was could have been checking out the horses in that area or backtracked to the house from there."

She crossed to the calendar on the bulletin board and pointed to the day in question. "I worked that afternoon. I figured since you guys were gone, I'd make some money, and the hospital needed coverage. Isn't that the access you gated and padlocked this morning?"

"That's the one. Joel's mom was showing a house north of here and figured whoever it was had a meeting with me or Dad. Where is Dad, by the way?"

"Resting."

His father never rested. It was a family joke and only partially funny because his mother wasn't on board with workaholic tendencies. On the other hand, she'd married his father, so that made some discussions loud and interesting. "Is he all right?"

She sighed. "He needs to lose fifteen pounds and eat healthier, but he doesn't want to listen to me. I'm pushing him to get his heart checked. His grandpa on his mother's side died of a heart attack at sixty-three. I'd like your father to take it a little more seriously. He'd like me to stop nagging."

"Would it help if I said something?"

She arched one eyebrow and looked straight at him, which meant he better stay quiet.

"I'd be glad to lighten his load. He still likes to prove he's got what it takes to do everything. Even with me and Kenny around." Kenny was the ranch hand who stayed on board all year. Two other guys worked part-time from March through June and then September through November.

"I set up an appointment, even if he doesn't like it. It's got to be done. And he'll be mad at me, so I figured I'd wait until after Christmas to tell him." She returned to stirring the stew. "It's on the calendar for the first week in January. But back to this Ned's relationship to Hal Cochran. Hal was a good friend to your uncle Nathan. Nate moved to Dallas when you were little, so you didn't get to know him real well, but he was such a good man. And a good congressman. Losing him to that plane crash was horrible. The state and this family suffered a loss that day."

"Joel thinks Hal might be the link."

She looked confused. "Link?"

"To Libby. If Ned Smith knows Hal Cochran, maybe that was the link that brought Libby here. Nobody picks a random couple out of the air and ships their baby to them. But Hal knows us, and the old guy knows him." He splayed his hands. "It doesn't make total sense. But it gives us a connection. Of sorts."

She set the spoon on the plate again and lowered the temperature beneath the big kettle.

Then she took a seat at the table. "When are those DNA tests coming back?"

He shrugged. "Not soon enough. Another week or two, most likely."

She bit her lip, then sighed. "I don't like being in limbo with the baby. There's a part of me that wants you to just sign the papers. It's clear this mother wants you to have her. How do you and Carolee feel about it?"

"We can't get beyond the obvious question," he admitted. "Why would a friend of Hal Cochran want to give us a baby? What is old Ned thinking? If that's his real name."

"Not a real common name around here. You'd remember if you knew someone named Ned, right?"

"Ned Peterson?" His father came into the kitchen just then. Despite his rest, he still looked tired.

Cole perked up. "You know someone named Ned?"

His father shook his head. "Not personally, but your mother's family talked about him now and again."

Cole's mother frowned. "I think I'd remember if—" She brightened. "Eddie Peterson."

"But—"

"Yes." His father fixed himself a cup of coffee and brought it to the table. "Only your father called him Ned a few times. When they were over for some potluck something or other. You made that weird dish with the crispy layers and spinach and some kind of cheesy thing."

"Spanakopita."

"Yes. That." He took a sip of coffee. "Hal said that Ned Peterson had given them the best spanak-stuff on the planet a few years before. His mother's recipe. Said yours was just as good and that was saying something. Said he'd never had better."

"But who was he?" asked Cole

His mother shook her head. "I just heard the name Eddie from time to time growing up. Ned's a new one for me."

"So are we thinking this Peterson guy might be Ned Smith?" Cole stood. "I'm going to head home and do some googling. At least I've got a name to go on now. Dad, everything's done outside."

"You didn't need to take it all on," his father said. But there was a hint of relief behind the gruff words.

"Was glad to."

"Come back for stew around four thirty," his mother called as he headed for the door. "I'm making those rolls that Carolee loves," she added. "They're perfect with stew, and we can all watch the late game."

His mother had been going out of her way to make Carolee feel welcome. And special. He appreciated it more than words could say. "Sounds good. We'll see you later."

He hurried home.

Carolee tapped her watch as he came in the door. "You've got time for a two-minute shower, and your clothes are laid out on the bed."

It took him a few seconds to catch her drift, but then realization took hold. "Church."

"You like the music at eleven thirty, and it's ten after now," she said. "I was just calling you to see what you were doing."

"I'll be ready in five."

He was too. Well, seven was more like it, but the church was less than ten minutes away, and she had the baby in the car and the engine running when he came outside.

She'd rarely gone to church with him. Sometimes, yes, but there were a lot of Sundays when she and Beau stayed home. R&R she called it, and he couldn't fault her. She was working full-time and had a child to watch and a busy husband.

To come home and have her ready for church, with the baby, wasn't just a surprise.

It had all the makings of a gift. The googling could wait.

She hadn't expected the church service to shake her up.

People were amazing, including one elderly woman who came up to them after the service and smiled at the baby. "She couldn't have found a better resting place," she whispered. Libby was asleep—a welcome respite during the service. "I'm so very happy for both of you. And her. God is good."

The words soothed and cut.

If God was good, why was Beau gone? Why would a woman feel the need to give up her child? Why would He break their hearts and now open them to grief again when Libby went home to wherever she belonged?

But the woman's perspective soothed too.

"She couldn't have found a better resting place."

The poignancy of the words described Carolee's feelings exactly, and when Cole began his internet search after they got home, she wanted to stop him. Maybe—just maybe—sign the papers and claim this perfect and beautiful child.

She brought him coffee as he typed Ned's name into the search engine.

Nothing came up, and Carolee couldn't deny the tiny spark of hope that flared within her.

He tried Ned, Eddie, Edward, and several spellings of Peterson. Nothing.

She felt guilty about being happy that they'd found nothing, which meant she was allowing herself to get attached. To fall in love. To let this feel real.

He called Hal Cochran next and put his phone on speaker. Halburt Cochran and his father had taken on the family lumber business in the midtwentieth century. He was a good man. "Mr. Cochran, it's Cole Lafferty. I heard you were sick—"

"Family don't hold on ceremony, Cole. And we're family, even if we have to go back a couple of generations to prove it. And I'm not sick. I took a tumble, and the wife put the kibosh on me going anywhere until my knee heels up proper. If there's one thing I've learned over the years, it's to abide by that old sayin'. 'Happy wife, happy life.'"

Hal's phrase made Cole smile, but he looked pensive too, and Carolee knew why. They were both growing attached—no, scratch that, were already attached—to that baby. And she was pretty sure a part of him didn't want to find out more than he could handle either. "Hal, I'm calling about the man who took your place last night."

"Ned."

"Yes, Ned."

Her heart beat faster as Cole glanced her way, and her hands went clammy.

"How can I get a hold of him?"

"He doesn't do Santa gigs anymore," Hal explained. Clearly, he thought they were hoping to hire the old man. "He did his share when he was younger. And he taught Santa school for a long while."

Carolee and Cole exchanged looks of surprise. "Santa school?" asked Carolee.

"Yes, ma'am. It was a great class too, because kids can spot a phony Santa or an unschooled helper right quick. They've got an eye for that kind of thing, 'specially when they get older and they're asking questions about this and that. One thing Ned taught in the class is that less is more. Let your face, your smile, your eyes, say more than your mouth. Good advice in a lot of ways."

"He's done teaching?"

"For eight or nine years now," said Hal. "Something like that, I think. 'Course, I took the class nearly twenty years back. I haven't seen Ned since your uncle's wake."

That meant Cole was right. There was some kind of family connection. Or maybe a political one, since Uncle Nate had been a politician.

"He was there?"

"He sure was. Nathan Sutton was loved by most and well-regarded by others. I remember seeing Ned there that day, but like I said, it was crowded, and we never got a chance to say anything. People don't linger at stuff like that. Not when so many turn out."

"You haven't seen him lately?"

"Not since then, but I knew he was still around, because we got a Christmas card a week or so ago."

Cole and Carolee exchanged glances.

"I gave his name to the committee when I got hurt at the last minute," he explained. "Any regular Santa would be booked for a December Saturday. I thought Ned might help. He needed to use my suit, but he stepped up to the plate for me."

"You saw him when he picked up the suit?"

"Naw. Penny Meyers came by and grabbed it from the missus. I was stuck out back with my foot up, though the knee hurts whether it's up or down, so I don't see a difference. Still, the wife knows best. Or thinks so, anyhoo."

So, they hadn't talked recently. The committee had reached out to Ned. "He's down in Houston?"

"He's got a few spots to hang his hat. But probably Houston right now if he's still got family around. Although roughed-up health sidelines us old-timers, so maybe he doesn't go from place to place like he used to. I knew he had a place up in Dallas and one on some island in the Caribbean. He came from money, and made more."

"He's rich?"

Hal laughed. "In my day, yes, but the word doesn't mean what it used to, now does it? He's well-set. Let's put it that way. And maybe rich. Like I said, I haven't seen him in a long time. But Ned Peterson is still a stand-up guy, from what the committee had to say about him last night. 'Course, we used to joke now and again about names. I mean, who names a baby Halburt?" He chortled as he poked fun at his own name. "I don't mind Hal at all, but Halburt sounds like someone who's not hifalutin tryin' to be hifalutin. Ned felt the same, because who goes around naming a baby Daedalus? He said he was just a kid when he decided to have everyone in the world call him Ned. Pretended his name was Edward, because being named after some fake Greek guy wasn't his cup of tea, but his mama and daddy—the Petrocokinos—were straight off the boat from Greece. They ran three or four diners in the city. Nice places, kind of Southern and Northern mix. Good eats. We stopped there a few times when we were young."

So "Ned" Eddie Peterson was actually Daedalus Petrocokino?

"Sounds like a good place to grab a bite," said Cole as he scribbled the name on a notepad alongside his laptop.

"Good and reasonable. The missus and I don't like to pinch every penny, but we do like our money's worth. She's calling from the other room, wanting to know if I need anything. Good talking with you, Cole. And best of luck looking for a Santa, even though it's kind of late. But who knows?"

Cole said goodbye and ended the call.

Carolee had typed the name Daedalus into her phone to find the correct spelling. Once they had it, Cole went back to the laptop.

Bingo.

Having the right name turned up all kinds of things under D. Peterson/Petersen, D. Petrocokino, Ed Petrocokino, Eddie Petersen, etc.

And there, on a search page, was a current address.

Cole stared at it, then shifted his gaze up to Carolee. "Got it."

CHAPTER NINE

Cole printed three pictures of Ned Peterson off the web, his address, and a picture of his house on Sewanee Avenue. He and Carolee arrived at the ranch early. He wanted time to show his parents the information before others arrived for Sunday supper.

His father whistled softly. "Some house."

"One of three that's listed under this name on the internet directory," Cole told him. "Once we had his real name, all kinds of links showed up."

"I have never heard the name Daedalus in my life," said his mother. "But a lot of people Americanized ethnic names over the years for a variety of reasons. Pronunciation, spelling, discrimination. It's interesting that he kept the Greek surname for business purposes."

"Smart marketing, if you're opening Greek diners in the Florida panhandle and Jersey. He's like a chain without the links of being a chain."

The Houston diners shared two owners. Ned, and a niece named Rula Marou. But the other diners were in his name only.

"So you're thinking he's Libby's grandfather? Or great-grandfather?" Cole's father frowned. "Why would a rich grandfather be giving away a child he could easily afford to keep?"

"Well, he's old." Carolee was stating the obvious, but she wasn't wrong. "And clearly there are other circumstances involved. So…"

She faced Cole. Her expression showed the war of emotions, but she didn't shy away. "When do we go?"

"Can you get a day off?"

"I'll make it happen."

"Tomorrow?"

She swallowed hard but nodded. "If your mom is available to watch the baby. I'm not taking her with us."

"I'm not scheduled for tomorrow, and if they call me, I'll beg off," said Cole's mother. "Adults-only makes perfect sense," she added. "Less chance of him making a baby grab that way." She set a tray of breads into the oven and arched a brow when they all stared at her. "I know it's not likely, seeing as how he's the one who brought Libby here, but don't pretend you all weren't thinking the same thing."

"Should we give him a heads-up?"

"Like he gave us?" His father made a valid point. "The old guy seemed nice. And playing Santa gives him extra points in my book, but we don't know what he's up to. We don't know what we don't know," he reminded them. "There's obviously more to this story. Go see him. If he's not there, leave him a note so he knows we've found him. If nothing else, that opens another line of communication. Then we'll see. Want me to come?"

Cole exchanged a smile with his father. "Not this time. We'll save you for when we need real muscle."

His father's smile deepened.

Despite his sometimes gruff exterior, Jim Lafferty was a solid negotiator. He knew when to let people think they were winning, and he knew when to walk away. Solid skills in the horse business. Solid skills in life.

A pickup truck rolled up the driveway right then. Cole's cousin was coming to supper with his new girlfriend. Cole's mom's older sister too.

He tucked the papers away.

There was already enough talk about the baby. Her arrival, her history or lack thereof, and their intentions.

He didn't want anyone to know their plans. Not because he was suspicious. He wasn't. But he was careful, and that was enough to zip the lid on talk about Libby's grandfather or great-grandfather and what he was doing playing Santa in Conroe last night.

Carolee snapped pictures of the neighborhood and Peterson's house, then added an address and texted it back to Cole's mother. IN CASE WE DISAPPEAR, was what she wrote, but she wasn't scared.

Nervous, yes.

Confronting the elderly gentleman might very well take that precious baby out of their lives, but since she didn't actually belong there, that was half expected anyway.

They parked on the street and walked up the driveway.

There were no cars in the drive. They climbed the steps and rang the bell.

Twin cameras recorded them from opposite sides of the opulent home, and the doorbell camera was pigeonholing them right now too. Carolee imagined that most everyone in this upscale neighborhood had similar security.

No one answered.

And no one responded via smartphone technology, although the doorbell camera was enabled. Was that unusual? Or simply guarded?

They tried again. Then they moved around to the rear of the house and tried knocking on the back door.

Still nothing.

Cole peered in the garage windows. "One car, off to the side. One empty space on this side."

Carolee saw that the guy had cameras here too. She wasn't sure that he didn't also have microphones secreted somewhere. "How about we go get coffee and come back?"

Cole nodded. They didn't hurry. By the time they returned to the house, two hours had passed.

Still nothing.

Cole left a note inside the door. "I don't know what else we can do."

"We left the note. He knows we found him. The ball's in his court, Cole."

He didn't look happy about that, but he accepted it. "I say we head back to the ranch, grab some takeout and the baby, and watch a Christmas movie."

"You never watch Christmas movies with me," she told him, and that was true. She had a list of every-year favorites, but he'd always veered away from them.

"I think walking a cranky baby, eating good food, and watching some guy realize his life made a difference—"

"A huge difference, and one of my all-time favorite movies," she assured him.

"Sounds like the best night ever to me, darlin'."

They climbed in the truck and headed for the expressway.

Cole. Libby. Barbecue and *It's a Wonderful Life.*

It sounded like a great night to her too.

Chapter Ten

Cole got a midday text from his mother later that week. SOMETHING CAME FROM ONE OF THE ANCESTRY SITES. IT'S HERE, AT THE HOUSE. RIGHT NOW.

He called her back straightaway. His mother wasn't a nervous person, but her voice on this phone call blended nerves, anxiety, and anticipation into one heartfelt cluster.

A part of him wanted to hop into the truck, drive up to the house, and rip the envelope open.

But he didn't, because he wasn't the only one involved. "I'll call Carolee and have her come straight to the house. We'll open it together when she gets there, okay?"

"That's two hours, Cole."

He added surprise to the emotions in her tone.

"I know. And none of your steaming tricks. I'll know if you did that. It turns the paper funky."

"Already have the teakettle on," she replied smartly. But then she sighed. "Of course I'll wait. I already tried reading through the envelope, but they use decent-quality paper. Go figure."

He laughed, although he didn't feel like it. He understood the anxiety wafting throughout the family. The results could be a big fat zero.

At least they'd tried, but Cole wasn't fooling himself. Their actions might look like attempts to find out more or return this baby to her mother, but their emotions, feelings, and choices weren't nearly so magnanimous. Each day that Libby was with them, fussing, smiling, cooing, blinking, and sleeping was a gift from God.

A gift none of them wanted to return.

He pulled into the ranch house driveway five minutes after getting Carolee's text that she'd arrived. She met him at the door. "I've been here five minutes, Cole Lafferty. Five extra minutes of waiting."

"I was afraid if I got here early, I wouldn't be able to resist ripping the envelope open. I hung back until I got your text. How was your day?"

He kissed her, and it was as natural as breathing. As if there hadn't been a year-long separation, as if they'd been happily married for the duration. And she kissed him back.

He kicked off his boots and followed her into the kitchen. Crockpot-barbecued chicken scented the air, and fresh coffee sat on the warmer. And there, on the table, was the envelope.

His mother poured coffee, Carolee set out the half-and-half, and then they all sat down, angling themselves in front of Cole's laptop.

Cole opened the envelope and removed the paper. Then he went to the heritage website and signed in.

His eyes went wide, and his mother gasped.

Carolee gripped his arm. "Libby is related to you?" Her eyes went wide. The informational link on the webpage indicated that Libby Smith was likely a close family member to Cole's mother. She and her two sisters had sent in samples years before.

Carolee's surprised expression turned to concern. "But how? How can that be?"

Cole's mother shifted her attention from the form to the laptop screen.

And then she took a deep breath as she faced them. "Because she's your uncle Nathan's granddaughter."

"Say what?" Cole stared at her. "Uncle Nathan had two sons who've barely reached puberty yet. Danny and Drew. So that's impossible."

His mother sat back and clasped her hands. "Nathan had a relationship with a young woman when he was younger. Probably nineteen—no, wait, twenty years ago now—and after they'd been dating for six or seven months, they realized she was expecting."

"That's been known to happen," said Carolee. "But who is she? Where is she?"

The sadness of old wrongs darkened his mother's expression. "I have no idea. It was a mess," she continued. "Her family was old-school. Straightlaced. They had plans and dreams for their daughter that didn't include Nathan or a baby.

"Nathan and Athena met at some Houston gathering and started dating. He was twenty. She was eighteen. They fell in love, but Athena panicked when she discovered the pregnancy. She didn't want to disappoint her parents."

"I can understand that," Carolee said.

"Nathan wanted to marry her, but when her parents cried—"

"They actually cried?" asked Cole.

"It was horrible. My parents and I were there. Her name was Athena Economides. She was brokenhearted, Nathan was hurt and angry, and my parents were distraught, but they tried to be a voice of reason.

"Mr. Economides didn't want reason," she said softly. "He wanted a do-over. He was furious that his daughter's future—and the family's good name—was 'forever made dark in the eyes of God.' His words. Not mine."

"I still don't get it," said Cole. "What happened to Athena? And the baby? I've never heard a whisper of this, Mom, and I'm nearly thirty years old."

"It wasn't my story to tell," she said. She lifted her cup to sip her coffee, then set it back down without taking a drink. "They took Athena away. Nathan fought for her, but in the end, they won out. As I said, he was only twenty then, and not the orator he became when he ran for Congress ten years later. He was one of the youngest congressmen ever elected, and he took the office seriously. He took life seriously, and I know he always wondered what became of Athena, but she asked him to stay out of her life, and he did.

"She claimed to have given the baby up for adoption. Based on this DNA report, it appears that Libby's mother—Mary Smith—is probably that child. Uncle Nathan's daughter."

"Which makes Libby your grandniece," breathed Carolee. "Look, there's a symbol that links to possible relatives."

Cole clicked on the symbol.

Several of his mother's relatives and ancestors popped up like a branching tree. And above Libby's name was another name, a name listed to likely be her mother.

Mary Smith.

"She used a false name?"

"A lot of people do that when they initially go looking for information," said his mother. "For privacy. Especially if there are family secrets."

"What family doesn't have secrets?" Carolee asked as she leaned forward. "And there's the link to you." She pointed to the branch above. "'Likely aunt.'"

"Don't these sites alert you when you get a new person that pops into your group?" asked Cole. "Wouldn't you have gotten some sort of notification when Mary Smith uploaded her DNA?"

"They send stuff all the time," his mother explained. "Most of it goes to my junk mail. I don't pay attention all that much. That must be how Mary Smith found you two." She frowned. "She must have gone looking for information about her birth family at some point, because it says she's been a member for a few years."

"Who are you, Mary Smith?" Cole posed the rhetorical question to the screen in front of him. "And how do you know Ned/Daedalus Peterson/Petrocokinos? I guess the better question would be, how did he find you?" He pointed to the screen. "Because he's right there, listed as Libby's great-grandfather. We were right about that. So they found each other—"

"And decided to reach out to us because we lost Beau?" The pain in Carolee's expression broke Cole's heart.

"Oh, I'm sure there's far more to this story than we know, Carolee." Cole's mother put an arm of support around Carolee's shoulders. "Whatever happened in Mary Smith's life, or is happening now, this tells me she looked for family for her baby. Only she can say how or why, but it looks to me like they reached out to family who would be a good fit for her baby girl. And that was you and Cole. Not because of what you lost. But because of who you are."

"Because of Mary's father? Nathan?"

Cole's mother nodded. "I'd assume so. She did do DNA testing, which means she wanted to see who she was. Who her relatives were. And that was a few years ago, so she's been looking and wondering for a while. Maybe when she discovered her father had passed away she gave up the search? Let things be? It looks to me like this baby pushed her to reach out so Libby would be part of the heritage Mary never had."

The sensibility of his mother's words struck Cole. "To embrace the Sutton side of the family because the Economides side couldn't accept her?"

"I don't know about that, but I know one thing," his mother said. "This child is family. She's a blessing. She's my brother's granddaughter. I'd be proud and happy to be her grandmother."

"How do we tell Aunt Allison about this?" Cole asked. His uncle had married Allison Teagarden shortly before his run for Congress. "How do we tell her about Libby and her mother and grandmother? What will she say? And how will she handle it with the boys?"

His mother's expression sobered. "We'll be upfront and honest. I know Allison. She'll want to know. We'll leave the boys up to her, of course. I never broached this subject with Allison before, but Nathan wasn't deceptive. She might have known all along."

"We need to find Ned," said Carolee. "If only to clear up the mystery of Mary Smith and her choices. It's even more important now, because we know her own birth mother was pressured to give up her baby. I want to make sure this isn't history repeating itself."

The baby began stirring. She flailed her arms in the swing, as if startled by a dream or their voices.

She soothed herself with her pacifier for a few seconds, but her puckered expression sent a clear message of dissatisfaction.

Carolee got up and warmed a bottle. Then she paused the swing and lifted the baby up into her arms.

Cole watched, enthralled by the look of love and contentment on her face, the warmth of compassion in his wife's eyes. She loved this baby, that was obvious.

Despite that, she wanted to make sure the baby's mother was sure of herself, of her choices, her decisions.

The three of them—him, her, and Libby—were a fragile dream right now. Like a mirror under stress of cracking.

But Carolee had come a long way since Libby was dropped off. She hadn't just reached out to help. She'd charged in, and maybe she'd stay. Not because he'd convinced her—he'd tried that a year ago, and it was an abject failure.

No, he wanted her to stay because she wanted to. She'd left on her own accord. He wanted her to come back the very same way.

᠗ CHAPTER ELEVEN ᠗

Cole wasn't an undercover type of guy.

He'd never yearned to be a cop or a detective or a local sheriff. He was a cowboy, pure and simple. A rancher. A horseman.

That made sitting west of Ned Peterson's place with little binoculars unusual behavior for him. Still, he saw no other way, so he'd parked up the road and shut off the engine. No one noticed him under the cover of darkness, so he sat, glad it wasn't a freezing cold night, as he watched and waited for the elderly man to come home.

He'd told Carolee to stay in Cut and Shoot, but she'd rolled her eyes and gotten into the passenger seat. "Let's do this. We've been trying all week to reach out to someone, anyone, who knows anything. We got nothing except another lecture from my mother about opening myself to more sadness."

She snapped her seat belt into place as Cole put her lower-profile car into gear. "Sorry, babe."

"Well, it's Mom, so it's rather expected and yet still ridiculous. You'd think, being my mother, that she'd have been around more after we lost Beau, wouldn't you? When she was so hyper about me when I was a kid? But that wasn't the case."

It hadn't surprised Cole, but he couldn't and wouldn't say that. "People handle grief in different ways, Lee. Some face it head-on. For others, it swamps them. I say we cut her some slack."

"I always have," she told him frankly. "I've had to because she shies away from a challenge. She put me in the spotlight, but she's a shadow-loving person. She doesn't deal with things well. And the distance between here and Florida gives her the space she likes now."

"She loves you. In her own way."

Carolee accepted that with a shrug. "But she doesn't get to call the shots, Cole. I told her that. And reminded her that you and I make our own decisions. Together."

The grace of that single word drove his pulse up.

"She cried and said that she just wanted to spare me pain. When she said that, I realized that life comes with pain sometimes, and it made me think about what you said."

"I've said a lot," he confessed.

"How you realized that even if you'd known what was going to happen, you'd have gone ahead and married me. Had Beau. Taken the chance on pain to have those years of wonderful."

"All true." He put his hand over hers. "He was worth every minute, Lee."

"I know." She leaned her head against his shoulder. "He sure was."

They'd actually talked about Beau. Connected. Something about having Libby in the house, another person to tend to, a tiny being who was dependent on them, made it easier to broach what had been left unsaid for so long.

They'd slipped into the empty parking space nearly two hours ago. Cole leaned back and stretched just as a large car rolled down the street from behind them.

It signaled left and turned into Ned Peterson's driveway.

They slipped out of the car, jogged across the road, and down the sidewalk. When Ned came out of the garage, they were striding up the asphalt.

He saw them, and his eyes went wide right before he waved them toward the door. "Might as well have that talk now as later, I suppose."

He unlocked the door and motioned them into a beautifully appointed home, gracious and inviting. He intercepted their looks of appreciation as he unbuttoned his tailored black coat. "My wife had great taste and knew how to stay on a budget. She was a rare breed for a wealthy woman."

He slung his coat over the back of a chair and moved to a seat. Then he indicated they should do the same. He didn't move smoothly like he'd done the day he dropped the baby off. He limped tonight. He winced slightly as he went to sit but didn't complain.

"Are you all right? Do you need help?" asked Carolee.

"Bad hip that's been fixed twice. Probably a foolish thing to fix it again at my age, but we'll see. I've been on a chair most of the day, and sitting is about the worst thing for it, but there were no options. So." He settled onto the firm chair with a grimace, then set his hands on his knees. "You found me."

"It took some doing." Cole reached out a hand to Carolee. "This is my wife, Mr. Peterson."

"Ned's good. I knew I should have said no to that Santa gig," he told them. "But I wanted to see if you'd show up. See how Libby's doing. Get a feel for things. A young person like Mary—"

"That's her real name?"

"Yes. Mary Elaine Cordis. That's her adoptive name. My grand-daughter was forced to give her up back then. It was an ugly time. A real tug of war. The adoptive family named her Mary Elaine. Athena wanted to name her Lindsey."

"And so she named the baby Lindsey Liberty," said Carolee. "We found the birth announcement and wondered if it was meant for Libby. Mr. Peterson—" She sat forward eagerly.

"Ned's good. Really."

Carolee acknowledged that with a nod. "We need more."

His expression went hard. "Of course. Babies are costly little things. How much?"

She frowned, then scoffed at his implication with a wave of her hand. "Not money. Facts. Information," she went on. "We discovered Libby's biological link to Cole's family, that she's Nathan Sutton's granddaughter, but Cole's mother made us aware that Athena wasn't given the choice of adoption. She was given an ultimatum. Neither one of us"—she squeezed Cole's hand in unity— "can overlook the possibility of history repeating itself here. If Mary is being pushed or forced into this decision, that's heinous. And we can't be a part of it."

His expression softened. He took a deep breath, but he didn't sit back in the chair. He stayed upright, leaning forward, and his earnest expression inspired Cole's confidence. "Nothing could be further from the truth, but let me ask you one thing. It's important." He drew his brows down and included both of them with his gaze. "If you're convinced that Mary is doing this of her own volition, for her own very good reasons, are you intending to keep the baby? To adopt Libby?"

"If it's as you say, wild horses and a team of rustlers couldn't get that baby away from us," said Cole.

Ned smiled. Then he stood. "I want you to meet me somewhere tomorrow. I'll text you the address. I want Mary to be able to tell you her own story, and there's not much time left."

Cole frowned as they stood too. "Because?"

"Because she's dying."

Carolee had been holding Cole's hand. Ned's words made her tighten her grip. Then she dropped Cole's hand, moved forward, and took the elderly man's hand. "What time should we meet you?"

"She's peppier in the morning. Nine thirty? She's at the Post Road Clinic. They've got a hospice house there, round back, tucked in the garden area. Mary's there."

Cole wasn't sure his heart knew what to do. Beat faster? Slow down? "We'll be there. Should we bring the baby?"

Ned's brows shot up, and he hesitated. His expression wavered, then he nodded. "I think she'd hate that and like it, so I'm not sure what to say."

"I'll tell you what," said Cole. "We'll have my mom ride along with us and Libby. If Mary wants to see Libby, we'll text Mom to bring her in. If it's not a good idea, Mary won't even know Libby was there."

"That'll work." Ned walked them to the door. When they got there, Carolee spoke the question that had been dogging both of them for nearly four weeks. "Why us?"

"Family. And people having a second chance. It's a winding road story, but it's not mine to tell. Unless we lose our girl tonight.

But they said that wasn't likely when they sent me home. Let her tell you tomorrow. It's best that way."

"Of course." Carolee reached up and hugged him. Cole spotted the compassion and the tears in her eyes. "We'll see you tomorrow."

She stepped back, and Cole extended his hand.

Ned took it, and he had a surprisingly strong grip. "Until then."

They retraced their steps to the car in silence, but when they got in, they both paused, gazing forward. Then Cole reached for her hand, and they prayed for a person they'd never known, a person they only knew through a baby's smile and others' words. They prayed for her to be comforted in love. No matter what the coming night or day brought.

When they were done—and the prayer was complete—Cole drove them home.

～ CHAPTER TWELVE ～

Carolee wasn't sure what she expected, but it wasn't the dark-haired frail beauty they met the next morning. The hospice bed looked like it belonged in a gracious room but had the conveniences of a hospital bed too. There was no trace of Christmas in the room, with one exception. A handmade Christmas card stood on top of a small dresser.

Ned stood and waved them in when they approached the door.

Carolee moved forward, but Cole didn't. He stood in the door, cowboy hat in hand, twisting the brim.

Mary looked at Carolee, then Cole. Then she swallowed hard, eyeing him. "We look alike."

Cole nodded. "I see it. I look like my uncle Nathan. My mom's side."

"Then I guess I look like my dad," she whispered softly. "I thought so when I looked him up on the internet. That's when I realized he was already gone, and I'd never get to meet him after all." There was no mistaking the sadness and disappointment in her tone. "Though I'll get to meet him soon now."

"He was handsome." Carolee spoke gently too. It didn't seem like a room for loud or even normal voices. Not yet, anyway. "And you're lovely," she added. "I'm Carolee. Cole's wife."

"Mary." The sick young woman didn't extend a hand. Carolee was pretty sure that was beyond her energy levels. "Not Smith, though. Cordis."

Cole moved closer. "I'm sorry you're sick."

"Well." She shrugged. "Things happen, don't they? Grandpa says that, and even though we never got to be together when I was little, he found me after I put my DNA online." She smiled up at Ned, and he smiled back. "If he hadn't, I would have been alone through all this. But I wasn't alone. And that's made all the difference. How's Libby? How's she doing? Is she all right?"

Cole and Carolee exchanged glances. Then Cole posed the question. "Would you like to see her?"

"Yes. Oh yes!" Hope and light filled the young mother's face, and a hint of color pushed into her pale cheeks.

Cole texted his mother as he said, "My mother has her. She's your aunt Eleanor. Norrie, she's called. Is it okay to meet her?"

"I have spent my life wanting to meet family. Wanting to know who I was, why I was given away. So yes. Please. I want to meet her."

When Cole's mother walked in with the baby, Mary held out her arms. But when his mom drew a quick, sharp breath, the young woman froze, stricken.

Norrie came forward, her mother-instincts in high gear. "I'm sorry, dear. So sorry. It's just, you look so much like your daddy that it took me by surprise. Your hair is darker, but your face. That beautiful face." Tears were rolling down her cheeks, and she didn't do a thing to stop them. "That's Nathan's face. His gray eyes. His nose, his brows. Oh, darling, I'm just so glad to meet you. I'm your aunt Norrie."

Mary reached up to take her baby daughter. She half smiled through her tears, then cried harder, gazing down, as if joy and sorrow lived in unison. "She's so big. And beautiful. And this outfit."

She stroked the holiday-themed onesie, her eyes locked with Libby's, wonder on her face. Then her demeanor changed. Her arms began to tremble, but she didn't take her gaze off her baby. "She's perfect, isn't she?"

"She is," Carolee breathed.

Mary's arms began to shake.

She ignored it a little longer as she gazed at the baby, then she lifted her eyes to Carolee. "She's slipping."

"I'm here." Carolee lifted the baby from Mary's arms.

Regret deepened Mary's features. Then she sighed softly and laid back against the pillows.

"Water, honey?" Ned held up a glass with a top and a straw.

She nodded, but when Ned put the straw near her mouth, she changed her mind. "No. I guess not. I guess not, Grandpa."

Carolee motioned to the chair. "May I sit down? Then you can lay your hand on her."

Mary nodded, and the color in her face faded. She swallowed, and it seemed painful.

Carolee helped her lay her hand on Libby, then asked softly, "Why us, Mary?"

"You're family. Right after I found out who I was, before I was pregnant with Libby, I saw that you lost your little boy. I was too scared to reach out. I wasn't sure what you would all say. Or do. But then when I realized I was expecting, her dad and I knew we needed help. That we needed you," she added specifically. "He's young too. In school. He's not ready to be a father."

"We would have loved you then like we do now," Norrie told her. "And like we'll love Libby."

Mary frowned. "I'm not an easy person to love."

"Ah, honey," Norrie said. "Who told you that?"

Mary hesitated. She glanced at Ned. Her left hand stayed on Libby's little chest. The right one picked at the blanket's satin binding. "I didn't always try to meet expectations. Let's put it that way. And when I was nineteen and discovered I was pregnant, they asked me to leave. They thought I was just like my mother."

"Kind? Sacrificial? Young?"

Norrie's words brought hope to Mary's expression.

"I met your mother several times," Cole's mom continued. "Her parents couldn't forgive that she and my brother fell in love and were expecting a child. Your grandparents were so full of disappointment—"

"My daughter and her husband," said Ned.

"And then I repeated the cycle." Carolee had to strain to hear Mary's soft words. "My adoptive parents couldn't get beyond that either. As if they gave me the only chance I had, and I blew it."

"No," Carolee began, but Mary interrupted her.

"That's what they said. They wanted me out of the house. A friend helped me get medical care. That's when they discovered the cancer. If I'd had treatment eight months ago, it could have extended my life. But the drugs would have hurt the baby. Maybe even kill her. I couldn't do that."

"And so you waited."

She looked up at Carolee. "I couldn't cure this cancer. Or change my past. But if there was one thing I could do, it was to give this baby the best chance at a normal, wonderful, and amazing life. And that's where you two came in. I knew how heartbroken you must be about your son. I couldn't even imagine what you went through, but when I found out I was going to die, I *could* imagine a little of how you felt. The helplessness."

Carolee didn't try to stop the flow of tears down her cheeks. "Yes."

"Grandpa found me nearly two years ago. When I reached out to him after my diagnosis, he took some convincing." Her eyes fluttered shut and stayed that way for a few long, drawn-out seconds. Then she blinked them open. "Not about you," she explained. Weariness was grabbing her. "About refusing treatment. But he understood. He's the one who helped me find you and then this place."

The big black SUV prowling around before Thanksgiving.

"Didn't have to like the choice to understand it." Ned used a white hankie to wipe his eyes. There was no mistaking the grief on the elderly man's face.

And then Libby peeped not once but twice. She wriggled, then sighed and collapsed back into sleep.

Mary smiled at the baby. "She was so totally worth it, Grandpa. A new beginning. You know that."

He blew his nose and bent forward to kiss her cheek. "She absolutely is, and you're an amazing mother."

She gripped his hand. "I'm tired, Grandpa."

"I know, my beautiful girl."

"Not so beautiful now," she said to him, smiling.

"Now and always, dear one. Like mother, like daughter, like granddaughter."

She sighed.

So did he. Then he moved away as she eased back into the pillows.

She looked tired. So very tired. And yet as Carolee stood, Mary's eyes flickered open. "Have fun with her. Okay?"

"Every day." Carolee leaned forward and kissed the young mother's cheek. "Every single day. Thank you. I don't have any other words for this, just—thank you."

Cole reached down and gently took Mary's hand in his. Her hand looked small and frail and pale in his work-roughened one. "We will love her and you all of our days."

Exhaustion took hold then. Mary fell asleep, but a tiny smile, a smile much like Libby's, tipped her lips up before they relaxed in slumber.

They tiptoed out.

Libby squeaked again, with more wriggles and momentum. Norrie reached out. "I'll feed her so you can talk."

"There's a little room just there." Ned indicated an anteroom off the hall. It was cozy and well-lit. "It's where families meet with staff and doctors. We can use that."

They sat around a small round table, and Carolee got right to the point. "Have Mary's parents been to see her?"

Ned shook his head.

"Has she blocked them?" she pressed.

Again, he indicated no.

"Do they realize how advanced the disease is?" asked Cole. "I know there are hard feelings, but if they know—"

"They know. And still they stay away. A choice like this is something I don't understand." Ned splayed his hands, his expression troubled. "How can the Cordises make that choice when they raised her? Said they loved her. And yet she said she often felt like a stranger with them. As if they waited for her to fail and weren't surprised when she did. That was part of why she insisted on you two," he said. "She knew you would love her child. She knew you would love Libby because you'd loved before and that meant you would love again."

Cole took Carolee's hand. Until that moment, she hadn't realized how much she needed his touch. That connection. "We'll love her, Ned," he said. "But I want one thing."

Ned met his gaze across the table.

"I want you to reach out to them one more time. Or I can, if you like."

Carolee's breath hitched, and she squeezed Cole's hand. "They've made their decision, Cole."

He met her gaze, and in that moment she knew he understood what she was thinking. That Mary's parents might change their minds. That they might show up and lay claim to their granddaughter. Carolee was sure she couldn't bear for that to happen. She couldn't lose another baby. Not when her heart was just beginning to open again.

He clung to her hand and her heart with his next words. "I don't think Mary will change her mind, darlin'. I don't think she's going to all of a sudden decide they're a better fit for Libby, but if they don't get one last chance to see her, then we'll always wonder if we did the right thing. And maybe they'd even like to be part of Libby's life someday. They raised her mama. I'm just saying I'd feel better if we crossed this T before it's too late."

"They'll likely refuse." Ned didn't beat around the bush.

"We'll at least know they had the choice." He leaned toward Carolee. "Is that all right with you, Lee?"

She wanted to say no.

She wanted to run out the door with the baby and know they were making a dying mother's final wish come true. That they were making it easier for her to go home to God and leave Libby here on Earth, with them.

She sighed and turned to Ned. "Try one more time."

He hesitated, then swallowed hard. "All right. I will."

∽ Chapter Thirteen ∾

Cole watched the sedan roll up the drive.

They weren't expecting anyone, and he didn't recognize the vehicle. And when a middle-aged couple approached the door, he didn't recognize them either.

He crossed to the door so they wouldn't ring the bell. Not because of Libby.

She slept through pretty much anything now.

But the half-grown golden retriever that had sauntered through a few days back, looking for a couple of square meals, was tucked in a large crate in the kitchen. Cole knew what would happen if the doorbell rang. The pup would start a full-on ruckus. Libby would sleep through the doorbell chime. But a big, goofy dog barking to beat the band might be more than she could handle.

Carolee had shampooed the dog, treated him for fleas, and called the vet for an appointment within two hours of the dog's appearance.

Cole knew what that meant. They'd have a Christmas dog cozied up by the fire if no one came to claim him, and so far no one had.

He opened the door.

The woman spoke first. "I'm June Cordis."

Mary's adoptive mother. And father. Here. On their porch. A week before Christmas.

His heart squeezed, and his chest went tight. He literally didn't know what to do. He'd had Ned make the offer but never wanted them to show up.

"And I'm William."

Cole's mind darted off in multiple directions.

Why were they here?

What did they want?

How did they know where Libby was? And could he kick them off his porch for abandoning his cousin?

"Cole?" Carolee had been out back. She came through to the living room. "It's too cold to hold the door open. The baby's fine, but I'm freezing." Then she stopped and stared, and her hand came to her throat.

She knew who they were.

He wanted a do-over. He wanted to return to that little room in the hospice home and snatch back his words. What was he thinking? Why didn't he simply leave well enough alone?

The Christmas tree twinkled behind him. They'd strung lights along the porch roof and around the door and front windows, and Carolee had bought a wreath for the door. For the first time in two years the house felt good and safe and happy.

And now this.

"May we come in?"

His first response was a firm "no," but he'd instigated the outreach, which meant he bore some kind of responsibility.

He bit back a sigh and swung the door wider. "Of course."

They stepped in.

"Would you like to sit down?" Carolee posed the question in a tight voice. Her angry, how could you do this? voice.

"Well—" William hesitated.

June moved forward. "Thank you. Yes." She settled into a chair. Carolee didn't wait for him to take the lead.

She came around the couch and took a seat not far from June. And then she surprised Cole.

She reached out and touched June's hand. "I'm so sorry about Mary. So dreadfully sorry. I know how you're feeling."

June choked up. Tears welled and spilled over, and Carolee thrust a box of tissues her way.

"We aren't terrible people," William said. "But we weren't good parents to Mary. I think we tried at first, but she was so different from what we expected. And then we didn't react to things well because it just seemed like no matter what way we pointed her, she went in the other direction. Not her fault," he added firmly. "She was a child, a lovely child, and I used to think she had a wild streak, maybe from her mother, and I couldn't get beyond that thought for the longest time. That it was her. Not us. And I was wrong."

"We were wrong," whispered June. She held a tissue to her face as her shoulders shook. After a few moments she managed, "Ned said she's given the baby to you."

"We're adopting her." Carolee kept her voice firm and strong, but Cole saw the tremor in her hands.

"Would you like to see her?" he asked.

"Yes. If that's all right. I—"

"That would be nice," said William.

Carolee got up and crossed the room. When she disappeared into the back of the house, Cole wasn't one hundred percent certain he'd see her again.

Then she returned, cradling the sleeping baby.

And then Carolee proved that she was far stronger and braver than Cole was. She reached out and offered Libby to June. "Would you like to hold her?"

June hesitated.

William didn't. "I would. Yes. If you don't mind."

The papers were signed and had been filed, but Cole knew the adoption wouldn't be finalized for months. The petition needed a judge's approval for Libby to be fully theirs. That meant the young father or these grandparents could still raise a fuss.

His heart beat faster, and his palms grew damp. Realism faced him as William accepted the baby.

When she squeaked and writhed slightly, William's mouth twitched. Tears slipped down his cheeks, but he smiled through them. And then his jaw quivered, and the smile disappeared.

This is it, thought Cole.

William looked up at him. Then down at Libby. Then back. "We brought her something," he said. "Something from her mother and then something for Christmas. If that's okay. We didn't mean to be bad parents." He was whispering now, choking on the words. "But it's so easy to think you know best. And when your mind is closed and your heart is only half open, it's a bad combination."

June had brought in one of those quilted purses, more like a satchel. She pulled a gift-wrapped box from it and set it on the table. "For Libby. If that's all right?"

Carolee nodded. "It's fine. Absolutely fine. I think it's lovely, June."

"And then this." She withdrew another box from the bag and handed it to Carolee. "It was Mary's. It came with her as a baby, and we were told it was from her family. It's been in a cedar box all these years, but I washed it to get the smell out."

Carolee lifted the lid. Then she laid back double sheets of tissue paper.

A quilt lay tucked in the box. An old quilt, done in large squares, with each square featuring a different flower. Texas bluebonnets and a vibrant purple iris flanked a bright pink peony. Friendly daisies added warmth and brightness to the hand-done piece.

Carolee lifted it out.

It was beautiful. Worn at the edges but not frayed. "It's lovely." Carolee ran a finger along the blanket's edge. "And old."

"I put it aside to give to Mary when she was older." June paused, staring at the blanket, but Cole figured it wasn't the old faded cotton she was seeing. It was the reality that Mary would never be older. She'd gone home to God two days before. "It's Libby's now. For later."

"We'll cherish it. And her," Carolee replied.

June nodded. Then she stood.

William looked surprised, but he stood too.

He handed the baby to Cole. "Can you let us know how she's doing? From time to time? If that suits?"

"I will."

"We'll be glad to." Carolee took a step forward. She put her hand on June's arm. "And we'd like you to come see her. If you'd like to, that is."

William seemed appreciative.

June looked torn, but she bit her lower lip and said, "We might. If it's okay. We might."

They'd never said a word about faith or hope or even joy when talking about Mary or their lives, so that's where Cole decided his prayers for them would focus. For the Cordises to find faith. It was never too late to make a fresh start.

After they left, he looked at Carolee. She crossed the narrow space between them and hugged him and the baby.

"Ours," he whispered.

"Yes." She whispered too. "And if it's all right with you, Cole Lafferty, I was thinking that Libby's going to need a brother or sister. Or two."

He grinned and kissed her. "Happy to do my part, ma'am."

She rolled her eyes, but then she got serious. "Me too. And if that happens, I'll be thrilled, but if it doesn't for some reason?" She kissed him. "We'll be fine. Just fine. Because we have everything we need right here."

She was right.

The baby squirmed and squeaked, for real this time. Her insistence went from low-key to high volume without much warning.

The big pup barked and whined, wanting to go out.

Cole kissed his wife, handed her the baby, and took the dog out back.

The moon was just rising over the clearing. It was big and full and glowing a pale yellow. It lit up the sky, making stars disappear. Planets too. Not much was visible this time of year, but when he turned and saw the Christmas lights from this side, from this angle, the little house was a beacon all its own.

The dog padded his way. He sat beside Cole, gazing at the house. Then him. Then the house again.

And then together they went inside.

The smell of simmering beef filled the air, and a tray of cupcakes sat waiting on the counter. White frosted, topped with red-and-green sprinkles.

And the Christmas station was playing in the front room where Carolee sat, head bowed, feeding the little miracle that had arrived less than a month before.

She looked up, met his gaze, and smiled at him.

And he smiled back.

Chapter Fourteen

Cole leaned the beautiful pine tree against the truck bed and slung an arm around Carolee and Libby. "We did it. Our first Christmas tree excursion, ladies. Done!"

"First of many," Carolee replied. She stretched her arm out to get a selfie, but Libby had other ideas. She lunged for the phone, arms reaching, hands waving. "Mine! Mine! Mine!"

Cole laughed, took the phone, and got the pic before Libby went into full-on meltdown because he wouldn't let her have the phone. "And next year it will be the four of us." He grinned down at his beautiful wife and planted a kiss on her forehead. "You. Me. The Libster. And little Jimmy."

The baby was due in four months.

A year ago, it took effort to climb out of bed and put on his shoes.

Not anymore. Not when a man had so much to live for. To be happy about.

"Trade you." He reached for the toddler and handed Carolee the phone, but he didn't miss the moment to kiss her as they made the exchange. He was of a firm mind to never miss a moment like that again. "I'll tuck her in. One of these days she's going to realize the car seat is not a mortal enemy."

"I'm not holding my breath," Carolee told him as she rounded the truck's hood.

They'd gotten her a toy phone, but she'd tossed it across the room, insulted.

It was a smart phone or nothing, it seemed, but when Carolee handed Libby a Velcroed little package, their daughter was enthralled.

She liked peeling Velcro.

Who didn't?

Cole lifted the tree into the truck bed and then climbed into the driver's seat. "Do we need to let the tree relax a little?" he asked.

Carolee shook her head. "Not with a homegrown Texas pine, cowboy. Nobody's netted or bagged that baby. We'll use it to light up the house now and feed the birds later. But first..." She patted the wreath between them.

He'd come prepared. He'd made a small tripod to be staked into the ground.

He turned onto the cemetery road a few minutes later. They climbed out of the cab, and he unhooked Libby from the seat while Carolee gathered the wreath and the supplies.

It was a beautiful wreath. She'd made it herself, weaving artificial fir branches around a metal frame. A real wreath didn't hold up well to South Texas weather, and she'd wanted one to last.

He set Libby down. Then he took the hammer and installed the tripod with sturdy ground stakes, and they wired the wreath to the tripod.

It was beautiful.

And heartbreaking because they didn't have their precious son to raise. To counsel. To hug and to hold.

God had taken over that task. As Carolee reached for Cole's hand, she sighed and looked up. "I know he's there, Cole."

Cole squeezed her hand lightly.

"I don't have to always like it, but I know it. And I know we'll meet again someday, but for now, Mary and Ned are up there with him."

Cole pressed a kiss to her forehead once more. "And I'd say they're having a grand time," he said. "Wouldn't you?"

Libby batted the wreath, then toddled their way over the uneven ground, arms out, laughing. Laughing out loud, loving them. In love with life.

And when Carolee swooped her up, she looked up at Cole and exchanged a smile with him. "I would, cowboy. I absolutely would."

Dear Reader,

The fun of setting a book in Cut and Shoot, Texas, is that it's Texas. ☺ As a Yankee, I love every opportunity I get to head down south, but what I love about Texas (besides its size!) is that it's unique in its own right. It's Texas. 'Nuff said. I've visited several times, and each time is different. I love it!

And what a bonus to find how many fun things they're doing in Cut and Shoot and Conroe for Christmas. Christmas on Main, the beautiful Living Nativity at the Baptist church, native Christmas trees alongside firs shipped in from the north. But what I particularly loved was writing a Christmas story about sacrificial love. A story that found beauty in ashes, a story that brought a young couple back together after tragedy pulled them apart.

Guilt is a wretched taskmaster. We often have an easier time forgiving others than forgiving ourselves, but God's timing is amazing. Technology has changed so many things in the last twenty years, and DNA testing and ancestry sites reveal new networks and family branches every day. And this time...it worked for the best.

Ruth Logan Herne

Dear Reader,

I recently took a drive to Cut and Shoot and was overwhelmed by the massive pine trees—still barren from the winter season. They loomed large all around me, their branches shooting out this way and that. Those sinewy branches served as a reminder of the many, many families that have come together over the years to make this small town a symbol of hope and goodwill. Many of those families still remain in the area, a testament to the truth of God's restorative power. He makes broken things whole again. He puts an end to division. He unifies even the most stubborn among us.

God truly can bring peace on earth, a message we all need to hear, especially during the holiday season. And while I love the idea of Christmas in the big city, truly, nothing can stop small-town celebrations. Carols around a tree in the center of town, gathering with friends and neighbors for wassail and cookies, joining together in worship at the local church—these are the things that small towns like Cut and Shoot are known for. And though this little town got off to a rocky start, God's grace and mercy caused the story of its resilient citizens to have a true happily-ever-after ending.

Janice Thompson

About the Authors

Janice Thompson

Award-winning author Janice Thompson has published over 150 books for the Christian market, crossing genre lines to write cozy mysteries, historicals, romances, nonfiction books, devotionals, children's books, and more. She particularly enjoys writing lighthearted, comedic tales because she enjoys making readers laugh.

Janice is passionate about her faith and does all she can to share the joy of the Lord with others. Her tagline, "Love, Laughter, and Happily Ever Afters!" sums up her take on life.

She lives in Spring, Texas (not far from Cut and Shoot), where she leads a rich life with her family, a host of writing friends, and three mischievous dogs. When she's not busy writing or playing with her nine grandchildren, Janice can be found in the kitchen, baking specialty cakes and cookies for friends and loved ones. She loves to blog about cakes, cookies, and other sweet treats on her *Out of the Box Baking* blog. No matter what she's cooking up—books, cakes, cookies, or mischief—she does her best to keep the Lord at the center of it all.

Ruth Logan Herne

Bestselling, multi-published inspirational author Ruth Logan Herne has published over seventy novels and novellas. She is living her dream of being a published author and in her spare time she is co-owner of a rapidly growing pumpkin farm in Hilton, New York. She is the baker-in-residence, the official grower-of-the-mums, and a true people person, so filling her yard with hundreds of people every day throughout fall is just plain fun!

She loves God, her family, her country, dogs, coffee, and chocolate. The proud mother of six with seventh daughter of her heart and fourteen grandkids, Ruthy lives in an atmosphere where all are welcome, no mess is too big it can't be cleaned up, and food is shared.

Story Behind the Name

Cut and Shoot, Texas

Nestled in the piney woods of East Texas, you will find the tiny town of Cut and Shoot. If you take a quiet drive through the area, you will discover a quaint community filled with loving people who all get along.

This was not always the case. In 1912 a big scandal almost tore the town apart. Back then, the area wasn't called Cut and Shoot. The name came as a direct result of a schism over religious differences.

The town had multiple congregations, and they all shared a common meetinghouse, which they called the Community House. It also served as the local school. An agreement had been struck that all would be welcomed to use the building except two groups—the Mormons and the Apostolics.

Then along came a man by the name of Stamps, an Apostolic. He wanted to make use of the building for a meeting. Unfortunately, Pastor Stamps had a bit of a history, one that involved saloons and dancing. So, half the town believed he should not be allowed to use the building for his meeting while the other half was all for it.

The situation escalated, and tempers flared. On the day of the intended meeting, townspeople showed up at the building, ready for a showdown! Guns and knives were rolled inside quilts, and when it was discovered that the Community House had been locked to Stamps and his congregation, those guns were drawn.

Fortunately, no one was wounded that day. Pastor Stamps and his group ended up meeting under a tree instead of inside the building. Crisis averted. But somewhere in the process of this bubbling brouhaha, the name "Cut and Shoot" emerged. Legend has it, an eight-year-old boy was so terrified at the goings-on that he cried out, "I'm scared! I'm going to cut around the corner and shoot through the bushes in a minute."

And that, my friends, is how the tiny town of Cut and Shoot got its name.

These days you'll find the people living in harmony, smiling as they tell the story of how their once-tumultuous town got its infamous moniker.

Tres Leche Cake

This Tres Leche Cake is always a good choice on any holiday dessert table. A delicious tender sponge-style cake drizzled with a milk sauce and topped with sweetened whipped cream, it can be dusted with cinnamon or graced with fresh fruit...but it's real fine all on its own too!

Cake Ingredients:

6 eggs, separated

1 cup all-purpose flour

¼ teaspoon salt

1½ teaspoons baking powder

1 cup sugar, divided

⅓ cup milk

1 teaspoon vanilla

Milk Mixture:

1 can sweetened condensed milk

1 can evaporated milk

¼ cup whole milk

Whipped Cream Topping:

2 cups heavy whipping cream

⅓ cup sugar

Directions:

Preheat oven to 350 degrees. Grease and flour 13×9-inch pan.

Separate eggs into two mixing bowls. Whites in one, yolks in another.

Mix flour, salt, and baking powder together and set aside.

Beat egg yolks and ¾ cup of the sugar until pale yellow in color. Add milk and vanilla. Blend this mixture gently with dry ingredients. Don't overmix.

In separate bowl, beat egg whites until foamy. Add the final ¼ cup of sugar. Beat on high speed until stiff peaks form. Using a rubber spatula, fold egg whites into batter gently.

Pour into prepared pan. Bake for 25–30 minutes until cake is golden in color and springs back when lightly touched with a finger. Cake is done when a toothpick inserted into center of cake comes out clean or with just a few moist crumbs.

Remove from oven. When cake has cooled, use a fork to poke holes through top of cake.

Combine the three milks and drizzle over surface of cake slowly, allowing milk to run into the fork holes.

Whip heavy cream at high speed until soft peaks form. Gradually add sugar; whip until stiff peaks form. Spread onto cake; dust with cinnamon if desired. Some people prefer nutmeg. Both are delicious!

Refrigerate for several hours to chill thoroughly.

Cake can be frozen, but you should wait until thawed to add the whipped cream topping.

*Read on for a sneak peek of another exciting book
in the Love's a Mystery series!*

Love's a Mystery *in*
Nameless, Tennessee
by Elizabeth Ludwig *&*
Leslie Gould

Fiddlin' with Love
By Leslie Gould

*Nameless, Tennessee
Monday, September 3, 1945*

Shifting the Bantam convertible into third gear, Iris Pitts kept her eyes wide open for Nameless, Tennessee. Mr. Scott Parker, president of the Nameless school board, had written in his offer letter, *Don't blink or you'll miss it.*

Iris had taken Highway 70 from Memphis to Nashville and then headed north. She'd driven on smaller and smaller roads, crossed the Cumberland River, and then turned onto an unpaved back road.

Now, as she gained elevation, the trees became thicker and the curves more frequent. Mr. Parker had called Nameless a "hilltop settlement," and that seemed accurate. Just ahead, the general store, with a gas pump and a shed, was on her right. On her left was a café. Then some sort of office. And a handful of houses. Mr. Parker had written there were fewer than two hundred people in the town. He'd also written, *I know you're wondering how Nameless got its unusual name. Our founding fathers couldn't agree on what to call the community, so the post office declared it "Nameless." And it stuck.*

There was the two-room school. *Her school.* At least for a year. She turned into the lot, shifted into first, and came to a stop. She'd never heard of Nameless, Tennessee, until her neighbor mentioned they had an opening for a teacher. The previous one left to get married. Four months ago, Iris thought she'd be marrying Will McCrae, home from fighting in Europe, by now—or at least soon. Instead, she was arriving in his car as a nobody from nowhere who had ended up in Nameless, Tennessee. On a wing and a prayer.

She climbed out of the convertible, untied the scarf holding her hair in place, and walked toward the school. She'd be teaching grades one through eight, all in one room. She'd spent the last two weeks preparing.

"Miss Pitts!"

She shaded her eyes. A man wearing a fedora came toward her. "Mr. Parker?"

"Indeed it is." He took off his hat, showing a head of thick, gray hair. His hazel eyes shone as he spoke. "I'm delighted to meet you."

He extended his hand, and she took it. His grip was firm but not too tight.

"You made good time." He nodded toward the convertible. "That's some car you have there. A '39 Bantam, correct?"

She smiled. "That's right. It's fun, but not much good in a move." Both the front passenger seat and the back area were packed with her belongings, as was the trunk.

"I'll show you inside the school and then your new home."

"Will my things be safe out here?"

"Oh my, yes," he answered. "We don't have any crime in Nameless. No one locks their doors even. You could have the Hope Diamond in that convertible of yours, and it would be safe."

She trusted that meant Will's beloved fiddle was safe in the trunk then. She doubted he was coming back—she would have heard from him by now if he was. Not knowing was as hard as anything she'd ever gone through. But just in case he did return, she'd keep his fiddle safe.

Mr. Parker turned the knob of the schoolhouse door and flung it open. He motioned for her to enter. She stepped into a large area with hooks for the students to hang their coats and a row of shelves for their lunch buckets. There was a stack of wood at the far end of the room. There were two doors across from each other and a third door to the right, at the end of the hall.

"As I told you in my letter, the school has two rooms, but we're only using one at this time. Quite a few of our families left during the war to work in cities. We'll gain some back over the next year, but others will go to the Jackson County schools in Gainesboro. In time, all our students will." Mr. Parker sighed. "But for the time being, we'll carry on here and do the best we can. As I said, you'll have all the grades in one room, thirty-eight students total. First through eighth grade, although several of the students are older than thirteen."

"Oh?"

"We don't have a bus to take them to Gainesboro, and their families don't want them to be out of school yet."

"How old are the oldest students?"

"Fifteen, mostly. Try to challenge them as best you can." He motioned to the door on the left.

Iris hadn't prepared for older students. She exhaled as she stepped through the doorway and then walked down the center aisle between the desks to the large teacher's desk up front.

Mr. Parker followed her. "I've put a list with the students' names and grades on your desk, plus the textbooks for each grade. The students' books are on the shelves over there."

Iris glanced toward the shelves along the wall. The books appeared old and ratty. She focused on her desk again. It was large, and the chair looked comfortable. There was a chalkboard behind it, maps to the right, and an iron stove in the corner.

"You'll notice we don't have electricity yet. Putting up lines in the mountains was slowed down by the war—hopefully, that will change soon." He glanced toward the south-facing windows. "The light is good in this room. There are lamps in the cupboard." He motioned to the far wall. "If you ever need them."

Charleston, Asheville, and Memphis had all had electricity.

"Do you have any questions?" Mr. Parker asked.

Iris looked around the room. There was a slate on each desk with chalk. She hadn't used a slate twenty years ago when she started school in Charleston, but Nameless was small and remote. "Are there paper and pencils available for the students?"

"Most families can't afford those for their children, so the school board provides the slates."

"I see." She glanced around the room again. "What about cleaning supplies?"

"There's a broom, mop, and bucket in the closet in the cloakroom. Plus a jug of ammonia. Work out a cleaning schedule for the students."

"All right." She smiled at him. "Thank you."

"Would you like a little background on the area?"

"Please," Iris said.

"The county seat is Gainesboro, which is ten miles from here. Traveling is better than it was in the olden days but can still be a problem. Many of our students live out in the country and will have a hard time getting to school when the weather turns. You came over the Cumberland River to get here—"

Iris nodded.

"There's good fishing in it and the Roaring River too—catfish and bass—and also in the creeks all through the mountains." Mr. Parker gestured to the windows. "The rivers used to be the main means of transportation, and there's plenty of people who still get around using them. Of course, the hunting is good too. Lots of deer and quail." He grinned. "Not that I expect you to hunt for game."

She smiled. "I'd be willing to give it a try."

"No need," he said. "No doubt the older boys will be bringing you a bird now and then. Most of the students live on farms. Tobacco and corn are the common crops. Lots of livestock. Lumber is another source of income, and there are several mills in the area."

It would clearly be a different life than Iris was used to.

"Some of our students lost loved ones in the war—brothers, fathers, uncles."

Iris blinked a couple of times, fighting back her own grief. No doubt, everyone had been affected in some way.

"How long have you lived in Nameless, Mr. Parker?"

"I grew up here," he said. "Then moved around quite a bit for business. I returned a couple of years ago to the family farmhouse, but I lease out the land. I'm no farmer." He smiled. "I'm ready for a quieter way of life, now that I'm growing older."

"Well," Iris said, "this is a lovely place to return to."

"That it is." He held her gaze for a long moment and then said, "I'm pleased you're here, Miss Pitts." Before she could respond he added, "I'll stop by tomorrow after school. I'm sure you'll have more questions then."

"I'm guessing I will."

"Now, let's take a look at the gymnasium and then go look at your new home."

When they returned to the cloakroom, he nodded to the door at the end of the hall. "That's where the gymnasium is. Basketball was king around here a few years ago." He chuckled. "We had students repeating eighth grade just so they could keep playing. During the war, as we lost students, the team hasn't done as well, but it's still the favorite sport."

Will had loved basketball.

Mr. Parker opened the door. The gym had a polished wood floor. "Of course, you won't be responsible for cleaning in here. Basketball practice won't start for a couple of months. We haven't hired a coach yet, but when we do, this will be his responsibility. When the weather gets cold, you can use the space for recess."

Benches lined the gymnasium, and high windows let some light in. There were five rows of bleachers on the far side.

"Now let's take a look at your new home."

Iris followed Mr. Parker out of the school. He pointed to a small building in a grove of white pines on the back property of the school. "Your cottage is right there."

As she followed Mr. Parker, Iris squinted. When they reached the building, it was clear it was a shack.

"I'm sorry the accommodations aren't better," Mr. Parker said. "I'll hire someone to shore it up a little before winter—repair the roof, clean out the latrine, that sort of thing." It had been a while since she'd had to use an outhouse.

He opened the door to the one-room shack and again ushered Iris in first. There was a small table with a lamp, two chairs, a kitchen area, and a bed with a bare mattress.

"Well," Mr. Parker said, "I imagine you have some unpacking to do. Like I said, I'll stop by tomorrow after school to see how the first day went." He started toward the door, leaving Iris alone in the middle of the room. But then he turned back to her and said, "If you have some extra time tonight, there's a gathering at the Nameless Grange Hall." He pointed east. "There'll be music, maybe some dancing. It's just a short way past here—but

I would drive. You don't want to walk home on the road in the dark."

"Thank you," Iris said. "I'll think about it."

As she unpacked the car, Iris felt unsettled. She'd grown up in Charleston, gone to the Teaching College in Asheville, and then moved to Memphis to be close to Will before he shipped out to Europe. Then, instead of getting a teaching contract, she'd taken a job at the Memphis Ordination Plant, determined to do her part. By the time the war in Europe ended in May, production began to slow and she'd needed another job—a teaching job. Although Nameless was small and out of the way, she was thankful for the opportunity.

Just yesterday, the surrender document for the end of the war with Japan was officially signed. It truly was over. And yet, Will wasn't home. She'd last heard from him in March, six months ago. She'd written the War Department but received a form letter saying no information could be released, since she wasn't kin. She'd tried to track down an uncle Will had mentioned by calling people with the last name of McCrae all over Tennessee, but she couldn't locate him.

Living in Nameless, a place with no memories of Will, would be the best thing for her. She carried in her clothes, bedding, and her few kitchen items—a Dutch oven, cake pans, a frying pan, and a kettle. Then a box with a few plates and bowls. And a box of staples—flour, sugar, spices. She grabbed the box of school things—her calendar and lesson plans and the books she'd kept from teacher's college—and placed it on the table, so it would be ready for the morning.

She decided to leave the fiddle in the trunk for now. At least it was secure. The shack barely had a doorknob, let alone a decent lock.

After making the bed, Iris glanced around, trying to decide whether to go to the grange hall or not. By the time she finished her supper of leftover fried chicken from lunch, she'd decided. It would be good to meet some of the people in the community.

She changed into her only new garment in the last four years. A navy-blue Kitty Foyle dress with a white collar and cuffs. She'd bought it last March, thinking she'd wear it the day Will came home. She might as well wear it now. She pinned her dark hair into a victory roll, two rolls on top and long in the back, and then slipped into her red pumps. She applied bright red lipstick. Had Will not contacted her on purpose? Or because he couldn't? Would she ever know if he had even survived the war?

Tears threatened. She grabbed a sweater.

As she drove toward the grange hall, a man stopped and stared. Then he shouted, "Where'd you get that car?" She was used to people—especially men—staring when she drove Will's convertible, and sometimes they shouted, mostly things she ignored, but no one had shouted a question before.

She kept driving. By the cars and trucks and buggies parked around it, she knew when she found the grange hall. She shifted down and made the left-hand turn. An older man started to wave but then his hand froze in midair, and he shook his head. What was going on? Perhaps someone in town owned a Bantam convertible— or had. It was sad to be the new teacher in town and have people already disappointed to see her.

She found a place close to the hall to park the car but couldn't hear any music. Once she turned off the engine, she debated about leaving the fiddle in the trunk. She wasn't worried someone would take it—but then, she was worried someone might take the entire car. She chastised herself. Mr. Parker had said the place didn't have any crime. She climbed out of the car and headed toward the front door of the grange hall.

Several people standing on the porch turned toward her and then stepped aside, allowing her to enter. Mr. Parker waved from the middle of the hall and motioned for her to join him. Just as she reached the group, three musicians took to the stage—an elderly man on the guitar, a middle-aged man on the banjo, and a young man—who was taller than the other two—on the fiddle. He wore a pair of patched overalls and had a surly expression on his face. He also had a boyish face. Perhaps he was younger than she thought.

The guitar player said, "This will be our last set. I hope you've enjoyed the music."

The crowd clapped, and the fiddler pushed his instrument against his chest as if he planned to drive it through his body. The music to "Medley of Reels" began.

Mr. Parker offered Iris his hand, and she took it as people began to pair off in groups of four. It had been a long time since she'd danced. Since Will had gone off to war. The music, the beat that came down from above and up from the floor, and the movement of dancing around the square sparked something inside of her. She bounced on her feet, pivoted, and sashayed around the square, smiling at Mr. Parker and the others as she passed. The faces of the musicians floated by—all three had smiles on their faces as they played, even the young man. As Iris twirled around, she felt a hint of joy. It'd been so long! It wasn't the harmony she'd felt with Will, but it gave her hope.

For just a moment. Until, on the closing note of the song, the fiddle groaned, and Iris turned toward the stage, reminded of how very quickly life could change. A war. A last letter. A move. An end to harmony and hope. And joy.

The fiddler held his bow out in one hand and his fiddle up in the other. Iris gasped. The back of the fiddle had cracked.

The other musicians stopped, and the guitar player put down his instrument and spoke softly to the young man. A few words were exchanged and then the fiddler stormed off the stage.

Iris's heart ached for the young fiddler.

The guitar player stepped to the edge of the stage. "Young Judson's had some bad luck. Say a prayer for him—we all know that was his daddy's fiddle." The man bowed his head and clasped his hands together. Iris thought he was going to pray out loud, but then he raised his head and said, "We need another fiddler." He squinted as he looked into the audience. "Do we have another? Anyone? You don't have to be that good."

Iris glanced around the group on the floor and those who stood along the sidelines. She hadn't played in public for years, but she practiced every day. She felt her hand go up, slowly, perhaps inspired by the music and the dancing and the hope she could feel something besides despair again.

The guitar player met her eyes. "Miss? Do you play?"

She nodded. "Give me a minute to collect—um, my instrument— and I'll join you on the stage."

When she reached the convertible, Judson stood at the hood of the car, the bow and fiddle still in his hands. Iris said, "Hello," and then opened the trunk and pulled out Will's case.

"Where'd you get this car?" Judson asked.

"It belongs to a friend of mine."

Judson's eyes narrowed.

"I'm sorry about your fiddle," Iris said. "Do you have someone who can repair it?"

He scowled, his dark eyes narrow and his chin down. Instead of answering, he asked, "Did you steal the car?"

"I did not." Iris pointed to the back of the grange. "Is there a door that leads to the stage?"

Judson nodded. "I'll show you."

She followed him up a few steps to the door.

"Go on through it," he said. "You'll see the stairs."

She made her way in the dim light up onto the stage. Behind the curtain, she took the fiddle out of the case, holding it tenderly for a moment as she gazed at the carving of hummingbirds and irises on the back. Will had the fiddle long before he'd ever met her. When she'd told him her name was Iris, he took notice.

She tuned the fiddle while the two remaining musicians played "Maidens Prayer." When they finished, she stepped through the curtain. Then she tucked the fiddle under her chin and joined in with the other two. As she played, she noticed one particular couple. The woman wore her auburn hair on top of her head, a red dress, red varnish on her nails, and black dancing shoes. The man was tall with his light brown hair cut short. He wore a suit and held his partner with a tenderness that made Iris's heart ache. As he turned, she thought, *Will!* But it wasn't. The man was heavier and a few years older. But still, he resembled Will.

As she kept playing, the music came to life and filled her soul. After eight more songs, the guitar player turned to Iris and asked, "Do you know 'Haste to the Wedding'?"

"Yes," she answered. It was one of her favorites. The guitar player counted out the beat, and Iris joined in. *Come haste to the wedding ye friends and ye neighbors.* As she played, she fought back tears as she searched the crowd for the man who reminded her of Will and his partner, but they were gone.

She closed her eyes as she played. The music coursed through her. It was time to let go of Will. *No Care Shall obtrude here, our Bliss to annoy... Which love and innocence ever enjoy.* She held the bow on the strings, drawing out the last notes as the crowd began to cheer. It was time to make Nameless, Tennessee her new home, at least for a season.

A NOTE FROM THE EDITORS

We hope you enjoyed another volume in the Love's a Mystery series, created by Guideposts. For over seventy-five years, Guideposts, a nonprofit organization, has been driven by a vision of a world filled with hope. We aspire to be the voice of a trusted friend, a friend who makes you feel more hopeful and connected.

By making a purchase from Guideposts, you join our community in touching millions of lives, inspiring them to believe that all things are possible through faith, hope, and prayer. Your continued support allows us to provide uplifting resources to those in need. Whether through our communities, websites, apps, or publications, we inspire our audiences, bring them together, and comfort, uplift, entertain, and guide them. Visit us at guideposts.org to learn more.

We would love to hear from you. Write us at Guideposts, P.O. Box 5815, Harlan, Iowa 51593 or call us at (800) 932-2145. Did you love *Love's a Mystery in Cut and Shoot, Texas*? Leave a review for this product on guideposts.org/shop. Your feedback helps others in our community find relevant products.

Find inspiration, find faith, find Guideposts.

Shop our best sellers and favorites at
guideposts.org/shop

Or scan the QR code to go directly to our Shop

Find more inspiring stories in these best-loved Guideposts fiction series!

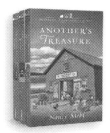

Mysteries of Lancaster County

Follow the Classen sisters as they unravel clues and uncover hidden secrets in Mysteries of Lancaster County. As you get to know these women and their friends, you'll see how God brings each of them together for a fresh start in life.

Secrets of Wayfarers Inn

Retired schoolteachers find themselves owners of an old warehouse-turned-inn that is filled with hidden passages, buried secrets, and stunning surprises that will set them on a course to puzzling mysteries from the Underground Railroad.

Tearoom Mysteries Series

Mix one stately Victorian home, a charming lakeside town in Maine, and two adventurous cousins with a passion for tea and hospitality. Add a large scoop of intriguing mystery, and sprinkle generously with faith, family, and friends, and you have the recipe for Tearoom Mysteries.

Ordinary Women of the Bible

Richly imagined stories—based on facts from the Bible—have all the plot twists and suspense of a great mystery, while bringing you fascinating insights on what it was like to be a woman living in the ancient world.

To learn more about these books, visit Guideposts.org/Shop

Printed in the United States
by Baker & Taylor Publisher Services